MACKENZY FOX

NITRO

BARREN RIDGE REBELS MC
BOOK 8

DEDICATION

To D, for always being there for me x

AUTHOR NOTE

CONTENT WARNING: Nitro is a steamy romance for readers 18+ it contains mature themes that may make some readers uncomfortable. It includes violence, coarse language, stalking, mentions of suicide, prison and kidnapping, and as always….LOTS of steamy love scenes!

BLURB

Bracken Ridge Arizona, where the Rebels M.C. rule and the only thing they ride or die for more than their club is their women, this is Nitro's story

NITRO

The way she moves.

The way she smiles.

Her face like an angel.

Like she has no care in the world.

But I know better.

She saved my life. She wouldn't remember.

But I watched her, for years.

I protected her, without her knowledge, or consent.

When I face her again, ten years on, nothing has changed.

Especially not the urge to make her mine.

If anything, it's only gotten stronger.

She's a complication.

One I may not let go of the second time around.

FRANKIE

He knows better than to lurk.

Until recently, I never knew he watched me.

Looked over me. Followed me.

I never asked him to.

He just hid in the shadows when he thought I didn't know.

The fact is, I liked it. Far too much.

He excited me in a way no man ever has. Not that I'd admit it.

But he took something from me, unbeknown to him.

And he can never take it back.

Even if my body, and my soul, are the very things to betray me.

I can't let him know he has the power to end me.

It's all I have left.

BRACKEN RIDGE
REBELS
ARIZONA
M · C
M · C

CHAPTER 1

NITRO

TEN YEARS EARLIER

I wake up and there's chaos all around me.

I can't make out the words, but people are shouting, and I feel cold.

I try to focus my eyes, but everything is hazy.

I feel a hand on my shoulder and when I look again, a woman's face comes into view.

She's like an angel. An apparition.

This can't be.

"Am I dead?" I mutter, even though I'm not sure if my mouth is even working.

She looks down at me, perplexed, and I've got a feeling none of what I just said made any sense.

"Don't try to talk," she tells me, her face kind and warm. "Just hold on."

What does she mean by that?

Where am I?

I've never been show kindness and compassion before.

All I've ever known is violence and terror.

Fast women.

Fast motorcycle clubs.

A fast life.

But I'm mesmerized by her. It's why this can't be real.

As if reading my mind, she goes on, "You're in the hospital, sir, and you've been shot."

I swallow hard, not sure why I can't feel my body. Maybe this is how it is when you're dying. Fuck that. I've got more to do, like this chick. I need to know who she is.

If I'm about to die, then I definitely want her face being the last one I see. I'll die a happy man.

Instead, I'm being wheeled down a hallway, and it's then I realize, she's got her hands on me.

I glance down.

She's straddled over my body, to be precise, but it's not that kind of straddle. Unfortunately.

Her riding me would be the gateway to the most exquisite Heaven, not the Hell where I'm headed.

She has a towel pressed up against my chest with blood all over it.

"Why are you on top of me?" I garble.

Even her voice is pretty. "I have to try to suppress the bleeding until we get you into the OR. It's quicker to sit while we move."

My eyes go wide… "No fuckin' docs…no surgeon…I

can't…"

She shakes her head, holding me down. Usually, I could overpower any woman, especially this slight little thing, but I'm weak. So weak, I can't even sit up. It hurts to blink my eyelids.

"Just don't try to talk," she tells me again as someone says something to her, and she nods. Then her eyes are back on mine. Her hair is like spun silk, her auburn waves tied back in a long ponytail. She looks young.

"Are you old enough to be doin' that?" I grimace. Fuck, it even hurts to talk.

She smiles again. "I'm an intern. This is my first gunshot wound."

"Try not to look too pleased about it," I mutter.

She presses down again as she looks up at someone and they say something, to which she shakes her head. What are they saying?

I stare at the ceiling, feeling the tightness in my chest. Wondering if we'll ever get to our destination, not that it matters. Heaven is here with her. Fuck anywhere else.

I would get shot all over again just to see her look down at me.

"It's my fuckin' birthday," I say.

She frowns. "It is?"

"Yeah."

"I'd say happy birthday, but I'm not sure it really is

one." She makes me laugh, and I start coughing, the pain ripping through me as someone shoves something into my arm. "It'll help with the pain," she goes on.

"Lookin' at you helps with the pain, sweetheart."

She ignores me. "Do you know who shot you?"

Club rules.

Nobody in the Phoenix Fury MC will be saying shit, and neither will I.

This motorcycle club is extreme, and they won't think twice about slitting my throat if I say anything about how I got shot or by whom. They did drop me here at ER after all, so at least there's that. They could've left me in the gutter where they found me.

I shake my head. "Got robbed."

I know the pigs will be all over this.

So, I'll do what I do best, fake amnesia. I did hit my head pretty hard, after all.

She purses her lips. I'm unsure if she believes me, and I'm not sure why it even matters.

"You're pretty," I tell her. "If I die, just know I'm happy that yours is the last face I got to see."

She frowns some more. "You're not going to die. What's your name?"

As she looks down at my vest, my dirty patch tells her my name.

"You can read."

She shakes her head. "Not your biker name, your real name."

I don't know why I feel the need to tell her shit; but this could be my last conversation.

I may as well not be a total asshole.

"Adam."

She smiles again, tightly this time.

"What?" I close my eyes and wince; the pain is starting to ease off. The drugs are kicking in, and thank fuck for that. It was better when I was passed out.

She shakes it off.

"What?" I demand.

She rolls her lips. "Adam is far too pretty a name for a man like you."

I snort, but that doesn't help. I end up choking and then I'm coughing up blood.

Fuck.

This isn't good.

She's now covered in it.

There go my chances of a first date.

"Sorry." I haven't apologized for shit ever in my life. It seems being shot agrees with me. Maybe if I stay long enough, she'll hear me confess.

"Don't worry about it."

Someone stabs something else into my arm as we swing through a set of double doors.

"What was that?"

"The drip just went in; it'll take hold faster."

"Wow, you can find a vein that quick?"

"We're here to please, Adam. You're not dying on my watch."

I fuckin' like this chick. "Wish you were ridin' me," I mutter, my eyes closing. I know that my words aren't coming out right. "Need to get out of here."

She shakes her head. "No, you need to rest."

"Tell me your name."

"You won't remember it. You're heavily sedated," she says.

I begin to see two of her.

"Tell me," I demand. "I want to hear it. Give a man his last, dying wish."

"Frankie," she says. "And you're not dying, like I said."

I nod, closing my eyes again. "Frankie," I mutter. "Fuckin' beautiful."

That was the night I almost died.

And that was how it all began.

My obsession with Frankie Stevens.

I lived.

And she became the object of my affection, from afar.

She nursed me back to health, so to speak, and checked on me every day after surgery.

She even kicked the cops out when they came to question me about the shooting. I faked amnesia and told the pigs I didn't remember anything. Safest way, really; that way nobody has to get hurt. Not me. My club. Or my girl.

Tex, the club President, wouldn't be too happy with me spilling my guts. I'd be better off having that bullet lodged inside my chest while I choke on my own blood, or better still, a bullet to the brain would be nice and quick.

The man is ruthless. But that's what you get when you enter a notorious 1% club and expect fucking Disneyland. It ain't gonna happen.

My other brothers like Smokey, the V.P., and Griller, the club's Sergeant at Arms, would have my back, but they weren't the ones who dropped me off at emergency. In fact, the club went into a major disagreement after I survived the shooting. It's not the first time that the committee members have disagreed with the decision of the club Prez. The truth is, Tex has been skating on thin ice for a long time, and everyone can see change coming.

I'm not part of the committee, so I don't get to sit in on the round table meetings, but you don't have to be a genius to guess when the V.P. isn't happy with the decisions being made.

I can smell trouble a mile away.

But for now, I'll watch my girl. I'll make sure she's safe because that's the promise I made to myself when I lived through the surgery that saved my life.

I didn't know that Frankie was an intern, but she may have told me, since I do remember her saying it was her first gunshot wound. Hopefully, it'll be her last, but this is a notorious part of town, and we're not the only motorcycle club in Phoenix with enemies.

Now I spend every free moment I have making sure she's safe.

At least, that's what I tell myself.

I also make sure she never sees me. It's better if she forgot I ever existed; first gunshot wound or not, but I can't seem to tear myself away fully.

Aside from the day I left the hospital, I've never run into her face to face. But I've seen her every other day, as I keep out of sight.

How could I stay away? I'm like a moth to a flame. She draws me to her like nothing I've ever felt before. It's not normal.

I watch her from the shadows.

I know her daily routine. Her days off. When she goes to the laundromat. When she has coffee with friends, none of them male. I'd be inclined to cut out any man's throat who could potentially take what's mine.

And she is mine.

She just doesn't know it yet, or at least, that's what I tell myself in my fantasy. Because in that world, the one where I get the girl, I can have anything I want.

In my fantasy, she loves it. She loves me watching. She gets off on it. Her skin is so soft, so delicate. There is nothing about her I'd ever want to change, except her frown. She frowns a lot.

Sometimes when I watch her, I'm reminded that we are all very complex creatures. She doesn't smile like she did to me that night when she sat on top of me and pumped my heart back to life. She seems off in her own world. Lost in her own fantasies.

Maybe she has good reason to. I guess a job like hers can't be easy.

Holding another person's life in your hands, the stress alone would be through the roof.

There's something oddly alluring about a woman you simply cannot have.

I want to go talk to her.

I want to follow her and have her invite me into her apartment.

I want her to want me.

It sounds fuckin' needy, but it's how I am.

I have needs that no woman could ever quench, except Frankie Stevens.

She's the epitome of perfection.

And there is no way in the world she's not gonna be mine.

I've been living in the dirty, stinking clubhouse for about six months. I've been proving myself to the club, trying to get patched in earlier than the required minimum of one year, and you'd think after getting fuckin' shot, that would count for something, right?

Not in this club.

Tex gripped me on the shoulder and told me I'd taken one for the team, then shoved a beer in my face. To say I'm disappointed is an understatement, but I know Smokey has my back.

He's a good guy. Fuck knows how he puts up with Tex and his array of bullshit, but they go back a long way.

I shouldn't be thinking that about my own President, but he doesn't make it easy. If anything, he goes out of his way to be a cruel, sick fuck.

Smokey's been disturbed by some of the shit he's pulled, and sometimes I think they're all waiting for him to snap, but I say; why wait?

He has no respect for women, which is not uncommon in a club like this one. A lot of the men don't. After the shit my own father pulled, you would think I'd be a woman hater too, but unlike him, I can think for myself.

I've never touched a woman in anger in my life. I may like rough sex; hell, the freakier the better, but I've never struck a woman or purposely treated a woman like shit.

Every time one of Tex's girls comes out of his private quarters looking a little worse for wear, I want to fuckin' smack the cunt for touching them like that.

I know he hits them. And I know that they act like they don't care. But honestly, how good could that actually be?

For some reason, bagging the Club Prez is measured as high as fuckin' a rock star. And I honestly don't get it. It's not like the fucker is Mick Jagger.

I'll bide my time.

He'll get what's coming to him.

For now, I have to toe the line.

If I get kicked out of here, then I'm done.

Smokey took me under his wing when I was down and out. I started tinkering around with motorbikes for fun. I've always been able to fix shit, and I don't find it hard.

I enjoy it. In fact, it's one of the few things I do enjoy aside from the other perks of the club; free booze and women. Not that as a prospect I get a choice, like the patched members do. Beggars can't be choosers.

Some of the chicks are better than others, that goes without saying. Some are more eager to please, and not that many are interested in prospects, but they've taken a shining to me because of my looks.

I inherited my baby face from my mother, according to my drunken father.

And it has served me well. I don't know what it is about my face, but women always want to save me.

When I was about ten, my dad remarried. I have two stepsisters, Tina and Lucy. I'm close with Lucy, or rather, I was. After three years, my stepmom kicked my dad out when she couldn't take any more of his drunken bullshit, not that she was mother of the year.

I went with him, but when I started getting into trouble and he started raising his fists, I went to live with her.

Things just evolved from bad to worse from there.

She hated my guts.

Lucy, though, she was like the mom I never had. Even though she was only eighteen at the time, she was always patient and kind, always asking about my day and taking an interest in me. I miss her. I wish things could be different, but when the shit hit the fan after I fucked up and got in trouble, I split. I was thirteen. I knew nothing.

Life on the street is pretty fucked up, but you grow up fast.

There's a loud banging on my door, breaking me out of my reverie.

I crack an eye open and turn over in my bed.

"What?" I yell out.

"Sun's up, fucker," Griller yells through my door.

I groan.

Griller is the Sergeant at Arms for the club, and whenever he comes calling, it ain't good.

"Surely there's someone else's life you can ruin?" I grunt.

"Don't make me come in there, fuckface."

I puff out my cheeks. "There ain't no rest for the wicked, right, bro?"

"You got it."

"Not even a gunshot wound counts for anythin' these days," I complain.

"You fucked two sweet butts as a reward. Should be thankful."

That's true. I should be. But I was still so doped up, I barely remember.

He stomps off, and I'm relieved that he didn't come in and drag me out of bed.

The sun isn't even up yet.

My duties as a prospect include anything and everything, and usually, it's the shittiest jobs in the world.

At least I've got hours before I have to go out.

My girl doesn't start work until tonight.

Whether she likes it or not, I'm going to watch over her.

I owe her. No matter what she says.

If I stop and think about if it's wrong to practically

stalk her, then I'll cuss myself out and realize I probably shouldn't be doing it. But I can't seem to stop.

She's put a spell on me.

One that I have no intention of coming out from under.

I like it here.

Seeing her, even like this, is the only fuckin' enjoyment I get in this godforsaken place.

And I'm gonna ride that high for as long as I can.

She needs to be safe, and the only way I can guarantee that is if I'm close.

Nitro

BRACKEN RIDGE
REBELS
ARIZONA
M · C

CHAPTER 2

FRANKIE

"Whatever happened to that guy?" Adele asks me as we eat lunch in the cafeteria.

I frown. "What guy?"

She rolls her eyes, like it should be obvious. "The one who got shot."

My heart skips a beat. Ah yes, him.

Adam.

I put on my no-nonsense face. Adele and I have gotten pretty close over the last few months, but I still don't feel right discussing him, and I don't know why. Maybe it's the trauma.

They lost him a couple of times in the operating room.

"Oh," I say.

"Yeah, oh. He came around here looking for you, remember?"

"Yes, I remember, he was…intense."

She snorts. "He's hot as fuck."

I glance her way. While I don't disagree with that, he does scare me a little bit. Or rather, what he's part of.

I've led a sheltered life. The ultimate little rich girl, some would say. And he's a walk on the wild side.

For one, he's part of a motorcycle gang, and not just any gang, the Phoenix Fury.

Everyone around here knows that club is trouble.

They're into all sorts of illegal activities, and judging by what he was brought into emergency for, I don't doubt that someone shot him for payback, or a deal gone wrong.

I remember the dirty worn patch that had his name on the front, then the words 'Prospect' on the back. I don't even know what that means in biker terms, but I can guarantee that it isn't anything good.

Even knowing all of that, I can't stop thinking about that night. About him.

That was my first gunshot wound, and it was terrifying.

The trouble is, since that night, I've questioned whether I am cut out to be a doctor in the emergency department, or any department.

I'm in my third year, and I finally get to be around real-life situations, and it's freaking scary sometimes.

Adele is still staring at me. "You're thinking about him now, aren't you?"

"No!" I whisper-shout. "I'm actually considering my options in the emergency department. That was pretty crazy. I've never seen so much blood."

She bites into her sandwich and shrugs again. I wish

I could just brush things off like she does, be strong, be courageous. "But you saved the guy, that's what it's all about."

I run a hand through my hair and tug on my ponytail, playing with the ends like I do when I'm nervous. "Yes, but maybe I got lucky. What if I did something wrong and then he didn't make it?"

She frowns. "You're an intern, Frankie, not a surgeon. You got him to surgery without croaking. Be thankful for small mercies."

I know she's right.

It's one of the first things they teach you, but trying to keep emotions separate is really hard.

I don't know how to separate the two.

If I don't keep my emotions in check and work out how to stay focused, then I may as well kiss my short-lived medical career goodbye.

I think about my parents and about how disappointed they'd be if I pulled out.

It's not like in my family, I could just do a normal job like be a hairdresser or work in a restaurant or be a flight attendant. No. All the Stevens have been to college, and have gone on to have successful careers that they deem appropriate. My mother is a lawyer, and my father is a doctor.

All of them have achieved great things.

None of them have failed.

My father is actually a surgeon at this very hospital, and not just any surgeon, he's celebrated. He was also the one to operate on Adam. He saved his life.

Imagining the shock on my father's face if I decided to quit is too much to bear.

Just as I'm thinking it, I feel a hand on my shoulder.

I turn and see my father standing behind me. He smiles and I smile back.

"Hey, Dad," I say.

"Hi, Kiddo." He glances up to Adele. "Hello, young lady."

Adele beams at him. "Hi, Doctor Stevens."

My father is very well respected and honored surgeon in Phoenix. He's at the top of his game.

To say he's a bit of a celebrity is an understatement.

I swallow the lump in my throat.

I'll never live up to his expectations.

He's my hero and my biggest supporter, but he's also the one person in my life that looks at me with rose-tinted glasses on. He thinks everything I do should be done with precision. With a goal in mind. His way.

And while I'm on board with most of that, I can't do things his way, because I'm not like him.

He's a wonderful surgeon, and he's not a bad father, but he has a confidence about him that I have not yet mastered at twenty-five. I know that will come in time, but all I see when we meet each other in the halls at work is how much I could disappoint him if I fail.

"How is your day going, honey?" And he still refuses to call me Doctor Stevens.

One day, I will graduate to that; I just don't know when that will be.

"It's going okay. We're restocking the medical supplies today, and then we're going to do rounds with Doctor Samuels."

He smiles at the first part, then frowns when I mention Doctor Trent Samuels.

From what I've heard, he's a well-known womanizer; or to put it bluntly, he'll screw anything that moves. But we're his students, and he's far from creepy. He's got a warm charisma and is actually pretty cool.

My father, however, hates him with a passion that I've not quite figured out the reason for.

"Hm. Well, let me know if you need anything, I'm only a phone call away."

I nod. "Okay, thanks." You can go now. People are starting to stare.

"Don't forget," he calls over his shoulder as he saunters off. "Taco Tuesday."

I face palm myself, and I don't even get the words out, when Carly and Olivia, two other interns, come skipping over.

"Was that Doctor Thomas Stevens?" Carly gushes as

she takes a seat next to me, Olivia following suit. They both have the same starry eyes.

"Uh, yeah." Don't they know this already?

I don't advertise who my dad is or that I'm his daughter. I want to make it in this field on my own merits without any influence from him. But I was also fairly certain almost everyone knows we're related. Maybe they didn't get the memo.

"He's so fucking sexy!" Olivia adds, peeking over my shoulder to watch my father leave the room.

I almost throw up in my mouth.

I hear Adele snicker next to me.

"Uh, okay." Please go away now.

They haven't even put two and two together yet that we have the same last name, but then again, they've only just been transferred to our program and haven't exactly cottoned on to simple things like last names.

"Don't you think so, Frankie? He's a fucking God around here."

Don't I know it.

My dad, the savior of Phoenix Memorial Hospital.

He is a God.

Everyone loves him.

Everyone wants to be him.

He saves people. His track record is second to none.

And I don't mean to sound ungrateful, because I can

learn a great deal from him, but I wish I'd been transferred to any other hospital where I get to just be a normal intern. Living in his shadow is heavier than I thought it would be.

Other doctors and my peers look at me expectantly whenever they fire out a question on our rounds, as if because I'm Thomas Stevens' daughter, I should also know everything that is lodged inside his brain.

It makes me feel a little inferior.

I stare at her, unable to form words.

"You look like you've seen a ghost," Carly says, her eyebrows knitting together. "Are you all right?"

"That's her dad, idiot," Adele butts in, subtle as usual.

At least one person around here has got my back.

Carly's eyes almost bug out of her head, a little insultingly, as she looks me up and down.

"Really?"

I fake smile. "Really."

"Holy shit," Olivia says, leaning closer to me, inspecting me like I'm some science project. "What is like living with him?"

Adele snorts again.

The girls ignore her, too fascinated with this new information.

Cheers, Adele. Way to go. Now I've got two new friends who probably won't leave me alone.

"Pretty boring," I reply, monotone.

Carly tucks her hair behind her ears. "Is your dad… married?"

My eyes dart up at her. "Yes," I snap. "Happily. To my mother."

She sits back in her chair, a mixture of disappointment and also awe crossing her face.

It's disgusting. Thinking about my dad like that.

I know he's a handsome guy and all, but fucking EW.

"This is so cool!" Olivia isn't good with social cues and clearly doesn't get that I don't want to talk about this.

I shoot Adele daggers as she tucks into her moon pie happily, shooting me a big grin.

Three. Two. One…

"Are you going to be a surgeon too?" Carly asks, her eyes searching mine like she's a federal agent, not an intern who should mind her business.

"I haven't decided yet."

"But he must be super proud of you, right? To be following in his footsteps?" she craps on.

I refrain from rolling my eyes. I don't want to be rude.

The Stevens family have a reputation to uphold.

We do not cause scenes. We keep the family name up there with the best families in Phoenix, like royalty. And it's all so goddamn fake.

My parents are far from perfect…

I shake that off.

"I guess so." Can't they tell from my tone that I DON'T WANT TO TALK ABOUT THIS?

"Hey!" Adele interrupts. "Pretty sure I just saw Doctor Samuels heading to the blood bank…don't we have him for our rounds…" She doesn't even get the rest of the words out as the girls are up out of their seats and are scurrying across the room like little lambs to the slaughter.

I turn to look at her as she smiles, taking the last bite of her pie. "You're welcome."

"You suck."

"I do, actually. Very well, in fact, but you wanted rid of them, right? Problem solved. Now I can finish this in peace without having dirty thoughts about your dad."

"That's so disgusting."

"For you, yeah."

I sigh loudly. "Not just about that. Why did you tell them he was my dad?"

She clucks her tongue. "Uh, duh, because he is? And they're gonna find out soon enough, sweet cheeks, so suck it up. You've got to get used to it."

I know she's right. "You've no idea what it's like. I've big shoes to fill, and half the time, I don't even know if I'm cut out for it."

She looks at me with sympathy in her eyes. I know we're going to be good friends. Anyone who can clear a room that fast deserves respect.

"You're just saying that because you're comparing yourself to him. You're your own person, Frankie. All jokes aside, your dad's great and all, but he's not a God. He's a man, first and foremost. You've got to put it into perspective, or you'll drive yourself mad."

"That's a little hard when he's getting the keys to the city in a few weeks."

She gives me a surprised look.

"Yeah," I mutter. "You were saying?"

She shakes it off. "That doesn't matter. You will achieve many things, Frankie. I know it. You have that look about you. But you've got to stop overthinking it. Accept it, because your dad isn't gonna let up, and neither are girls like Carly and Olivia, who will want to know you because of your family connections. Use it to your advantage."

I shoot her a look. "And how do I do that?"

She shrugs. "Easy. Use it to pick up hot guys."

I snort a laugh, and she follows suit.

"Is this what I have to put up with for the rest of the year?" I groan.

"What? My charm and honesty? It could be worse; your intern buddy could be Carly who wants to fuck your dad right after she fucks Doctor Samuels."

"Please refrain from talking."

She laughs again. "I don't know who I feel sorrier for."

I do not need those thoughts in my head.

"My dad. Doctor Samuels is a well-known womanizer who screws anything in a skirt, but you didn't hear that from me."

She leans in, her interest piqued. "Even his students?"

I give her a pointed look. "Is your mind always on the pepperoni?"

"Yes. He is pretty hot, so sue me. I'm just stating the obvious."

"He's also very good at what he does," I remind her.

We pack up our trays, lunchtime almost over.

"Though," she adds, walking to the bin. "I'd still do your dad over him."

I shriek and throw my balled-up foil wrapper at her head. She ducks, and it skits across the room, hitting someone else in the head.

"I'm so sorry!" I call out, as Adele falls about laughing, and I tug onto her arm, dragging her out of the cafeteria, not even waiting to see who it was I hit.

"You are so gross," I add through gritted teeth.

"That's why you love me, babe."

I can see what they all see in Doctor Samuels.

We've only had a couple of rounds together, and I was busy taking notes.

But as I study him, I know why everyone flocks to him like he's the shepherd.

He has a sunny, tan complexion, sandy blonde hair, good cheekbones, and the bluest eyes I've ever seen. He's probably not a day over thirty-five.

He's like California sunshine, and doesn't he know it.

He doesn't make a big fuss, but manages to keep all our attention on him as he makes jokes and tells us to call him Doctor Sam.

I can see why my dad takes offense. He's not serious enough.

My father takes his job very seriously; it's not play time.

"Doctor Stevens," he says, snapping me out of my reverie. I realize he's asked me a question.

Shit.

Of course, everyone turns to look at me.

I glance at the patient in the bed, who has also turned to look expectantly at me, too.

"Uh, I would offer an EKG and then wait for the bloodwork to come back. That way, we could rule out the possibility of a stroke, and in the meantime, keep the patient calm and monitor their blood pressure." I think.

The corners of his mouth turn up.

"Very good," he drawls, his eyes dancing with amusement. "Of course, you come from a long line of exemplary doctors, so I wouldn't expect anything less."

I smile tightly. At least he didn't go on about it.

I already feel like I've got a target on my back as it is. I don't need any more arrows.

We move on, and I follow behind as Adele eyes me, her smile knowing. She waggles her eyebrows and makes a blowjob gesture with her fist and her mouth.

I give her wide eyes.

Now is not the time or the place, but she still laughs at my annoyed face.

At least this is a distraction from her talking about my dad, or about Adam nonstop.

That's the one thing I really just can't handle, and I've no reason why.

BRACKEN RIDGE
REBELS
ARIZONA
M · C

CHAPTER 3

NITRO

I don't like him.

He watches her too closely, more closely than I do, and when she turns to leave, his eyes drop to her ass. That gesture alone makes me want to slit his throat.

He's one of the doctors here. I've seen him in the halls, his students following behind him like faithful little servants as he walks high and mighty, like he's God's gift to the universe.

Whenever I see Frankie, she's trailing behind, her friend prattling on as she pretends to listen.

There's something about the way she holds herself. Her shoulders slumped. Her head hanging down. Her whole demeanor, it's like she's trying to not be seen.

I don't understand it.

She's beautiful on every level, but so much more than that.

When she was sitting on top of me, her hands covered in my blood as she kept me from bleeding to death, she had that look in her eye. The look that told me I was gonna be okay, no matter what. That she's got this. That she wasn't letting me go, not on my watch.

Those were her words, and I believed them.

I'm shocked, and saddened, to see her in this state. I wonder what has happened.

The woman I watch, walking with her body slumped over, is not the same one who kept me believing I wasn't going to die.

It throws me.

It pisses me off.

It makes me want to choke whoever did this to her, whoever put a frown on her face.

Is it the doctor she follows on her rounds?

Is it just the pressure of the internship? That shit can't be easy.

I watch her with her friend, the one who never stops talking.

I don't know why, call it a gut instinct, but I get the feeling this girl has her back.

I can't be the only one who thinks she doesn't light up the whole world.

My phone goes off. I quickly grab it from my pocket and hope I don't get called back to the clubhouse; I haven't had my fill of her yet. I want to watch her a little longer, make sure she's okay.

I haven't even had the balls to face her. Aside from when I left the hospital, all patched up.

I see it's Hoax, one of the other prospects. "Dude, Tex is lookin' for you."

Fuck.

"What the fuck for?"

"Dunno. Didn't sound good."

When does it ever?

I run a hand through my hair, torn. I clear my throat. "I'll be there in ten."

"Better make it five. He's pissed about something."

"Thanks for the heads up."

I snap my phone shut. Fucking piece of shit.

I can't think of what I've done this time, aside from being shot. But he can't be entirely pissed about that. I didn't squeal, and the pigs don't know shit, and, oh yeah, I almost died.

Tex doesn't give a shit.

I'm a nobody.

A fucking piece of shit prospect who's disposable.

Even this gig, as much as I grin and bear it every goddamn day, is better than being on the streets. I get a hot meal or two every day. A dry, warm place to sleep, and for the most part, a club of brothers who look out for one another.

The jobs I have to do are no shittier than what I'd be doing on the street, In fact, the streets are far worse.

At least when I got shot, they managed to get me to a hospital.

I know Smokey is still pissed about that whole thing. He and Tex had a massive disagreement, and it's shaken the core of the club. The instability is proving to be taking a toll on everyone.

It's like watching the Titanic about to sink.

But Tex doesn't seem to give a shit; it's his way or the highway.

I wish things could be different in the club. I wish I had respect for my Prez, but I just don't.

I'll bide my time. Work my way up in the ranks, and maybe in time, things will change.

Maybe Smokey will finally get his chance at running the club, and Tex will get run out.

Something tells me that Tex isn't the kind of man that would go down without a fight, but if a unanimous vote goes to the table with the executive committee, then he will be voted out.

I wish I didn't have to go back to the club just now.

I shouldn't be thinking like this. My club comes before pussy.

Everything else comes before pussy.

But with Frankie, nothing is normal.

My connection to her, even though one-sided, to me, feels like the only thing that is keeping me fixed to the ground.

Just the fucking thought of her.

I watch her ponytail swaying as she walks. She's cute in her white overcoat.

As ridiculous as it sounds, my attraction isn't completely sexual with her. It's everything else about her that keeps me hanging around here.

I've never felt this strongly about a woman.

Yet, I know I can't lurk in this hallway for the rest of the day, not when I have club shit to go and see to, and probably get the shit kicked out of me for.

If anyone finds out this is what I've been doing, even if it is on my own time, they will want to know about her. I can't have that. But I do need to get some more information about Frankie Stevens.

I know nothing about her aside from her car, her workplace, and where she lives.

Yeah, I'm not above following her home to see where she resides. And I was surprised to learn she has a new apartment on the edge of town in one of the new complexes. It's in a good neighborhood. She also drives a nice car, one that is far too nice to be purchased on a intern's wage. Something tells me her family has money.

Maybe she's a trust fund baby. It would explain a lot.

Material shit doesn't matter to me, it never has. But that's easy to say when you have nothing.

I hope I'll start making some good coin once I'm patched in, then I'll get a cut, but let's face facts, I'm never gonna be in the same circle as Frankie.

I'm not gonna be the man giving her what she needs. She wouldn't look twice at me on the street, much less take me to her bed.

I'm scum to her, like I am to most people.

And I'm okay with that.

This fantasy I live in is mine and mine alone. I've made peace with it.

Just to get to see her is like some fucking mirage. Yeah, I've got an obsession.

She's the only thing I look forward to when I've had a shit day. Sometimes I sit on my sled, idling outside her apartment, looking up to the window, waiting until the lights go out.

I don't honestly know what I'd do if a man came over. I couldn't let that happen.

I'd have to fuck him up.

I'm depraved, but I want her to want me. Somewhere in the deep, murky depths of my fucked-up mind and mangled heart – what's left of it – I want her to look at me like she's glad to see me. Like she fuckin' cares.

She's some kind of angel, not like the women I know. Not like any person I know. Maybe aside from my sister, Lucy, she's the only other women I've looked up to and respected. And I haven't seen her for so long. I've thought about looking for her, but coming back into her life now would be a wrong move.

I've got my own demons, and I don't need to drag them up and upset my sister, the one I look up to the most.

I close my eyes.

So many regrets.

I take one long last look at the back of my girl, disappearing down the hall, and I feel my heart in my chest lurch at being dragged away from her.

I know this is wrong.

Watching her like this. But I'm not leering at her like that fuckface doctor.

Yeah, I need to find out more about him too.

When I get back to the clubhouse, I walk straight to the office where Snitch is working on the computer. He's the club's hacker, and while he looks like he needs a hot bath and a decent, hearty meal, he's smart as fuck. And for some reason, he likes me.

Being a prospect means I don't get shit at this club, and Tex will kick his ass if he finds out I'm getting favors, but if I ask him for something, I know he'll get it for me. We're buddies.

He gives me a chin lift when I approach. "Hey, fucker."

I give him a smile. "How's it hangin'?"

"You hear Tex is lookin' for you?"

I run a hand over my face for about the tenth time. I do that when I'm stressed. "Good news travels fast."

"What d'ya need?"

"Anything you can give me on Frankie Stevens. Works at Phoenix Memorial Hospital as an intern."

"The doc that kept you together?"

"The very one."

"What exactly do you need?"

"Personal stuff."

"Financial?"

"Nah, just family life, friends, who she's seeing…" I say that last part with gritted teeth, and I can't for the life bring myself to say the words, who she's fucking.

From what I've seen, it seems that Frankie Stevens is all work and no play, and that makes my mood feel a little better, though I need concrete details.

"Also, there's this other doctor who she does her rounds with, Trent Samuels." I managed to get his name off the registrar as I left. "I need to know what his deal is. I don't like him."

"This is gonna cost ya."

I can't help my smile, though I rarely show any emotion to anyone. "Yeah? What this time?"

"Gotta try and get one of those pretty fender fluffs in here, under the desk."

I can't help the laugh that leaves my lips. "Are you fuckin' serious? I don't have any say with the sweet butts, Tex will kick my ass."

"Not sweet butts, the chicks that hang off you. You've got enough of them. How about sharin' the love?"

He's right, they do hang off me, but I've got to keep a lid on it around the brothers. They see it as a challenge and get shitty when women pay me attention.

I'm dog shit.

And if they hang off me too much, they beat the shit out of me.

"I'll see what I can do." I look down at his dirty t-shirt and torn vest. "You know, it may help if you tidy yourself up a bit, bro. Chicks dig a dude who looks a little less… disheveled."

He gives me a strange look, then looks down at himself, as if he's only just considered it.

"I suppose…"

I shake my head. He really is fuckin' hopeless.

"But then again, what would I know?"

I hear his footsteps before I even get to turn around.

Tex is a big man. Not someone I'd intentionally get into a fight with.

I turn just as he gets to me, then the king hits me in the face. It's so hard, he knocks me over. I wasn't prepared for it, and that's not like me. I'm becoming complacent.

Shit.

I didn't bang his ol' lady or anything. In fact, I haven't banged anyone since I got fixed up.

It's been over six weeks.

I don't say anything. I just hold my jaw and move it a few times, glad it isn't broken.

I really wanna fly up and punch the shit out of him. I've been gaining muscle and working out; I'm not where I need to be yet, but I'm getting there.

"Wanna know what that was for?" He glares down at me, and I don't know if he's going to kick me in the head or shoot me.

I don't dare answer, I just nod.

He stands for a few more moments, then he reaches a hand down to help me up.

I frown, taking it as he hauls me to my feet, then he slaps me hard on the back, almost knocking the wind out of me.

"You're gettin' patched in, fuckface."

I stare at him; I can't believe it.

"Really?" I ask, as if I've misheard.

He grins. "Takin' a bullet for one of our own counts in this club, and not snitchin', even fuckin' better."
He grips my shoulder as I take in his words.

No more prospecting?

This is very unexpected; I have six months to go, at least. Usually, they'll make you grovel longer just to prove a point.

"Party this weekend," he goes on. "You know the drill.

Make sure you bring your knuckle dusters because I know Griller wants a poke at you before you're patched in."

It's a ritual. Smack the shit out of the prospect to initiate them.

I don't care about that. They can fuck me up. Nothing could ever be as bad as getting shot.

And if it means I get sent to emergency again, all the better I'll be for it.

Then I'll get to see my girl again.

Fuck.

I need to make a move on her. My feet move in her direction, but my head won't let me close the distance. I know I can't.

Even being patched in, this isn't the life for her.

She wouldn't want me like that anyway. I was her patient, not her fuckboy.

Though I'd let her use me any which way she wanted. I'd take anything she wanted to give me, even the crumbs.

One thing is for sure, I've got it bad for Frankie Stevens. And she doesn't even know I'm alive.

BRACKEN RIDGE
REBELS
ARIZONA
M · C

CHAPTER 4

FRANKIE

Today dragged on. But I think I'm becoming Doctor Samuels' new favorite student.

It isn't lost on me that he pays me more attention than some of the others in our group, but some of them really don't know what they're doing, nor do they brush up on their homework. And this is our third year. There's no excuse for laziness.

People think it's so easy for me because my father is a surgeon, but I have to work twice as hard. Not just to appease my peers, but also my father; if I can't hack it, that isn't something he'll be able to understand, or recover from. With my parents, appearances are everything.

Such as tonight's charity dinner.

The last thing I feel like doing is going to a stuffy, over-priced dinner, and rubbing shoulders with high society, fake smiling while people pay hundreds of dollars for a plate of food. I remind myself that it is for a good cause, but I don't like the fact my father insists on dragging me along. I even have to dress up for the occasion.

I have plenty of nice clothes, but my favorite thing to wear is jeans or sweats and a t-shirt. After being in pants and sometimes scrubs all day, I just want to climb into my loungewear and veg out. My downtime is precious because I have very little of it.

When my parents collect me at 8pm, I've managed to pull myself together in a fitted, classic black dress, with heels and a small clutch that barely fits my phone.

As I climb into my parents' car, my mother is on the phone. She gives me a wave as my eyes meet my father's.

"Hi, sweetie, how was your day?"

"Good," I say as I plant myself in the backseat. "We did rounds and visited the maternity ward. I'm in emergency again next week." I want to add Doctor Samuels is happy with my progress, but I bite my tongue. Every time I mention him, Dad's nostrils flair.

He pulls out into the evening traffic.

"You really won't learn anything in the maternity ward." He scoffs, almost like it's a joke. "Your hands are skilled for surgery, Frankie, just like mine. You come from a long line of prestigious doctors and surgeons, none of them bothered with the maternity wing. What is Doctor Samuels thinking?" He fails to mention that everyone in that long line were men.

Then, because he's annoying me so much, I say, "He's

actually a really great teacher, Dad. I'm learning a lot from him."

His eyes meet mine in the rearview mirror. "I told you I don't like him, and trust me when I say I did everything in my power to get your name on another list.

My eyes go wide.

My mother spares him a glance, even though she's still talking, and I can't decipher the look on her face.

He ignores her.

"What? Why?" I ask, dumbfounded.

Trent Samuels is a great doctor. Warm. Encouraging. He doesn't dismiss me or make me feel stupid, unlike my father. He takes a genuine interest.

"You know why. Those rumors about him are true."

My mom still talks on the phone, holding one finger to her ear to block out my father's rising voice.

"What rumors are those?" I play dumb, but I'm not stupid. I know all about it.

"He's a womanizer," he says finally. "You already know this."

"Dad, I'm an intern, do you really think he's going to try something with me? Is that it?"

"I wouldn't trust that asshole as far as I could throw him," he mutters.

"If he's so cavalier, then why hasn't he been fired?"

Dad shifts in his seat. "Money talks, Frankie, don't ever

forget that."

I don't really see Doctor Samuels as being a creepazoid. Sure, he's got the looks, nice car, money, a perfect job, and probably a body to die for under his white coat. He's got it all.

I doubt there is anything that he can't just get by clicking his fingers. There is certainly no shortage of minions at the hospital that run around for him, doing whatever he says.

I'm one of them.

But he's never hit on me, and as far as I know, any of my fellow interns.

He's anything but a creep.

We ride the rest of the way in silence.

I'm furious with my father. I don't get why he drags me along to these things, says stupid shit about my mentor, and then ignores me for the duration of the journey.

When my mom's off the phone, she turns to me. "Frankie sweetie, it's time we went shopping."

Translation: she doesn't like what I'm wearing.

It's Calvin Klein, for pity's sake.

"Hello to you too, Mom," I mutter.

She's an attractive woman. Well dressed and intelligent. I have the look of my father, while mom has chestnut hair cut into a simple but elegant bob and her makeup, as usual, is perfect with nothing out of place. She's more like my brother Christopher.

That reminds me, Christopher tried to call me earlier. I don't know why he gets out of coming here tonight, and I'm about to ask, when Mom glances at Dad and shakes her head. "You've put her in a bad mood, Thomas, and we haven't even gotten to the party yet."

I love it when they talk like I'm not even here.

"I'm not in a bad mood," I shoot back. "I'm fine."

Mom isn't satisfied. She smooths one side of her hair down and checks her phone with a sigh.

"If the mayor approaches, for God's sake, someone rescue me after five minutes if he's still talking. If he's drunk, he gets too friendly and starts to touch," she goes on, scrolling through her phone.

She's right, I am in a mood…

"Why do you insist on rubbing shoulders with these people if they're so horrible?" I ask out of nowhere.

Dad's eyes flick to mine again. Mom doesn't even look up from her scrolling.

"The same reason you have to put up with Doctor Samuels," he says. "Because the overall goal is much larger than just showing up, Frankie. It's important to maintain relationships with people of importance, people who can open doors for you."

I want to gag.

Of course, he's right, that is how it works, but I have no

interest in these people, and the only reason they brought me here tonight is to brag about me in front of everyone they secretly hate. Because I'm my father's new pet project.

I fear for Chris. He's only fifteen, but I just know that my father will have complete control of his life by the time he's even graduated high school.

I secretly hope Chris will defy my parents and tell them he wants to play in a rock band.

Wouldn't that put a rocket of fear up their asses.

I don't bother answering. My silence echoing through the rest of the journey.

When we roll up to the town hall, the valet takes the keys and we climb the stairs, my parents stopping several times to kiss the cheeks of other high rollers. My father makes a big show of introducing me to some of them, and I smile and shake their hands like a good little daughter.

All the while, I'm seething about the comments in the car. I feel so suffocated.

When we get to the main floor, we mingle around the room while my parents act like the most perfect people in the world. I walk behind them with my orange juice while they drink champagne and laugh at bad jokes and talk shit about politics.

When I can't take it anymore, I excuse myself to the ladies' room.

I don't even know how I am part of this family

sometimes. I just never feel good enough in either of their eyes. I think that's what it is.

Telling myself I can do this, I reapply my lipstick and take a couple of deep breaths. As soon as dinner is served, I'm out of here.

I exit the ladies' and smack right into someone.

My hands fly to my mouth as he turns; I've just drenched Trent Samuels with his champagne.

"Oh my God, Doctor Samuels. I'm so sorry!"

He jerks back in surprise, but doesn't get mad. Instead, he gives me a lopsided grin, his eyes dancing with mischief.

"Frankie?" He peers at me, as if I could be mistaken for somebody else. "Is that you?"

"In the flesh," I reply, feeling embarrassed.

"My apologies." He holds one hand to his chest. "I rarely recognize anyone out of their hospital scrubs, and you look…very beautiful."

Warmth pools in my stomach.

He smiles kindly, and I smile back. "Thank you, that's very, uh, kind of you to say."

I feel a pinch of excitement when I think about my father rounding the corner and seeing us together. As innocent as it is, it would outrage him.

He leans in. "I don't know about you," he fake-whispers behind his hand, "but I hate these old fuddy duddy parties, full of rich snobs with nothing better to do on a Wednesday night."

"You're forgetting it is a for a good cause," I reply, trying not to laugh.

He points as he takes a sip of his, now half glass, of champagne. "That is very true, but I wish we could just give money and forget the rest."

He looks dashing in his black suit, and handsome as hell.

"Where are my manners?" he says, waving his arm toward the bar. "You don't have anything to drink."

"I can't," I protest. "My parents wouldn't like…"

"They won't know." He winks as I step ahead of him, and I feel his hand on the small of my back. "And anyway, you're twenty-five years old, not a child."

He's a womanizer, Frankie. Money talks, you should know that.

I can see now why Doctor Samuels has that kind of reputation.

He has the single, hot, bachelor doctor down pat.

He swipes a champagne off a passing tray and gestures toward the side entrance. "Fancy a breath of fresh air?"

"I'd love that."

We walk across the room together, and I look around for my parents. I don't see them anywhere.

A part of me is thrilled that I might get caught talking to him. I can just imagine my father's face if he catches us. I don't know why, but that thought makes me roll my lips to keep from smiling.

When we step out, he gestures toward the end of the balcony where there are less people.

"So, Frankie," he says, turning to me, his tone mocking. "How are you enjoying your internship?"

I sip the champagne. I'm not a big drinker, never really have been, even in college. But I feel suddenly nervous around him.

"I'm loving it," I say, looking everywhere but at him. "It's a great hospital, and we've got one of the best programs in the country."

My eyes finally meet his, and he watches me with interest.

He's actually paying attention when I talk and not interrupting me like everyone else in my life does.

"Glad to hear it. What about your stick-in-the-mud mentor. Bet he's a pain in the ass."

I smile too, unable to hold back any longer. "He's not so bad."

He feigns shock. "Not so bad? It seems I'll have to up my game."

I take another sip, needing the whole damn glass.

My cheeks flush, and I feel…different. Alive, almost, which is pathetic. I've had two sips of champagne.

"You know," he goes on, as if he's deep in thought. "You are one of the standouts in the class, Frankie, and not just because of who your father is."

He thinks you're the world's biggest creep.

"Thank you, Doctor Samuels, that means a lot."

He brushes a hand to my arm and touches my elbow. "It's Trent."

I take another sip, but this one is more like a gulp. He's touching me.

"What do you like best about being an intern?" he asks, his hand leaving my arm.

"I like learning new things, doing rounds. I also did a stint in emergency, and I had gunshot wound about six weeks ago. I kept the patient stable and performed CPR."

"Of course you did. You're very talented."

Out of the corner of my eye, I think I see movement, but as I turn to look, the bushes rustle, and I'm dying to laugh. Someone's probably in there doing the nasty.

I shrug. "I try."

"Give yourself more credit. Your first real patient is always scary, especially someone who's been shot, and you managed it like a pro."

"He was from a motorcycle gang," I say.

He makes a face, and I laugh.

"Are you here with anyone?" he asks in a low tone.

He's not interested in me in that way. He's just being nice.

"Yes. My parents."

I feel like a child even saying it, even though I'm twenty-five.

A smile tugs at his lips. "Of course."

I don't know what he means by that, but as he sips his champagne, I suddenly feel a little cavalier myself.

"What about you?" I ask. "Are you married?"

He smirks. "Why, do I look married?"

I shrug. "I don't know…I was just…"

He waves a hand, cutting me off. "I was kidding. No, Frankie. I'm not here with anyone. It is recommended that you have a date, but half of the things I get invited to are last minute. Hence, I'm just a lonely, old, pathetic bachelor."

"You're not old, Doctor…" I'm about to say when he holds up a finger in warning, his eyes teasing. "…uh, Trent…" It feels so weird calling him that.

"Now you're just being nice." He winks as he downs the rest of his champagne, his eyes watching me. I follow suit, even though I'm already feeling a little lightheaded.

He grabs the attention of a nearby waitress and takes two more glasses of champagne off her tray; he takes my empty glass, and his fingers brush mine.

He doesn't seem to notice, but I think I may have suddenly developed a little crush on my mentor. Or maybe it's the booze.

When his eyes gaze back to mine, he raises his fresh

glass toward me. "A toast," he declares as I hang onto his every word. "To raising lots of money for whatever we're here for…and to getting completely shitfaced while doing it."

My eyes go wide, then I burst out laughing, raising my glass to his as they clink.

His smile could light up the whole world.

A moment later I hear, "Frankie!"

Oh shit.

I know that tone anywhere. My father.

I want to shrink into myself and wither away.

We both turn at the same time as my father marches over the threshold, glaring at Trent.

Staring at him, he barks, "What do you think you're doing?"

I glance at Trent and watch as he leans one hand on the rail behind us, holds up his champagne glass, and says, "Hello, Thomas, such a pleasant evening, wouldn't you say?"

My father stands protectively in front of me, still looking at Trent as he says to me, "We're leaving." Then he turns and takes the champagne out of my hand and tips it over the edge of the balcony, the fury rolling off him in waves.

What the hell is his problem?

My mouth hangs open at how rude he's being, but

Doctor Samuels isn't pissed off. If anything, he looks amused.

He rubs his chin and assesses my father. "You know, Frankie and I work together, Thomas. I was just filling her in on some of the dos and don'ts of the hospital." While he did no such thing, his main goal seems to be making my dad pissed.

I feel his hand on my elbow.

When he doesn't answer, Trent's eyes meet mine, and he says, "She's very smart, talented, and obviously beautiful." My dad's spine goes rigid, then he adds, "Just like her mother."

My father lets go of me and pushes Trent in the chest. I stand there, aghast, with no idea what the hell is going on or why my dad is going over the top.

"Dad!" I yell. "Stop it!"

People are starting to notice, and heads turn our way.

Dad points in his face. "Don't fucking go there, or I will end you!"

He has hold of his suit jacket by the collar, his face hot and angry, all the while Trent just laughs in his face.

"Calm down, old chap. You're going to have a coronary, then it'll be up to me to save you."

As if realizing where we are and what's going on, Dad lets go of him.

I frown as my eyes follow his movements, and he drags

a hand through his hair.

"Frankie," he says, grabbing me by the arm. "Let's go."

He yanks me away, and I turn and mouth, I'm sorry, as he drags me off.

Trent runs a hand through his hair and shrugs, like it's no big deal.

I'm so angry that I yank out of my dad's grip and whirl on him.

"What the hell was that?" I scream.

Only now do I see the ferocity in his glare.

Something has happened between them. Something truly awful.

She's very smart, talented, and obviously beautiful.

I frown as I remember the last part: Just like her mother.

Could it be the oldest reason in the book?

I can't…I can't go there…but my mind does…Did my mom have an affair with Trent Samuels?

I all but shudder. Surely not.

"Don't make a scene," Dad scolds.

I snort. "I think we're way past the point of making scenes, Dad."

I stalk off, passing nosy on-lookers as I head back into the main hall.

I'm so over this family.

I'm so over being treated like a child.

I just want to run away and never come back.

Nitro

BRACKEN RIDGE
REBELS
ARIZONA
M · C

CHAPTER 5

NITRO

Doctor Trent Samuels needs his throat slit.

I don't recall a time I've ever been so angry.

I almost blew it and charged over there and fucking choked him.

Lucky for me, Frankie's dad stepped in and pulled her away from the creep.

Another revelation: Frankie's dad, aka, Doctor Stevens Senior, was the surgeon who operated on me. I was pretty out of it when the surgeon came to check on me after surgery, so I had no idea he was the one who saved my life, and she never mentioned it.

Snitch surprised me with that revelation.

What doesn't surprise me is Doctor Fuckface hitting on my girl.

First, at every turn when he's in the halls of the hospital, and now, at this fancy fucking dinner where I had to scale the fence to get in.

They don't let people like me into these things.

I had to get a look at her tonight, all dressed up with her auburn hair in loose waves.

She was a sight for sore eyes.

Elegant.

Beautiful.

Though, she'd look good in a paper bag.

I've no idea why this jerk thinks she'd be interested in him. She's his fucking student, and he's probably old enough to be her dad.

A nauseating thought occurs to me; could she be into older guys? Or worse, she's only into other doctors.

I might only be nineteen, but I'm no dummy, and I know that he only has one thing on his mind. When she's not looking, he sneaks subtle glances at her breasts, her legs, her ass.

Oh, he's all in, even if she is clueless to the fact.

She may not seem to get along with her father, especially tonight, but I'm with him on this one. I would've liked to have seen Dear Old Dad mess him up and wipe that smug smile off his face.

I ride back to the clubhouse furious.

The second I get there, I know I'll have questions about where I've been, but since tonight's the night I officially get patched in, I doubt it really matters.

The party is in full swing, and nobody even realized I've been gone.

I feel an arm sling around my neck, then Hoax shoves a girl in my face.

She's one of the sweet butts, Cindy. Sweet, beautiful and, until now, completely off limits.

"Brother," Hoax slurs as I turn to look at him. "Been lookin' everywhere for you."

I try to seem enthusiastic, but the rage I feel is simmering. "Now you've found me."

Cindy slinks closer to me, her hands running up my chest. She's almost as tall as me and has a nice rack to boot.

She smiles as our eyes meet.

"Is she an offering?" I add, my eyes skating to Hoax. He slaps me on the back really hard, laughing.

"You could say that."

She leans closer to me and whispers in my ear, "I've been waiting for you for a while now, prospect."

I wish she interested me, but sadly, I've only got eyes for one fuckin' woman in this town, and it's messing with my goddamn head.

Still, appearances are everything in this club. I can't help that the only woman I want to sink my dick into is currently being pursued by her mentor, a man who will wake up tomorrow to find his most prize possession vandalized, his flashy red Porsche. And if he pulls any more stunts, I might hit him where it hurts, literally. Or at least kneecap him so he won't be able to walk.

It doesn't matter that I haven't busted a nut since before I got out of the hospital. The only woman I have my sights on is her, even though I've not really planned to confront her or do anything about it just yet.

Well aware I have Frankie on a pedestal, I meet Cindy's eye. "The other chicks in the club been braggin' about me, sweetheart?"

Her gaze travels down to my dick. "They sure have."

She tries to kiss me, but I don't kiss on the mouth. I turn my head and grab her hair, bringing her head to my lips as I whisper. "You take cock down your throat?"

Her eyes go wide, her hand squeezing my pec. "You bet I do."

I smack her on the ass. "Good, wait for me. I'm gonna need patchin' up soon."

She jumps up and down with glee, her large tits bouncing. I rarely sink my dick into women from the club. For one, Tex would have my ass on a platter. I could do with a blowjob, but I really just want to get rid of her. By the time I'm done getting the shit kicked out of me, she'll have moved onto another brother.

I need to get this ass kicking underway. It's the last chance the committee members, and anyone else with a patch, will get to treat me like shit.

To think they will go easy on me is laughable. If anything, some of them will go harder.

I rub my chin, unable to fathom where the fuck my mind is at.

I'm turning down a fuckfest with Cindy, and whoever else she may bring along, all because I don't want to fuck another woman, unless it's Frankie. I'm fucked.

Maybe something happened to me when I got shot?

Maybe I've got limp dick now or something. I don't fuckin' know. All I know is that this ain't good.

Hoax continues to sway and smile at me. At least he's a happy drunk, not like some of the brothers. Some of them really should never touch the bottle, nor should they indulge in heavy shit they can't handle. A couple of the dudes I hung with on the streets OD'd and it wasn't pretty.

I don't touch the stuff now, but I did plenty when I was a teenager, too young. I got high with my friends and didn't give a shit about anything. It took all the pain away.

Then I lost one of my best friends to heroin, and I knew I didn't want to end up like that.

Cold, broke, and alone.

Nobody even came looking for him. Nobody gave a shit. Then and there, I decided I wasn't going to be another statistic. Sure, joining an MC may not be everyone's lifelong dream, but they're my club, my brothers. I took a bullet for them, and most of them appreciate it.

"Fuck her now, man," Hoax goes on as she keeps her hands on me, her eyes eating me up.

"Sounds like you wanna watch, sick fuck," I say, slapping him on the back.

He laughs, taking another swig of beer, and I know he's about five minutes away from passing out. "Wouldn't say no."

It's no secret some of the brothers share women. Some even like to share at the same time, but that doesn't appeal to me one bit. Two chicks at once? Sure, but I don't want to see Hoax's dick, for example. Hard pass.

"Keep fuckin' dreamin', bro."

Before we can say any more, I feel a thud on my back and turn to see Smokey looking down at me.

"You lost, prospect?" he says, though I can see there's a glint in his eyes as his brow furrows.

"Nope," I reply. "I'm right where I need to be."

"Is that so?"

I meet his eye.

Me and Smokey go back a ways. Like I say, I owe him a lot. But I also know he's probably been dying to kick the shit out of me just once. And now he'll have the chance to do just that. He's one of the few that have been good to me. He may give me a hard time when I don't pull my weight, which isn't often, and only when I'm hungover, but that's no big deal. He's one of the reasons I'm still here and haven't shot through.

"Yeah."

"That all you got?" I see the challenge in his eyes.

"You mean, do I have a death wish?"

He chuckles. "Come on now, Nitro, we'll leave you breathing. Plenty of pussy here to help you upstairs afterward."

Yeah, just not the girl I want.

I hope I'm not that fuckin' transparent. "It's a rite of passage, isn't it?"

He drops his hands to his hips, assessing me, then he leans a little closer. "Not sure you can handle some of these bitches, they can be pretty crazy." His gaze lands on Cindy for a moment. "Right, sweetheart?"

She gazes at him longingly as he slings an arm around her neck.

"Smokey," she purrs.

He grins. "I know I'm not as pretty as this fucker." He points at me, jabbing me hard. "But I'll bet my cock will look better down your throat than his."

I know what he's doing, but I don't give a fuck. He can have her. I've no interest unless her name's Frankie.

I laugh. "Whatever you say, brother."

It's just a face. I'm lucky because I don't have much else going for me.

It's one of the reasons my dad hated me, I'm sure. I reminded him too much of the wife he lost. My dear, sweet mom. I look like her. We have the same unusual green eyes, and I have her olive complexion and dark hair.

Just to piss my dad off, I grew it long when I was thirteen, right before I left home, knowing that it was the one thing he hated. Sure, I wasn't an easy kid to deal with, but no kid deserves to be beaten. Most of that stopped when he remarried, though he did strike my stepmom a few times before she kicked him out. I've no doubt if he was violent toward a defenseless child, he would be toward a woman, too.

Even though I never liked my stepmom, she didn't deserve that. At least she tried to shield it from her daughters.

Some people say the apple doesn't fall from the tree, but that couldn't be further from the truth. If I were anything like him, I'd slit my own throat.

I look down at my wrists, covered by chain bracelets, and try not to think of that dark time in my life when I did something stupid.

Smokey walks off laughing, Cindy by his side. Hoax slaps me on the back again.

"Better luck next time, asshole." He chuckles.

"Plenty more pussy," I say.

It hasn't escaped me that I'm getting a lot of female attention tonight. Word must have got around that I'm no longer off limits. But the fact remains I haven't been patched in yet, so they wait at bay like bulls at the gate.

Not a bad problem to have, and I'm not complaining, but oh how I wish it were a different pair of eyes that gazed at me.

I've got her on a pedestal. I know that. And not for the first time, I realize that it'll be my downfall.

Weeks go by.

I drop by the hospital a couple of times a week. Now I have more spare time on my hands, I'm freed up a little bit. Plus, I've got the added bonus that I don't have to answer to the entire club about where I'm going or where I've been. That's a new experience.

I've always had someone breathing down my neck.

I don't know what ever happened with Frankie and her dad and the argument that they had that night at the charity dinner, but I see the air thick with tension whenever he's close by in the cafeteria, or when they pass by one another in the hall.

Her affections have dulled somewhat toward Doctor Fuckface too, much to my delight.

She's still the apple of his eye, that much is clear, but the way she looks at him has changed. I should know. I notice every little detail about her. The only thing I don't like is the frown she still wears, and I don't know why.

The beating I got after being patched in still shows on my face and bruised ribs, so I get strange looks from the hospital staff as I walk around, and I know for a fact I'm going to alert security if I don't try to keep a low profile. I don't want to, but I take my cut off before I go inside the doors.

If my club found out, they'd probably shoot me all over again. On the other hand, if security haul my ass out, it'll make things harder to try to get back in and make sure my girl is all right.

This way, it just looks like I belong here, with the bruises and all, so I can use it to my advantage.

Until…

"Hey, Adam, right?" I hear a voice behind me.

I spin as I turn to face the chick that hangs around Frankie all the time. I don't know her name, but they spend every waking moment together.

How the fuck does she know my name?

I should just ignore her and make for the exit, but then I'd look like a coward.

Fuck.

This wasn't supposed to go down like this. Now she's going to tell Frankie I was here, unless…

"Yeah."

A playful smile tugs at her lips as she gives me a nod. "Do you usually hang out in the hospital for kicks?" She tilts her head, taunting me.

I rub my chin, unsure of what to say to her. Nosy fuckin' bitch.

"I'm here to see someone." Well, it's not a lie. I am.

"You're in that motorcycle gang, right?"

I roll my eyes. "It's not a gang, it's a club."

"Right." She draws the word out for like five minutes.

I push off the wall, ready to leave. "Wait," she says, snagging my arm.

I look down to where her hand clutches onto my shirt, and she removes it quickly.

She's either really fuckin' brave, or really fuckin' stupid.

"Not a good idea, sweet cheeks," I say, feeling like I need to make a run for it before she works out what I'm really doing here.

"You like her, right?"

"Who?"

She gives me a pointed look. "Frankie."

I glance down at her. "She saved my life. I owe her."

If she knows I'm not really here visiting someone else, she doesn't say anything to contradict my lie.

"So that's why you come here?"

"Told you, I'm visitin' someone."

"Who, exactly?"

"Fuckin' nosy. Don't you gotta be somewhere?"

She smirks, clearly not afraid of me, and also not affected by me.

I don't go out of my way to charm women. In fact, I never do. I'm an asshole most of the time. But that still doesn't stop them.

It's the fuckin' baby face.

"Hey, I'm just looking out for my friend," she states as I turn to leave.

The comment has me halting in my tracks as I turn back to face her. "What do you mean by that?"

"Exactly what I said. You've been here a few times, I've seen you."

"I've got a lot of people I know that come in this shithole like a revolvin' door, sweet cheeks."

"Perks of the job?" She quirks a brow, and if I didn't know any better, I'd say she's enjoying this.

I move closer to her. "You're not afraid of me." It's not a question.

Her breath catches in her throat, but she doesn't step back. "Should I be?"

I smirk. "Probably."

"So, we're clear, then?"

"On what exactly?"

"You're looking out for her, and that's it?"

She fuckin' knows.

"I can't promise that. But to answer the first part of that question, I will always look out for her. I owe her a debt that money can never repay. I owe her my life. Simple as that."

"What about her father. He's the one who removed the bullet."

"She's the one who kept my heart pumping before I even made it to the operating room."

She shakes her head, but she looks far from horrified. If anything, I get the feeling she supports my overall goal.

While I don't like her questioning my intentions, it's also a good sign that she's looking out for her friend. Respect. There aren't many people around like that anymore.

She's good for Frankie.

"I guess that makes her flavor of the month, then?"

"No, sweetheart, that makes her fuckin' God." I turn and leave this time. Marching straight down the hall and toward the exit.

I don't want Frankie to see me, even though there's a good chance her friend will tell her everything.

My fuckin' cover is blown.

I fucked up.

Royally.

BRACKEN RIDGE
REBELS
ARIZONA
M · C

CHAPTER 6

FRANKIE

"What the hell are you talking about?" I say to Adele as I bite into my sandwich.

"Adam," she goes on, like I'm an idiot. "He was here."

"What does that have to do with me?"

"That's just the thing, he didn't have his motorcycle jacket on. It's like he was trying to go incognito. It was shady as fuck."

"Shady, like how?"

She leans forward, lowering her voice, like anyone around us in the cafeteria would even give a shit what we were talking about.

"He said he was here visiting someone, but I didn't believe him."

"Why not?"

"Because he was so checking you out. I was running late this morning, and when I ran past him, his eyes were glued to your ass as you were doing rounds. I saw the whole thing."

"That sounds royally creepy if you ask me."

"Not if your stalker's hot."

I shake my head. "I cannot believe you just said that."

"What? Like you're not thinking it."

"If he was a real-life stalker, that would be far from funny."

"Okay, smarty pants, how do you know he isn't?"

I stop mid-bite. "Because I think I would know if someone were following me and watching me all the time."

She gives me a pointed look. "Cleary, you've never watched late-night true crime stories. I suggest you don't, by the way, if you ever want to sleep at night ever again."

"So, you talked to him?" Obviously, if he said he was visiting someone.

"For a few minutes. He had bruises on his face, and he was recovering from a black eye; he could have a fractured socket. Looks like he got banged up pretty good."

"What the hell?"

She shrugs. "Sons of Anarchy, baby, it could be any number of things."

"I don't think romanticizing a motorcycle club is very cool, Adele, they're real-life criminals. Need I remind you that he was in my care because he got shot, and then the police came to question him about it."

Adele is kinda boy crazy, and that's an understatement.

"I'm not saying you need to marry the guy, for Christ's

sake, Frankie, but a roll in the hay with a sexy fuckboy like that, count me in any day."

"I do not understand why we're having this conversation."

"Because you're in denial that Adam has a major jones for you, and it's not the first time I've seen him hanging around, long after his checkup appointments have passed. Admit it, he's a walk on the wild side. All that muscle, those cheekbones, that ass…the only reason you're not jumping him is because he's in a motorcycle gang."

"Club," I mutter.

She chuckles as I glance up, giving her daggers. "What's so funny?"

"That's another thing he said when I called it a gang. He corrected me and said it's a club, exactly like how you just did. Aww, you guys are already saying the same things, that's so cute!" she gushes as I shake my head in disbelief.

"You're insane."

"Yes, but you still love me."

My mind is reeling at what she's telling me, even though I don't believe it's true.

He's not following me, or stalking me, as Adele put it.

"So, is that all he said?" I go on after a few moments.

She just about falls off her chair laughing. "Can't stand him, huh?"

"I just want to know so I can prepare myself. If he really

is going to be a problem, then I need to make sure I have all the facts."

"You don't need facts when you're riding his face."

I slap a hand over my forehead and keep it there. "Adele!" I whisper-shout.

"What?" she whisper-shouts back. "Jesus, he'd be into it. You can tell he's a deviant."

"You cannot tell someone is a deviant from one look at them."

She gives me a smirk. "I can. It's like this sixth sense I have."

"Any other words of wisdom, Obi-Wan?" I tease.

"No, but he also said that he owed you because you saved his life."

I give her a look. I may have only known her a short while, but we've become fast friends. And I seem to always know when she's keeping things from me.

"What else?"

She shrugs.

"Adele!"

"Fine! I asked if he was just looking out for you, or was it something else?"

"And what did he say?"

"Basically, that he can't promise that, and then he said that he owed you a debt. It's kinda romantic, really, when you think about it. You saved his life, and now he's got a

big ol' crush, and he's fighting other men off in your honor."
She fans herself as I stare at her agog.

"That is ridiculous."

"Is it? He didn't look too pleased with Doctor Samuels. Has he been a little bit off, by the way?"

Ever since the night of the charity dinner, things have taken a turn.

My father wouldn't admit to anything that night, but the thought of Trent Samuels and my mother…please God no. I can't think of any other reason my father would just hate on someone so badly. It's just a feeling.

I know doctors don't have to always get along, but Dad hates him with a passion. The way he was yanking me away from him said way more than he was actually willing to tell. And Mom just drinks herself into oblivion to numb herself from ever having a real conversation with anyone.

The way Trent was all smug to my father, though; She's very smart, talented, and obviously beautiful, just like her mother. It wasn't what he said, it was the way he said it.

"Off, like how?"

She shrugs. "I don't know, he just seems, like, a little less jokey."

I didn't share with Adele what happened at the dinner. It's too personal, not to mention embarrassing.

He even apologized to me the next day at work, saying he never should have given me champagne, and commandeered my attention.

Then he asked me if I'd be interested in doing a case study for extra credit, along with some of the other classmates who were invited. That's what we've been doing ever since.

Except, some of the classmates decided to switch their days, so it's been just us for a few weeks.

And…he has been super attentive, not that he's made any moves or anything. He's just…everything my damn father isn't, in terms of a doctor. He actually listens to me and says all the right things when he's supposed to and genuinely seems interested in my learning.

My own father just wants me to keep up the pretense that we're the world's happiest family and nothing bad is happening in the Stevens' household. It's all so fake.

I know my parents have been having problems for some time; they fight a lot when they think neither myself nor Chris can hear. I just don't know why or what's going on, or what to do to help them. My parents don't air their dirty laundry.

Both of them live busy lives, so that could have something to do with it. They barely see one another, and when they do, it always leads to bickering.

Today, things took a bit of a turn. Trent Samuels and I had a moment.

Kind of like on the balcony at the dinner when he

touched my elbow. I felt something, only, I can't stop thinking about the fact that he may have slept with my mother and how repulsive that is.

"He seems okay to me," I reply, because I can't let Adele know just yet that things are, in fact, a little off with him. "Maybe he's just got a lot going on?"

Something else thrills me even more than Trent Samuels.

Adam.

I should not feel one bit elated that he was here. Even if he's managed to escape my thoughts for a few weeks because I've thrown myself into work and had the night shift again; things have been a little hectic.

But it doesn't change the fact he's in a motorcycle club. A dangerous one.

Those bikers scare me a little bit. Well, he doesn't scare me, per say, but that club is notorious for illegal activity. Plus, do I need a reminder? HE GOT SHOT!

Sometimes I wonder if I was dropped on my head at birth.

"Is everything okay, Frankie?" Trent asks when he corners me after rounds a few days later.

I look up at him and try hard not to chew my lip.

My parents had a huge fight last night, and my father is talking about moving out.

That was one argument my brother and I unfortunately overheard, as did our neighbors and probably most of the neighborhood. At least Dad and I made up a few nights ago, and he's back to talking to me again. His fury now aimed solely at my mother.

"Everything's fine, Doctor Samuels," I reply, hoping he doesn't ask me anything more.

"No, it isn't," he says, leaning back on the desk as he studies me. "You've had a frown since the night of the dinner. I'm sorry your father hates me, but I can't exactly help that."

"What happened between you two?"

He shrugs. "Search me."

He seems honest enough, his face passive as he watches me.

For some reason, I don't buy it. He knows exactly, but just doesn't want to say.

"You have absolutely no idea?" I press.

He meets my gaze. "That's what I said. It happens in this field of work, Frankie, it's just how it is. Ego plays a big part in being a surgeon. I don't want you to hate me for it."

I know his words are deliberate, but also very true. He pushes off the desk as I slide my satchel over my shoulder.

I shake my head. "I could never hate you."

He watches me and then he lifts one hand to my chin and grips it. I'm stunned that he's touching me and looking at me like that…

"Frankie, it's important that you know, I'm not the kind of man who hits on his own students…" I try not to think of my father's words as he says it and about him being a womanizer.

My breathing is shallow and rapid when I reply, "Is that what this is?"

He smirks. "No. You know that would be crossing a line. It would put my reputation and my job on the line."

Why do I feel like there's a 'but' coming up?

I stay quiet. I've no idea what to think. Only, I don't want this…

A few weeks ago, I had a mild crush on him, but now I don't know what to think.

"I'm sure you have women throwing themselves at you all the time," I whisper.

He moves the pad of his thumb to my lower lip as my heart races in my chest. "You've no idea," he mutters. I don't know, but it feels like he's about to lean down and kiss me, when there's a knock at the door.

I spring back as he steps away and calls out for them to enter.

"Trent…" another doctor begins, then his eyes fall on me. "I can come back, if you're busy."

"Uh, no, not at all. My intern was just leaving." He turns to me. "Thank you, Frankie. We'll reconvene and study the test results tomorrow at the same time, all right?"

I nod and quickly leave the room, hoping that our close proximity wasn't noticeable to his colleague.

All the while, I feel the scorch of his touch, only this time, I know I didn't just imagine it. Now, though, in the light of day, I don't want it. I want to learn from him; he has a great mind and he's charismatic, but I don't want to get involved with my teacher.

I don't know why I didn't tell him to leave me alone, to not touch me like that. Then I realize, that I liked the attention. Just not from him.

But he's the great Trent Samuels. I'm sure he was just being…nice? I'm sure he's not really interested in me. Maybe I misread the situation…

The pounding in my heart as I walk away tells me I didn't.

I don't end up seeing Doctor Samuels the next day as planned, since he got called away last minute.

It only gave me more time to think and go over exactly what happened in my head, like a continual replay.

He's far too old for me, and he's my mentor. No. I must

have it wrong; he's just a flirt.

Cocky, with too much to say for himself. And far too good looking. If he hit on his student, he'd get his license revoked.

That still doesn't stop me from dropping by his office unannounced with his favorite soda before rounds. I need this extra credit, so I don't have to keep doing extra night shifts.

He's made it clear to all his students that he has an open door policy, so I don't think this would be weird. Plus, we're supposed to be studying the test results from a few days ago, so I can make a diagnosis.

When I get to his office, the door is slightly ajar. I knock quietly and when I don't hear him, I knock again, then, pushing the door open a little more, I walk inside.

He's not at his desk. I try not to let the disappointment flood through me. These days, seeing my mentor, who may or may not have hit on me, is the only thing I really look forward to.

Aside from potentially running into Adam in the hall, though I don't believe Adele when she said he was here to check me out. I'm sure dozens of his club members are here every other week with gunshot or stab wounds.

Then I hear Doctor Samuels' voice.

There's a small bathroom adjoining his office space, so figuring he's using the bathroom, I wander toward his desk and set the soda down and wait.

Then I hear a groan. My ears prick up, I listen more intently…there it goes again.

Then I hear the slapping of skin and a woman moaning.

Oh no…is Doctor Samuels…

I don't know what possesses me to move closer to the bathroom, pure curiosity, I suppose, but I do, and through the crack I see them in the mirror.

"Fuck me harder…" a girl's voice cries out, then she tips her head back, and I see her breasts hanging out of her top.

Unable to move my feet, I stand there like an idiot, watching.

Doctor Trent Samuels is screwing Carly, the girl from my class who sat with us not long ago, ogling my own father.

She's bent over the sink, resting on her elbows, her skirt rucked up to her waist and he's slamming into her from behind, his pants hanging around his ankles.

He doesn't say anything back, just grunts as he thrusts harder, one hand resting on her hip, the other gripped in her hair.

She's certainly enjoying every second of his pounding.

My hand flies to my mouth as I quickly move across to the wall, hoping it will swallow me whole. My heart thrums in my chest so loud that I feel the blood pounding in my ears.

Trent is fucking Carly?

Bile rises in my throat. I actually feel like I might throw up.

I have to get the hell out of here.

I make a mad dash, leaving the same way I came in.

Running all the way to the bathroom stall, I lock myself inside and sit on the toilet with the lid down to take a moment.

I take a few deep breaths. Then I slap myself on the forehead.

Stupid!

Stupid, stupid, stupid!

The fact that I could ever think Trent Samuels was interested in me or my academics, when clearly, all he is interested in is fucking his students.

What an idiot I was to believe I was anything special or that he'd taken an interest in me because he thought I "had great potential." Barf.

And the worst part of it all?

My father was fucking right.

BRACKEN RIDGE
REBELS
ARIZONA
M · C

CHAPTER 7

NITRO

I stare up at her apartment. It's clouded in darkness.

She left tonight upset.

I don't know why.

She went straight home, and the lights never went on.

I want to bang her door down.

Call up to her to let me in.

Let me take care of her.

Then I'm reminded that I can't do any of those things. That she isn't mine, and as if that couldn't be any worse, she doesn't even know I'm alive, no pun intended.

I want to hurt whoever made those tears. I want to fucking cut them.

I'd drag them down to their knees and then ask her what she'd like me to do to them. Anything to get her to smile again.

I feel the urge to climb the fucking drainpipe, but I stop myself, because if I keep thinking of ways to get into that apartment, I know that I will, and she won't fucking appreciate it.

I don't know how long I sit there, until it begins to rain, but then I snap out of my reverie.

I start up my sled, the engine roaring to life, not even caring if she hears the fuckin' thing.

I want her to.

I want her to come down here and drag me inside and use my body. Use my mouth. Use anything she wants, as long as it takes that pain away.

I've been there. I know what it's like.

I never lived up to my father's expectations either. Little did I realize, at thirteen, that it didn't fucking matter, none of it did.

I've learned to please myself and nobody else. Sure, it took several years of groveling at the club and taking any shitty job I could, but I had an end game.

Anyone in their right mind can see that Frankie isn't happy. I can see it, and I barely know the girl.

I take one last look and just as I do, the curtains above move.

Suddenly, she's there, staring down at me.

I stare up at her, my Queen. My fucking Queen.

Her eyes watch me, assessing me, confusion spreading across her pretty features, but she doesn't look away. I could look at her for a lifetime and it wouldn't be long enough.

She'd send me to my knees with one command, and

while that may be seen as weak in my club's eyes, they haven't been left for dead at the doors of emergency.

They've got no fucking clue what death's door looks like. I do.

My angel was there to take care of me; she was covered in my blood, that's gotta mean something.

The rain pelts down, but I don't even notice. All there is, is her.

The woman I can never have.

The woman that haunts my every waking moment.

The woman I want to give everything I have, even when I have nothing to give.

I'll never be good enough, it's just a fact.

I don't have a college degree. Hell, I didn't even finish high school. I also don't eat at the country club or own a fucking blazer or even cut my hair.

She deserves a man who is at least on the same playing field, not light years away.

But I'll be fucked if I ever let that happen.

Like tonight.

I'll find out.

And when I do, they'll wish they were never born.

I run a hand over my hair as it falls in my eyes, slicking it back. I rev my engine as she still stares at me, and I don't tear my eyes from hers.

She places a hand up to the window, her palm facing it,

and I don't think I've ever seen anything so sad in my entire life.

I want to rip the glass pane from its foundation and take her in my arms.

As usual, my body stays motionless. The cold seeps into my bones as I kick the stand up, rev once more, and with one last, longing look, I skid off from the sidewalk and screech down the street. My motorcycle tires sound like they're in pain. Good.

I want the whole fuckin' neighborhood to hear me.

My heart pumps in my chest hard as the adrenaline courses through me.

She saw me.

She saw me, and she didn't look away.

She didn't even look horrified.

I don't know why that makes me feel any better. It shouldn't.

It means she now knows a few things about me.

One, that I know where she lives.

Two, I'm staring up at her window like a freak.

Three, I meant to be there and didn't give a shit if she saw me.

I ride back to the clubhouse and park my sled in the lot, then saunter inside.

I'm dripping from the rain, but I don't care. Making my way to my room, I'm glad the clubhouse is quiet. It's late, not even the prospects are up.

For once, the clubhouse is still.

I shrug my cut off and lay it over the back of a chair, then pull off my boots, then my clothes, and make my way to the bathroom.

I take a hot shower, reveling in the heat from the boiling water. I only wish I could wash her from my brain, but she's engrained in there, whether I like it or not.

Why don't I have the guts to take her? Claim her. Make her mine.

I'm no longer a prospect, I'm a patched member, but even as I think it, I know that's not it.

I know the reasons why, and she never will be, because protecting her from the evil in this world is far more important.

I know what people are like. I know how scum think.

I've been on the streets. I've hung around bad people. I fuckin' know.

And most of the monsters out there look normal, that's the scary part.

If I get her into bed, then I know I'll be consumed by her. I know that when she rejects me, it'll be the final nail in the coffin. So, I tell myself that it's better this way.

To watch her. Observe. Make sure that nobody gets in her way.

Tonight, I dropped the ball.

I didn't protect her, and now she's hurt.

Anger rages through me that somebody made her upset. That she shed tears and stayed locked up in her apartment all night with the lights off.

My Queen shouldn't be locked away like that…the way she looked at me. Like she was almost…hopeless.

I can't have that. I won't stand for it.

I wash myself, ignoring my dick. Thinking about her always has me hard, that's no secret, but jerking off in the shower angrily won't help my cause…then again…it could help me relieve some tension.

My hand grasps my cock, and I sheath myself a couple of times, my cum practically leaking out of me when I picture her face at the window.

I let the spray hit my body, cascading down my chest as I pull my dick harder. Bracing myself against the tiles with one hand, I imagine that she let me in, we go upstairs, and I crawl into her bed. She spreads wide for me as I taste her sweet, wet cunt and fuck her with my tongue. Enjoying every one of her moans and pleads for me to take her. And take her I do. Her tight little pussy strangles my cock while she calls my name over and over as I pound into her relentlessly.

It takes all of a few minutes before I'm spurting violently over myself, draining every drop as I try to slow my breathing. Fuck.

I wash myself clean and turn the taps off. Stepping onto the cold tiles, I dry myself and wrap the towel around my waist.

Sleep won't come for a while yet.

And no, jerking off didn't relieve any tension, if anything, it only made me want to ride back to her place and bang the door down so I can fulfill my fantasy.

When she saved my life, she also fucked it.

I was capable of all kinds of things until she came along. Now I can barely get through the day without seeing her.

It's like she's a drug and I can't get enough.

Even if I know now that she'll hate me. That she'll know.

But facing any backlash will be worth it if I get to see her again.

That's the part that stabs my heart the most.

Several things transpire over the next couple of days as I spy on her, unable to stay away.

It gnawed at me for days whether I should fuck the hell off.

Added to the fact her friend now knows about me and would have told her, now she's seen it for herself.

My biggest fear isn't her calling the cops on my ass, it's her being mad at me.

But even as I watch her now, I know something has changed.

There are times, depending on her mood, that I've seen her almost bouncing along, a spring in her step as she walks, and I've also seen her shoulders curved, her eyes down, as if she's avoiding anyone noticing her at all.

Frankie Stevens is a conundrum that I haven't quite figure out yet. And I need to know what makes her tick.

For some reason, she's hanging at the back today, doing anything except looking at that asshole doctor. What's going on there?

She's usually happy to vie for his attention, much to my annoyance, and he laps it up like a fucking dog. While I imagine all the things I could do to him with my blade, he calls on her for a question, and she stumbles and flusters over it, instead of answering confidently, like she usually does.

I took a risk today. I even snagged an orderly's jacket so I look a little less conspicuous.

Try to stay focused. I tell myself. I just need a few more minutes to try to figure out if someone at this hospital is the culprit, and, even as I think it, I'm pretty sure I know exactly who has been making her cry.

The doctor's eyes assess her face like he's almost…

concerned about her. That would be hilarious since I know the only person he's concerned about is himself and where he sticks his dick next.

Frankie eventually gets the answer out and when she looks up, he gives her his best I'm puzzled, was it something I said? look as he starts explaining about blood cells and anemia.

She looks down, biting her lip.

Peculiar.

When he finishes, they move on. He waves the students off, but as they file past him into two lines, he leans toward her and asks, "Everything okay, Stevens?"

She looks up at him with those big round eyes; eyes he doesn't deserve to have on him… "I…umm…yeah, everything's fine."

"Really? Then why can't you look at me?"

She links her fingers and fiddles with them as I take in this very different side to her.

I hate how she hangs off his every word, like he is in total control, and doesn't this asshole know it.

"I am looking at you," she whispers.

"When did you come to my office?"

They begin to walk as I loiter, trying to keep as close as possible.

"…how…how did you know?"

"You left a soda can on my desk."

Fucking prick.

"...oh, I...I don't remember."

"Frankie." I do not like how he's using her name, it's too familiar. "Well, when can we reconvene our study for the extra credit?"

Both my hands make fists as I fight the urge not to jump over there and choke him.

Is he actually kidding right now? Extra credit?

Oh, for fuck's sake, Frankie. I thought you had a little more fire in you than that.

I thought she was a woman who took control of what she wanted, who wasn't afraid to speak her mind. It seems all of those things that I've grown to adore about her have taken a backseat.

The only satisfying thing is seeing Doctor fucking Samuels at a loss for words.

It's him. I realize.

I don't know what exactly, but he did something.

"I...uh...I'm not sure at the moment. I might need to take a raincheck. I've got a lot going on."

She's definitely off.

He looks puzzled. Honestly, it's like fucking gold as I follow behind them.

He struggles with not being able to figure her out.

I've been obsessed with her for months now, fuckface, and I know more about her than you ever will.

She only looked at him like he was a god because she believed a lie.

I can see straight through him. I know he's not a good guy.

I know he's shady as fuck.

He's got it written all over him, and it's not even sour grapes. He just has this air of I'm so much better than anyone else about him that I'm truly surprised people seem to respect him.

I wouldn't be happy about anyone going near her, much less touching her, but him?

Over my dead body.

I know I'm close to being sprung, but Frankie is too caught up in her conversation to bother to notice me.

Each day that passes, I get bolder, and I know that at some point, I'm going to slip up.

A lot like the other night. Except it'll be worse because we'll be face to face and then there is the very real possibility she won't be happy about me following her and watching her outside her apartment.

"I was hoping we could catch up; you don't want to get behind, Doctor Stevens," he goes on. "Getting ahead should be your top priority in this hospital, or you can be like everybody else and flounder through this internship and get average grades that are passable but won't gain you any respect or recognition, nor will it win any brownie points with the honors board."

"Respect," she snorts.

My ears prick up.

I see him turn to look down at her. "Why is that funny?"

"Oh, no reason, Doctor Samuels."

He frowns, clearly unhappy with that response.

Normally, Frankie is usually a little doe-eyed when it comes to this creep, so to see her look at him with almost… contempt, makes me realize that she's not kidding around.

"Least of all, you don't want your father thinking that you're going to fail, do you, Frankie?"

My hands clench into fists as she gasps, looking up at him, shocked.

She shakes her head, and I think he instantly regrets the jab. "You're just like everybody else," she whispers, stopping in her tracks as she turns and begins to head my way. "I was stupid to think you were different."

He catches her arm as she tries to storm away. "Frankie, wait."

"Let go of me!"

A few people walking the halls turn to look at them.

I move before my brain catches up. "Are you deaf and stupid, fuckface?" I push him backward, and his hand releases from her grip.

"Who the hell are you?" He frowns, regaining his footing.

Frankie's eyes are wide when she turns to look at me. "Adam?"

I ignore her. "A friend. And she said to let go of her."

She pushes me in the chest, trying to get me to stop.

The other interns stop walking and turn to look at the commotion. The good doctor decides to not make a scene as he looks down at Frankie.

"You're expected to conduct your rounds, Doctor Stevens," he says, eyeing me at the same time. "And that means; move it, now!"

"I'm feeling a headache coming on," she says, reaching out and yanking me away.

I'm about to punch him in the face if one more word comes out of his mouth.

He turns and stalks back to his students and tells them off for stopping. They scurry ahead like little ants going this way and that.

When we're far enough away, she whirls around to face me.

"Adam, what are you doing here?"

The only thing I can think of in this moment is, she knows my name, and she's still touching me.

I palm the back of my neck.

I wasn't expecting to have to confront her, not like this.

"I know you've been following me," she adds when my mouth doesn't work.

"I'm visiting a friend," I say, knowing she won't buy it.

She shakes her head. "No, you're not."

"You're right, I don't have any friends."

"So you just made that up?"

"Which part?"

Her nostrils flair as she lets go of me. People are still staring, so I do what anyone in my situation would do when the object of their desire yells at them in a public place for stalking them; I grab her arm and yank her into the nearby cleaning closet so we can talk in private.

Slamming the door behind us, her eyes are like thunder. "What are you doing?" she shrieks.

"Calm down," I say. "You're making a scene."

She points in my face. "You followed me."

I let go of her and palm both hands behind my head.

I notice her eyes travel the length of my chest up to my arms where she flinches briefly. I don't know what all that's about.

I'm a big guy, but surely, she's not afraid of me?

She takes a step back.

"Listen, I was actually visiting a friend," I lie, but I have to. If she thinks I've really been stalking her, she'll call the cops. "But then I saw you having an argument with Doctor Fuckface back there, and that's when I followed you."

She frowns. "That doesn't explain what you were doing outside my apartment."

She's right, it doesn't.

Someone yanks the door open and then stops the minute they see us arguing.

"Fuck off!" I bark over Frankie's shoulder.

The dude turns on his heel and slams the door closed.

Frankie facepalms herself.

I wait in silence for what feels like an eternity.

"Please, just tell me what you were doing there," she whispers, unable to face me. "Outside my goddamn apartment."

I open my mouth, then close it again.

Do I go with the truth?

She's smarter than me, and she'll figure out pretty quickly I'm lying, so I go for some version of the truth and say, "I admit that I followed you, and before you go gettin' all weird about it, I was makin' sure you got home safe. I saw how upset you were when you left the hospital."

She brings her eyes to mine.

I see such sadness in their depths that I want to take away.

I want to make her forget all about whatever it is that's troubling her. I want to bury her pain, so she never remembers what it's like to suffer.

I realize that I don't like her being upset or worried.

She's young and beautiful; she shouldn't have all this weight on her shoulders.

"Was that when you were visiting your friend?"

"The very same one."

She doesn't look impressed. "Isn't that against the law?"

"What? Drivin' down the street?"

"Following someone and then hanging around outside. Stalking them!"

"I told you; I was makin' sure you got home safe. Nothin' else, I swear it. Scout's honor."

We stare at each other, and I've no idea if she believes me.

If she were smart, she'd hightail it out of the closet and run back to her friends. I'm bad news and she knows it. But I'll never hurt her. I'll always look out for her best interests.

The more time I spend around her, the more intoxicated I become, and that ain't good, not for either of us.

Something's got to give, and I fear that more pain is headed my way.

Nitro

BRACKEN RIDGE
REBELS
ARIZONA
M · C

CHAPTER 8

FRANKIE

I have no idea what the hell I'm doing in here with him. The one thing I can't shake, despite the fact I should give him his marching orders, is the intense look he's giving me right at this moment.

His eyes…they are beyond the most beautiful color I've ever seen. Green, with little flecks of hazel.

His face is the most perfect damned face; bikers are not meant to be this pretty. I don't even mind the long, messy hair. Since it's tied back today, I can see him in all his glory, and while I should run a mile, my eyes wander all over him, like I'm seeing him for the first time.

It's a far cry from the bleeding, dying man that lay on the gurney as I pumped his chest and told him he wasn't going to die.

I remember his chart, he's not even twenty years old yet.

I know for a fact that nobody has ever looked at me like he is right now. It's slightly unnerving, and I think he knows it.

I also can't mistake the frantic beating of my heart.

"How gallant of you, making sure I got home safe," I snap back at him. "But I didn't ask you to do that, Adam."

His eyes drop to my lips. "It's Nitro."

I know I'm off kilter. After what I saw Doctor Samuels doing to Carly in his bathroom, it has me shaken up and on edge. I shouldn't be so fricking naive. Sometimes I just want to scream at my own stupidity.

I should have known exactly what he's like after my own father told me point blank. It's not like he would lie to me. He may be many things, but steering me away from Trent was my dad being the most fatherly he's been in a long time, and now I know why.

The sick feeling of him potentially having an affair with my mom, while hitting on me, makes me want to shrivel up and die.

"Nitro? What kind of a name is that?"

He shrugs. "One that stuck."

I palm my forehead. "I don't even know what I'm doing in here with you."

He's still staring at me. "Gettin' away from that douchebag?"

"Very funny."

"You asked."

I jab him in the chest. "Stop following me."

"I only followed you once." His eyes dart down to my finger, his eyes blazing.

Even if I believed that, which I don't, and not just because Adele already told me she ran into him another time and he was watching me…the thought sends a shock wave right through me, and I frown when I realize it's not an entirely unpleasant feeling.

Then again, I was previously crushing a little on Trent Samuels, so I can hardly trust my instincts on this one.

"I don't believe that."

"Believe what you want." He shrugs. "You saved my life, the least I can do is look out for you from time to time."

"That doesn't mean you can just hang around my workplace and follow me. Maybe I'm not happy about you knowing where I live."

He frowns. "Why not?"

I give him a duh look, and he steels his jaw.

"If you think that I would ever hurt you…" he trails off, like he's testing the words. Like they're new to him.

"I don't know you, that's the point." Even as I say it, my body's reaction to him feels nuclear. He's affecting me in all the wrong places, and why does he smell so fucking good? Like Brut mixed with oil and cigarettes. That should not be attractive!

"Why was Doctor Fuckface trying to get you alone?"

I stare at him, agog. Is he freaking kidding me right now?

"Are you seriously questioning who I talk to now?"

Again, he does not look fazed. "It's not a bad idea if the guy's only after one thing."

My eyes go wide. "How dare you!"

"What?" He shrugs. "It's the truth, and you know it."

I flush beet red.

Why is he doing this to me?

"That is the most ridiculous thing I've ever heard."

He moves toward me as I step back. The closet is small, but big enough to maneuver around. He towers over me as I gape up at him.

"Really?" He smirks. "Well, since you just yelled at him in front of his students, and he put you down in return, I'd say that's a sure enough sign that he isn't worth your time, wouldn't you?"

I want to slap the smirk off his face.

All the while, I also notice those perfect lips, and the top one curves up, like he's fighting a smile.

Why are you thinking about his lips? Snap out of it already!

Maybe I'm just overtired and overworked but I feel like I'm a on a rollercoaster, hurtling toward the ground at top speed, ready to crash land.

My mentor, and the man I've grown to respect, is fucking another girl in my class.

I'm still digesting all of that and I don't know what to do with it; I haven't even told Adele.

I take a steadying breath. "You don't need to come here and defend my honor."

He narrows his eyes. "You weren't sayin' anythin' like that when you were on top of me, pumping on my chest that night, Doc, so why the hostility now?"

"Are you actually serious right now?"

"Deadly."

We have a stare down and he comes closer still. I back up until I hit the wall.

"I'll scream," I say. The minute the words leave my mouth, I regret them.

Does he back up, though? Not on your life.

He cages me in, his face only a few inches from mine. "Nobody will hear you."

"Wanna bet?"

He trails a finger up my throat, over my clavicle and up to my jaw, holding my chin as his eyes glare at me. "Yeah, Doc, I'll bet the only screamin' you'd be good at is when I'm buried inside you, balls deep."

My eyes go wide. I open my mouth, then close it again. Then, "You…you can't talk to me like that!" It sounds feeble, but in my defense, he is the one standing over me in a closet, with nothing between us except charged tension.

"Told you when you saved me, I like the idea of you on top."

"You have a disgusting mouth."

Again with the smirk.

"You know I won't touch you until you're begging me for it."

"Well then, you'll be waiting a long time, Adam."

"You know, it doesn't have to be this way."

"I actually have no clue what you're going on about. And I'm leaving."

He steps back and motions toward the door. "Be my guest."

My traitorous feet do not move, earning me another smile.

I have to admit, even though he has a dirty mouth, he still has the power to render me to a pile of mush. And I hate myself for it. I hate that I'm always attracted to the wrong kind of guy; it's the story of my life. In my two previous relationships, and every other fling in between, not that there's been that many, and there hasn't been any lately. Work and study consume every waking moment.

"Since we're being honest with each other," I blurt before I can stop myself. "You might think the caveman, pound my chest thing works on all women, but I'm here to tell you that in the real world, women want a lot more substance than a man who's only good for one thing."

He does an odd thing; he puts his hands on his hips as I steel my back, ready to bout with him if that's what it takes. My parents didn't raise me to be a stick in the mud. The one thing I did learn from my mom was that it's best to speak your mind and speak it good, or say nothing at all.

"Is that so?"

"Yes, and I can tell by looking at you that you probably are only good for one thing, but I'm not interested."

"You don't like sex?"

I blink rapidly. Shoot.

I got myself into this mess, now I have to try to dig my way out of it.

"That isn't a subject I'm discussing with you."

"Well, it's a simple question, Frankie."

The way he says my name… "It's not a question that you ask a complete stranger!"

He holds a hand over his heart as I watch the movement, realizing I'm still plastered against the wall, and I'm unable to peel myself off right at this point. "And here I was thinking we've shared so much."

"You're crazy."

"I've been called worse."

"I don't doubt that."

He taps his chin. "Do you know what I think?"

God, he was so much cuter when he had a bullet in him, and wasn't trying to get inside my head…or my pants.

"Am I going to be able to stop you from telling me?"

He ignores me. "I think that you're not pissed at me at all."

I shake my head. "You're right! I'm mad as hell!"

His eyes…Jesus Christ, I can't…

"No, you're not. You're mad at Doctor Samuels because he's an asshole and probably hit on you more than once, but because you're his dutiful little student, you brushed it off, or maybe even wanted it, the attention, at least, until he fucked up."

I open my mouth, gaping at him, and I've never wanted to hit someone in anger in all my life.

The trouble is…he's right. I'm not even mad at Adam at all, not even for spying on me outside my apartment, and I should be. I should call the cops…

"You're wrong, he's…he's not like that."

"Frankie, you're a smart girl, you'd have to be to get this far into your internship, but you have to open your fuckin' eyes and don't let people walk all over you because they disguise themselves as your 'mentor' or even a friend. Just because they're highly respected in their field, doesn't make them a good person. His eyes are all over your ass, and not just yours, anything in a long coat and a stethoscope. It's written all over him. What he's doing is wrong; you're his student."

He's right about Doctor Samuels, but I'm not going to let him get the better of me.

"Oh, and you are a good person?" I snicker.

"No, but I'm not pretending to be." He holds his arms out wide. "This is all of me, like it or not. I don't pull any punches, I don't pretend to be a fucking saint, but I also don't lie and chase skirt just to prove something to my own ego."

It sounds awful, and extremely judgy, even in my own head, but I've just realized that he's a lot smarter than he looks.

I look down his body and as I bring my eyes back to his, he shakes his head.

"I don't know you," he says, his voice low. "But I don't want to see you get hurt, and I don't know why I care…or maybe I do…it's because you brought me back, but it's also much more than that…" He runs a hand through his messy hair, like he's trying to find the words.

"To anyone else, you'd sound like a complete lunatic."

"But all that matters is how I sound to you."

I want to scream at him to leave me alone. To get the hell out of here and stop following me.

Tell him he's wrong about Doctor Samuels and the fact I'm not feeling anything at all for him…but that would be a lie. And somehow, in the last few minutes of being in his presence, I don't want to lie to him.

"Messed up," I reply, trying to digest his words and letting them sink in. "Like you've got some sort of Nightingale Syndrome built around what happened to you."

"Maybe I do."

"It's not healthy…to follow people, even if you mean well."

"Most people would have called the pigs, or at least go get security, but I'm curious as to why you haven't, Frankie."

I meet his eyes. "Because I know you won't hurt me."

"How do you know?"

I shake my head, unsure how to answer, so I just simply say, "Because I can feel it."

"Is that something they teach you in medical school?"

I shrug. "Instincts? Yes, but I've clearly never been a good judge of character."

"Well, you can start now. Not all guys are asshats wanting to get into your pants. Some of us want more than that."

I bite my lip. Is he saying that he does? I'm so confused.

"Some guys also know all the right things to say to get sex. I'm not stupid, Adam."

"Call me Nitro."

"Why don't you like your name?"

"Because Adam died a long time ago."

I stare at him, perplexed.

I'm about to ask what he means by that when the door abruptly opens. Two security guards stand there, and I push off the wall.

"What's going on?" one of the men asks, both eyeing Adam with the same abhorrent expression.

I don't like the way they're looking at him, and again, I

internally scold myself for being such a sap.

"Nothing," I mutter.

"Did he hurt you?" the other one asks me.

"No!" I shake my head. "He's my friend…"

Adam's eyebrows shoot up, but in all of a few seconds, the security are on him, hauling him out the door as they grab onto his arms and he struggles against them.

"Leave him alone!"

"This isn't over, Frankie," he says, and as I try to grasp onto his arm as he passes by, the security guy swats my hand away. "This isn't over!"

"Adam!" I cry.

I watch in horror as they cart him off out of the room and down the hall.

All the while, I can't stop thinking about his words and what they meant. As much as I want to hate him, I can't bring myself to do it.

He was honest.

I know that may be dumb and naive, but I can't help feeling that when he's around, everything is better.

The chaos in my life is forgotten. The people who cause me stress don't matter. Everyone else around us is a blur. It's just us.

My whole body tingles when I think about his close proximity and the way he touched my chin.

It shouldn't feel like that. I barely know him, and what I

know of him isn't good.

I have no idea what the hell I'm going to do about Doctor Samuels, my parents, or the feeling inside me that gravitates toward Adam, but the one thing I do know is that I'm not going to be a doormat anymore.

Not to anybody.

Starting right fucking now.

"What do you mean you can't come to the dinner?" I stare at my mom in the kitchen as she hunts through her briefcase. "We've been planning this for months."

She doesn't look up when she says, "I'm sorry, sweetie, things are hectic right now at the office. You know I just got made partner, and I can't take the extra time off."

"It's one in the afternoon."

The Martins, a prestigious family from Phoenix, put on a charity auction at their estate every year to raise money for the hospital, or the local shelter, or the drop-in center. This year, the theme is mother and daughter. We're supposed to go as a team. Make a speech about how we got into our prospective fields, and how proud we are of each other's accomplishments.

I thought that it would be a good way for us to bond. We haven't been close for a number of years, and I've always felt like having kids hindered mom's career. Maybe that's why she's so hell bent on ruling the world now.

I've no problem with powerful, strong working moms; I respect it. I know it's hard to juggle life, family, and a job, not to mention dogs, PA meetings, and sports after school.

But my mom hired people to do that.

She never even took me to speech therapy when I was a child. My nanny, Eliza, did.

My gut begins to churn.

After the day I had with Doctor Samuels, and then Adam, and seeing him hauled off by security, I thought it just couldn't get any worse…until now.

"I'm sorry, Frankie, I really am, but I have this huge case…"

"There's always a huge case," I mutter, going over to the fridge and taking out a soda, the blood pounding in my ears.

"Don't pout or sulk, it doesn't suit you."

"So am I supposed to go alone?" I fire back, slamming the fridge closed.

It dawns on me then…she expects me not to go at all.

"I'll make it up to you," she says, her eyes finally meeting mine.

My mother is an attractive woman. There is never a hair out of place. If there were a gold medal in keeping up appearances, she'd win hands down.

"No, you won't."

"Frankie." Her tone grows more terse. "I'm not going to fight with you about this. I said I'm sorry. I can't help that I've got a lot going on at the moment."

"And I can't help that I have a woman who looks like my mom, talks like my mom, but certainly doesn't act like my mom."

She narrows her eyes. "Don't take that tone with me."

"I'll take any tone I want. I'm right! How stupid of me to think that you might actually be proud of me for following in Dad's footsteps…or is that it? Did you want me to be a lawyer like you?" I try not to gag as I say that last part.

"Frankie, you're acting very childish. I'm not going to engage in this conversation."

"Why not?" I spit back. "Is it because you know that you're being a shitty mom?"

She turns on me, her face every bit the cool, calm, controlled lawyer, but I know better. "You love to rub it in my face, don't you? Does it make you feel better thinking I'm a shitty mom because I have a busy job and juggle a family, along with other commitments that don't revolve around you?"

"Just once it'd be nice for it to revolve around me."

"This attitude is very unbecoming," she says. "I thought I'd raised you better than that."

"You didn't raise me," I fire back. "My nannies did."

We stare at other as I see the anger rise in her face. "That isn't fair."

"No? Then why do we never do stuff together? Why are you always too busy or too engrossed in work to do something with me, just for once?"

Why can't she see I'm crying out for her, for an ounce of something from her, to be finally in a good place where we can talk, hangout, and I don't know…be civil to one another. Is it asking too much?

Clearly, it is, as there is no emotion on her face at all. Am I even her kid?

"It's not all about you," she snaps, annoyed. "You sound exactly like your father, whining and being all needy. Now I know where you get it from."

Anger rises in me like it never has before.

"Did you sleep with Trent Samuels?" The words are out of my mouth before I can stop them.

Finally, I've struck a nerve. All the color drains from her face. Then her expression contorts like slow motion; it starts off as shock, then horror, then disbelief.

"What did you say?" she whispers.

I know from the look on her face, lawyer or not, that she's trying to figure her way out of this.

She fucking did.

She had an affair with my mentor, and this is why Dad

hates him with a passion.

"That's it, isn't it? You screwed him behind Dad's back, and you're pissed because he won't even look at you anymore, and now he only goes for younger girls who are my age and not washed up old has-beens trying to resurrect their careers!"

She smacks me across the face before I can even realize what's happening.

I gasp in shock, my hand flying to my face. "Oh my God."

She takes a step back, her hand presses against her mouth like she can't believe what she just did. "Frankie… I'm sorry, I didn't mean to…"

"Feel better now, Mom?" I spit back. "Maybe you can add this to your list of achievements as a shitty mom; hitting your kid because you can't take the truth."

I stalk off, holding my cheek in one hand and my soda in the other.

"Frankie!"

"I hate you!" I yell back at her.

This is the last day I'll ever set foot in this house.

It's over between us, not that we ever had anything anyway.

I can't even stand to look at her, and maybe I never will again.

BRACKEN RIDGE
REBELS
ARIZONA
M · C
BRACKEN RIDGE
REBELS

CHAPTER 9

NITRO

TWO WEEKS LATER

I toss and turn all night thinking about what happened. I can't shake it.

It makes me want to go to her, plead my case. I don't like her being mad at me.

All I can picture is her shocked face as those security asshats dragged me away.

I didn't care; they can't keep me from her. Nobody can.

I decided to cool it and stay better disguised, which means staying away from the hospital until I can change my appearance and sneak back in unnoticed.

My thoughts circle around everything that happened in that closet.

Her close proximity; so close I could smell the scent of her fucking shampoo.

The look in her eyes.

The way she stood her ground. I like that. I like that she had a backbone.

As much can't be said when she's being accosted by that fucker, Doctor Samuels.

I just wish she wasn't so trusting of people, me excluded. She's older than me, yet she's still naive.

I know that's mostly because she's a daddy's little rich girl, one where she's had everything handed to her and has only grown up around certain types of people. People that are nothing like me.

I grew up fast. Living on the streets rough does that to you, but I learned a shit ton, and I learned to read people.

I can read anyone.

It's got nothing to do with the fact that she saved me.

She has a kind heart.

She's honest.

She's fearful at times, but she has a fearless side too; she just needs to let it out.

I know what it feels like to be stunted by the people closest around you, to feel like you aren't loved by your own family. Sometimes I mourn for that little boy I once was and all that I lost when my mom died. Maybe she took the best of me with her.

Sometimes I know that there will never be a happy ending for me, and I've grown to accept it. It's why I live life every day like it's my last.

I just never expected to care about anybody.

I've always flown by the seat of my pants, done what

I want and, even when those decisions were bad ones, I've always taken risks.

Frankie Stevens is a different kind of risk.

One I have no business fine tuning or even being around.

But this isn't about sex. It never has been. I can get sex anywhere.

It isn't like that with her. We're connected.

Whether she wants to admit it or not, there is something between us and it's not just one sided. If I felt that it was, it would be hard, but I'd try to leave her alone.

But I'm reminded that she didn't leave when she had the opportunity. I don't know if she's attracted to me or hates my fucking guts, but I do know she's intrigued by me. Like she doesn't know which way to take me.

I also didn't let any of that shit slide with Doctor fucking Samuels.

I fucked him up good.

Let's just say, he'll think twice before trying to hit on Frankie, or any other student under his supervision ever again.

I made it look like a robbery.

He's lucky I left him breathing. He's lucky about a lot of things.

If the chicks around the hospital thought he was handsome before he met with my fists, that's all changed since I landed blow after blow to his face. I know how much he thinks of himself, so I made sure I broke his nose.

I chuckle.

Hoax looks at me. "What?"

"Nothin'."

"You fuckin' that doctor yet?"

How is he always so fuckin' observant?

We're sitting in the van, checking out a lead Smokey got on some punks running drugs on our turf.

"Nah, man."

"Then why do you hang around the hospital so much?"

I sigh. "Just to check on her."

He's the only one who knows what I'm up to and he only knows because I confessed one night when I was drunk.

To anyone else, it would sound pathetic, but Hoax has always been pretty cool.

The one I don't trust, other than Tex, is Rachet. If he gets wind of anything to do with Frankie, he'd go after her just to prove a point. He's like that. Sick in the head.

It's why I won't share who she is to anyone.

Now I'm patched in, it means I can bring whoever I want to the club, but unless she's claimed, she's fair game if another brother wants in.

I can't let that happen. It's why she can never come to church, not that she ever will.

Frankie wouldn't understand any of this shit, and that's what makes me like her more than I should.

She doesn't know the life. She's innocent, and I haven't been with or around an innocent woman in God knows how long.

"And you still got no pussy?"

Another thing they don't understand and never will. Maybe I'm just made differently.

Sure, I love pussy as much as the next guy, but imagining Frankie so much as looking my way is enough to give me a wood. I can't even imaging fucking her. It's not my main goal.

My main goal is to protect her, make sure she's safe. Anything else that may happen is just a bonus.

"Nah, man, it's not like that."

He laughs. "You got it bad, bro."

"Maybe she's right. I looked up Nightingale Syndrome."

He spurts out his coffee all over the table as I frown. When he recovers from choking, he gives me a side-eye. "Are you fuckin' serious?"

"Deadly. It's a thing."

"Jesus H. Christ."

"He ain't gonna help me."

"You need to fuck her, get it out of your system, this…" He waves his hand at me. "This ain't healthy, bro."

"What isn't?" I look down at myself, confused.

I don't think I'm dirty like some of the brothers. I shower. I put on a fresh shirt every day, and even though I don't shave as much as I used to, I'm not a fuckin' grub.

"You mopin' around here like the cat who didn't get the fuckin' cream."

"Mopin'? Is that what I'm doin'?"

He gives me a pointed look. "You ain't gettin' pussy anywhere. This chick is fuckin' with your head. So you need to get some and move on before it fucks with you even more."

I shake my head with a laugh. If only it were that simple.

There ain't no moving on from Frankie Stevens.

"I've got it under control."

He points in my face. "Where were you last night?"

"What are you, my mother?"

"Answer the question, asshole."

Oh, I know exactly where I was last night. Outside her apartment again, only I stayed out of sight because she may have thought better of it and called the cops this time.

When I don't answer, he shakes his head and takes another sip of his coffee. "That right there is the why this is a bad idea."

"Christ, you're at it again," I sigh.

"Like I said; she's fuckin' with your head. Next thing you know, you'll be followin' her around everywhere she goes—if you're not already. She'll be callin' the shots, makin' demands, and rulin' the roost. This is a woman who you won't even be bringin' around here to party, never mind claimin' her at the table."

Everything he said is probably right, except her calling the shots; she won't be doing that. But it would be nice to see her stand up for herself with other people in her life. If I can help bring that out in her, then that'll make me happy.

"Says you, who's pussy-whipped by half the sweet butts, or anythin' in a skirt who shows any interest." One sure-fire way to get the attention off me is to get it back on Hoax, because he loves talking about himself.

"Least I get pussy, bro."

"I get plenty." Usually, not lately.

He snorts. "Sing another song. You're fucked either way."

He's probably right.

"Then again," he goes on. "It could be good for when you finally break free from her. Least with that pretty boy face, you'll get any chick at church to suck your dick."

Just not the one I want.

"Bet you wish you were pretty, huh, fuckface?"

He elbows me in the ribs hard as I shove him away. "Doesn't matter when I've got a big cock, bro."

I shake my head. "Thanks for that visual."

"How long you think we're gonna be sittin' out here?"

He looks over to the house, with still no movement.

"It's not like these punks have any idea we're here," I reply. "Could be all fuckin' night."

"Should've brought food," he complains.

"I thought these shitty jobs were over once we're no longer a prospecting?"

"Tex doesn't trust any prospect to do this. They'd find a way to fuck it up, no offense, since you're newly patched in."

I think about a couple of the other prospects in the club, and I know he isn't wrong.

They're a little too wet behind the ears.

"None taken, I get it. Long as we get somethin' out of it and aren't just sittin' here all night, watchin' a vacant fuckin' street."

"Especially when the girls cooked up a big fuckin' storm tonight."

"What's the occasion?"

"One of the girl's birthday or some shit."

"How come we don't get a cook up for our birthdays?" I groan.

"Fuckin' pussy, that's why." Hoax shakes his head.

The rest of the night is spent watching an empty fuckin' house.

I'm tired, but still restless by the time we get back to church.

At least they left us some food.

In the kitchen, two giant pots of stew sit on the stove, and it smells delicious.

"Help yourselves," Gem, one of the sweet butts, says as she puts icing on some cupcakes.

"What the fuck?" Hoax says, watching her carefully pipe pink icing all over the dainty, fluffy cakes. "You seein' this shit, bro?"

I chuckle. "Seein' it. Smells fuckin' good too." I reach to grab one and Gem smacks my hand.

"Not before the birthday girl blows out her candles!" she scorns.

I frown. "Fuckin' kiddin' me," I mutter.

Hoax gives me a knowing look. He just spent the better part of two hours complaining that the sweet butts are slowly taking over the club and we're just all falling into line without even realizing it.

"You suck cock with that mouth, Gems?" He smacks her on the ass as she looks up at him with devil eyes.

"Desiree never had a proper birthday party before." She scowls, going back to her duty with precision. "It'll be nice for her to have a cake and blow out the candles, so could you stop doing that? You almost knocked into me, and I want this to be perfect."

"I'll fuckin' knock into you in a minute, woman." He grabs her ass with both hands as she shakes her head and tries to smack him away.

"After, Hoax! I'm busy!"

"Fuckin' woman!"

I roll my lips. "What were you sayin' about pussy?" I quip, helping myself to a giant bowl of stew. I take the entire plate of biscuits with me, since they look like they're going to waste.

He knows if he interrupts Gem again, he'll probably wear the piping bag full of pink icing.

Gem seems pretty hell bent on getting this finished and making it look pretty.

"Are we gonna sing happy fuckin' birthday next?" he grumbles.

"Don't pout, baby," she says with a smile. "I'll make it up to you."

He rolls his eyes as he goes to grab himself some food and joins me at the dining table.

I haven't eaten properly in a few days. It's been hectic.

Tex has us all on high alert. When someone comes into our territory, trying to take a cut, shit can get messy.

Plus, Smokey won't let up about the dudes who shot me. If revenge is a dish best served cold, then I may be waiting a while where Tex is concerned. Sometimes in clubs as big as this, we retaliate quickly, but sometimes it can drag out, waiting for the right moment.

Personally, I can't wait to gut the bastards.

Since I was shot while a prospect, it didn't really matter then if I lived or died. Prospects are disposable, the least important members of the club.

I wonder if I'd been shot a month or so later, would things have been any different?

I guess we'll never know.

A few moments later, Rachet comes barreling through the door.

"What the fuck is this?"

Gem rolls her eyes. "Don't you start."

He sneers at her in that way that I don't like, and I clench my fist on the table.

Hoax gives me a look, but I know he's thinking the same thing.

Ratchet is a loose cannon and one of the brothers in the club that hangs on every word from Tex. I wouldn't be surprised if he was his little bitch, but at the very least, he's a snitch.

"What's up, fuckers?"

"Gettin' a feed," Hoax answers as I ignore him. "What's it look like?"

He gives me a nod. "What's the name of that surgeon, the one who took the bullet out of your chest?"

I don't want him knowing shit, especially about Frankie. But I don't give a shit about her dad.

"Stevens. He's one of the best surgeons in the state."

He snickers. "Or, he was."

I look up at him, wondering if he's joking. "What the fuck happened?" I ask, dropping my fork on the bench with a clatter.

He shrugs, helping himself to a cupcake. Gem has the good sense not to slap his hand. I know what would happen to her if she did, and it makes me want to lay into him like I did Trent Samuels.

"It's all over the news." He takes a bite of the cake like an animal. "Dropped dead. They're sayin' it's an aneurysm. Let's be thankful he was still here when you got shot, brother. Could be singing a different tune."

Thomas Stevens is dead?

What the fuck?

I type a quick search into Google and read the first thing that comes up, not even bothering to hear what Hoax is saying next to me.

Breaking News: Highly esteemed and well-respected Phoenix surgeon, Doctor Thomas Stevens, has reportedly suffered a brain hemorrhage and was pronounced dead on arrival at Phoenix Memorial Hospital at approximately six pm tonight. He leaves behind his wife, District Attorney Helena Stevens, daughter, Frankie, and son, Christopher…

I stare at the words in utter astonishment.

A few moments later, Ratchet fucks off without a backward glance, licking his fingers clean as he does.

I turn to Hoax. "This is a big fuckin' problem."

Frankie will be devastated. Her father is the one person on earth she looks up to.

I hope to God they made up after the fight at the Gala, which I never ended up getting around to asking her about because I wasn't meant to be there.

A sinking feeling creeps right through me as Hoax meets my gaze.

"Jesus, fuck," he says as I show him my phone. "You got her number?"

I nod.

Snitch got it for me, not that I've ever texted or called her, for obvious reasons.

I just had it in case I needed it.

For the first time since I met her, I've no idea what to do.

BRACKEN RIDGE
REBELS
ARIZONA
M · C

CHAPTER 10

FRANKIE

I stare at the casket, unable to comprehend anything.

He's gone.

My father.

The Great Doctor Thomas Stevens.

To me, he was indestructible, larger than life. A man who helped people. With his bare hands, he saved lives.

He can't be gone; it just can't be possible.

But I'm sitting here, in the church, and people around me are crying, shuffling their feet and listening to people talk about what kind of man he was.

I feel like I'm having an out of body experience.

This can't be happening.

My mother sits next to me, unmoving. She dabs her eyes every now and then with a tissue.

She looks stricken. Like she can't believe he's gone.

None of us can.

My brother, Chris, sits on the other side of her. It's the first time I've seen him in a suit.

My father…he was fifty-two years old.

I look down at my hands, tuning out the words. Unable to look at the casket any longer.

I just want to run far, far away and never come back.

Everything this week has been a blur. I wasn't able to go to work. A couple of my friends called and Adele too, but I can't face anyone.

I think back to the night that we fought at the charity dinner, and I want to scream. He was so angry with me, and I defied him on purpose because I was being a child and wanted to be right. I wanted to prove him wrong about Doctor Samuels, and I ended up being completely out of my depth.

And my dad knew.

We didn't speak of it again, and it was a long week with the two of us avoiding one another and being awkward. I realize now that he was just protecting me. And he probably realized that I figured out what really happened with my mom and the man he hated so much.

Getting through the sermons is a nightmare, and then having to face everyone when they leave the church is pure torture. I can't even speak about the wake a few days prior.

Mom and I barely say two words to one another. It's not like I don't want to comfort her, I do, but she's not the sort of woman who allows it.

Now she just seems so blank, and I don't know how to

reach her.

I don't even want to think about the fight we had, or how our family seemed to be hanging on by a string. Now that string has snapped and all that's left are the frayed edges.

I want to be there for my mom, though, even if we aren't getting along, and she hit me. I close my eyes.

I never thought she'd be capable of striking me, but I guess I pushed her too far.

What does any of it matter now?

I sit in stunned silence, feeling a coldness in my bones I've never known before as family members take their places at the podium and speak about their brother, uncle, friend. All the while, I'm dying inside.

I spare a glance at Chris. He's openly crying. Mom holds his hand and a moment later, she reaches for mine.

We don't look at each other. I just take her hand in mine and wish I were somewhere else.

Anywhere else.

At least this way we get to pretend we're a strong family unit and that all is okay in the Stevens household. It's what Dad would have wanted.

The rain pelts down on the roof.

I haven't slept since the funeral yesterday.

Everything is a blur.

Chris is a mess.

Nobody tells you how grief will smack you in the face, then continue to run you over again and again until it's done with you. Until the next time, that is. There's always a next time.

I get up and go downstairs to boil the kettle and make some herbal tea.

I don't even dare check the time.

I stayed at my parents' house last night after the funeral, so Mom wasn't alone. It was difficult being there without my dad around. So very strange.

I don't know what to do or how to fill this hole in my heart. There's an ache inside that won't go away.

I've run out of tears; my body is literally dry.

I make the tea, then slowly drag myself upstairs. I don't know why, but I stop over at the window and look out.

The rain cascades down the window as I take in the street. There's no traffic, so it must be late.

I take a sip of my tea, then I glance my eyes down to the street.

Adam is sitting in the rain, on his motorcycle, looking up at the window.

My chest jolts as my eyes find his.

What the hell is he doing here?

I haven't seen him since that day at the hospital when security dragged him away. That isn't to say he hasn't been watching me without my knowledge, like right now.

I don't know what possesses me to do what I do next; but I set my cup down on the side table and go downstairs.

Before I can change my mind, I open the door and run out toward him.

When I reach his motorcycle, he's still sitting in the same position, soaking wet.

"What are you doing here?" I garble.

He runs a hand through his wet hair. "Checkin' on you."

I swallow down every single warning and red flag that's going off in my brain.

"Come inside," I whisper.

"I can't do that."

"Yes, you can." I tug on the sleeve of his jacket. He looks down at my hand curiously. "Please, Nitro."

I've never used his biker name before, and I can tell he likes it by the look in his eyes.

He looks back up at me, as I plead silently, while we both get drenched.

As if he's reluctant, he stands, then I step back as he swings one leg over the bike and dismounts.

I grab his hand and almost drag him toward my front door…and he follows.

When we get there, I shut the door on the rain as he

stands on the welcome mat like he doesn't belong. Running off to get a towel from the upstairs bathroom, I dry myself off as I go, and when I return, he's still in exactly the same position.

"Didn't anyone ever tell you it's dangerous bringing strange men into your apartment?" he asks, quirking a brow.

I ignore him, holding the towel in both my palms as I reach for his head. He bends toward me as I ruffle dry his hair. Next, I tell him to shrug off his jacket, which he does. It's then I notice his t-shirt clings to his skin as I work the hem out of his jeans and lift it, rolling it up his body as he lets me drag it off him. I dump it unceremoniously on the floor where his jacket lies.

I stare at his body.

He's broader than I remember. Muscled with pecs that go for days...then there's his abs and that smattering of hair that leads down into his jeans. His chest has a black raven tattoo spread across it.

I roll my lips.

"Yes, but you said you won't hurt me," I reply when I've had my fill of him. Then I add, "Take off your jeans."

"Aren't we supposed to at least have a date first?"

I smile. It's the first real smile I've managed to form in days. "I'm not having sex with you; I'm trying to make sure you don't catch pneumonia."

His eyes blaze as he says, "You first."

I look down at myself and see my sweats are in a similar state to his clothes.

I tug off my sweater, and his eyes dance with mischief.

"I shouldn't be here," he whispers. His hand comes to my face, his knuckles grazing down my cheekbone. "You should kick me out, if you know what's good for you."

"Maybe I don't know what's good for me," I whisper back.

He cups my face. "I'm sorry…about your dad."

As he looks me right in the eye, I swear my heart kicks up ten notches.

I nod. I can't say anything because I've nothing left in the tank. No tears. No words. Nothing.

"Thank you," is all I can summon.

Then, I don't think. I grab his hand and yank him toward the stairs. He doesn't protest when we head up and enter my bedroom.

"Frankie…"

I turn on him. "I just need you to hold me, Nitro."

He swallows hard, and I see the challenge in his eyes as he fights whatever it is he was going to say. I don't want to hear any of it. I just want him wrapped around me.

Around him, everything feels warm. Everything feels so much better, even if it's wrong on so many levels. We're from two completely different backgrounds, with absolutely nothing in common, and I don't even know him.

But none of that matters tonight.

Reaching down, I undo his boot laces, then he kicks his boots off, pulling off his socks too and discarding them.

I undo his belt buckle as he watches me. My deft fingers do everything I can not to brush the bulge front and center, but it's a little difficult; I can see he's rock hard. I shove his jeans down and find that he favors underpants. I can't say I manage to keep my eyes on his while doing it, but I'm only human, after all.

He's standing there at the foot of my bed, with no clothes on aside from his underwear, and I've never wanted to jump somebody so much in my entire life. The feeling that comes over me startles my every being.

As if reading my mind, he reaches for me, brushing the hair back off my face as he looks at me like he's staring into my soul. "I came for you, right after it happened…"

I frown. "You did?"

He nods. "Yes."

"Why didn't you…say something?"

"After the last time I saw you?"

I look down at my hands, but he brings his fingers to my chin and lifts it again. "You'll get through this, Frankie. It seems hard now, and I promise you, it's going to test you, but you're strong, so much stronger than you think."

It's like he really can read my mind. And it's not just him saying the things I want him to say. I know that this is just the beginning of the grieving process. I know I have a long road to go down, the whole family does.

"I wish I could believe you," I whisper.

"I didn't come here to get you into bed," he says, though it's barely audible. We're so close.

"I know that. You're the only person that's ever straight with me, Nitro, and I don't even know you."

"We have a connection. You don't have to know me."

But I want to, so very much.

"Come to bed."

I pull back and lift the hem of my shirt because it's a little damp. I was only wearing a thin tank underneath my sweater. As I push down my sweatpants, he watches every single movement like it's the first time he's ever seen a woman undress before.

He fascinates me. Everything about him. And I can't get enough of his warmth.

I grasp his wrist and tug him toward the side of the bed. He's slow to move, almost reluctant. I've never had a guy look at me this intently and not even try to fuck me.

He's got every opportunity. I'm right there, all the signs right in front of him, even when I told him I didn't invite him in for sex. That part was true, until I got him undressed.

I flip the duvet aside and climb in. He towers over my bed, watching me.

A thrill goes through my body as I pat the empty side of

the mattress.

He's so damn fine. His body tanned, muscular, and those abs…hot.

Bending forward, he slides in next to me, then pulls the duvet over the two of us.

He reaches for me, then says, "Turn around, your back to me."

I feel a tinge of disappointment that he really does want to just cuddle and nothing else.

But I don't argue. I turn over, and he pulls me to him.

He's warm, his chest presses against my back as we spoon and his arm comes over my hip, effectively caging me in.

I can't even describe how he smells. If I had to, it'd be something similar to perilous danger, mixed with Brut and cigarettes. Whatever it is, it's doing things to me that shouldn't be legal.

I grasp his hand in mine as he cradles me, then I feel him press a kiss to the back of my head.

He really isn't trying to have sex.

This strange sensation comes over me.

He's protecting me, just like he said.

With all the courage I can muster, I ask, "Did you fuck up Trent Samuels' face?"

I close my eyes, waiting for him to reply, not that I need him to. I know it was him.

Signature stalker move.

"Yes," he replies softly.

I swallow hard. "Why did you do that?"

His thumb starts to stroke my hand gently. "Because he disrespected you."

"You broke his nose."

"That was for hittin' on you. Asshole needs to go find women his own age and stop preying on his students."

It really hit a nerve with him.

The fact that he's in my house, in my bed, holding me…and I don't even know him, just goes to show that I'm clearly not thinking straight.

Yes, there's something about him that smells like danger, but I somehow know that he won't do anything to hurt me. If he wanted to, he could've done it by now.

"Are you in the habit of beating people up who annoy me?"

A few seconds go by before he replies. "No, but I am in the habit of keeping my promises."

I don't even want to decipher what any of that means.

I snuggle back into him, pressing my ass against his hard length.

"Frankie," he warns.

He has a wood like nothing else. It makes me dizzy just thinking about it.

How I wish I were brave enough to turn back around

and touch it, rip my tank off, and let him see my body. I want him to take the pain away.

"What?" I ask innocently.

"I know what you're doin'."

"So, you're saying no to sex? Just so we're clear…"

He chuckles. "Fuck no. But this wouldn't be right. Not like this."

I feel like I've swallowed cement when I ask, "Why not? We're practically naked."

He kisses the back of my head again. "Because it would be a mercy fuck." My eyes ping open as I try to digest his words. Was that an insult? Then he adds, "As in, you're only givin' me the time of day because you're sad."

I turn in his arms and sit up on my elbows. "Is that what you really think?"

"I think grief does things to people. I can't take the pain away, not permanently."

"I never asked you to!" I snap, then I immediately feel bad.

He reaches for me and tucks one side of my hair behind my ear. "I don't want to take advantage of you."

"You wouldn't be. I want this."

He hesitates. "You want this?" Why does he sound so disbelieving?

"Yes," I reply. I reach down and grip his cock as he hisses at the contact. "And this."

"Fuck, Frankie…"

Just like in my fantasy, I become even more bold, and I start to massage it. Feeling his length, his hardness, and loving every moment of it.

"What, don't you like that?"

I feel his chest rumble as I try not to come undone just at the sound he makes.

"Of course, I like it, but…" he trails off as I lift the elastic and shove my hand down the front of his underpants.

He hisses again, one hand reaching to my hair as he grasps it with one hand, looking down at what I'm doing.

I tug his underpants down his thighs so his dick springs free, and my eyes go wide. I've seen a few, not that many, but Nitro is big. And thick. Of course, he had to be well endowed. The man has it all in the looks department.

Heat rises in my belly as I stare down at it and begin to jerk him off as he grips the side of my tank.

"You're gonna make me come," he growls. His eyes find mine, and I know exactly what will ensure victory. I move my head down to his cock and lick the tip.

The groan he makes sends a shiver down my spine, so I do it again, enjoying the sounds and the taste of him.

When I look up at his face, he's got his eyes closed, his expression nothing short of euphoric. It only encourages me. I take him farther into my mouth, gripping his base as I begin to bob my head and suck him, working my mouth up and down.

"Jesus fuck, Doc."

I love his nickname for me, especially when he says it like that, when I'm taking him with my mouth.

All of a sudden, I'm being hauled off him. He rolls me onto my back and pins my arms above my head. I yelp as he presses his body into mine.

"Nitro," I whisper.

He stares at me with those green eyes that I know, no matter what happens between us, I'll never forget the way he's looking at me right at this moment.

It's like he's ripped down my walls without even trying. Like he really can see to the heart of me.

"Shouldn't have done that, Doc," he says. "That pretty mouth…"

I have no idea what this man is doing to me, or how I let him into my bed and got into this predicament, but I don't care. It feels too damn good.

"Shut up and kiss me," I whisper.

I need him like I need air.

As if sensing my need for him, he smirks. "Nah, babe, I know where your mouth's been."

Nitro

BRACKEN RIDGE
REBELS
ARIZONA
M · C

CHAPTER 11

NITRO

She's like fuckin' heaven.

I know I shouldn't be here.

I know I shouldn't have let her pull me inside, not that I put up a fight. I'd let her drag me anywhere, to Hell if that's what had to be done. None of it stops me.

I willingly crawled into her bed and felt her up.

It doesn't help she's being a cock tease, rubbing her little ass against my wood.

I really did just come here to try to catch a glimpse of her, to make sure she was safe and sound. I never in a million years thought we'd end up like this.

Even if she is using me because she's in pain, I don't mind being her battering ram. I'll be whatever she wants me to be.

Now that she's here, underneath me, almost naked, I feel like I hit the fuckin' jackpot.

I slide her tank off her body and her tits, round and full, come into view. She's so beautiful.

Then I'm shoving her panties down until she kicks them off, and my heart beats so loudly in my chest that I'm sure I'm gonna see God tonight.

She's a vision, naked under me, at my mercy. Not that I'd do anything she didn't want to.

I almost don't want to speak in case this is really just a dream and I'll wake any moment.

"You sure you won't regret this in the morning?" I nudge her entrance with my cock.

She shakes her head. "Condom," she breathes.

"You got any?"

She shakes her head.

I kiss her on the nose. "Good. Let's keep it that way."

I lift off her and hunt around for my jeans on the floor. Rolling on a rubber, hardly daring to believe it, I mount her body once more.

Fuck, she feels good, and I'm not even inside her yet.

Her auburn hair splays out on the crisp, white pillows like a fuckin' angel. One I'm corrupting by even being here.

I bring my knees up, along with her legs that wrap around my waist. Bending down, I suck one nipple into my mouth. She groans and cries out, and grasping the other breast, I fondle her as she rubs against my cock.

I want in so badly. I've dreamed about sinking into her hot, sexy body ever since the day she was on top of me, pumping my heart. I wanted her to pump my dick with the same vigorous movements, and I've jerked off so many times imagining it. Now it's really happening.

"You're a fuckin' angel," I rasp, moving my mouth to the other peak as she writhes against me, grinding herself, our bodies tangling together.

I want to play with every inch of her, but my cock's begging me to bang her hard. I can feel cum leaking out of my tip already, but I want this to last.

She wraps her arms around my neck and grips my hair in her hands.

I don't remember when I've ever been so hot for a woman. Having her look at my cock like that and wrapping her lips around me…Jesus, I almost blew my load down her throat.

"I need it," she groans. "I need you, Nitro."

Hearing my name turns me on. I pull out of her grasp, moving down her body as she gasps at every kiss and nip I give her.

I open her legs as she spreads them for me, and I'm delighted to see how wet she is.

She's bare, smooth, and fuckin' gorgeous. I bend and suck on her pussy lips as she bucks underneath me, holding her legs apart. As they come toward my head, I run my tongue through her folds.

"Oh, God!" she cries out.

Yeah. I'm good at head. I like to make a meal out of it.

I do it again, this time licking her clit as she moans. I know she's close.

I want to taste her first orgasm on my tongue.

I begin to eat her out, shoving my tongue inside her as she gasps, then I lick her soft, luscious cunt all the way to her clit, knowing I'm driving her mad. I eat like a man possessed, because that's how she makes me feel.

When I latch onto her clit, she cries out, her hands in my hair again as she pushes my face into her pussy. Fuck yeah.

She starts to come, grinding against my face as she moans her way to an orgasm that goes on and on. When she's done, I lick her arousal and gaze up as her eyes meet mine.

"Taste so fuckin' good, baby," I say. I insert a finger inside her, and she groans.

I finger her pussy as she watches me, my cock so hard it may explode. As I insert another finger, she grips the sheets, her breathing erratic and heavy. Curling them inside her, I lean down to her clit again and suck it into my mouth as she grinds against me, chasing her second release.

She's so responsive. So hot for my touch.

She comes again quickly, so loud that I can't hold on anymore. I move up her body, position my cock at her entrance, and I shove inside her full tilt. She gasps as I groan.

"Nitro," she moans.

"Yeah, babe?"

"You're fucking huge."

I chuckle, pulling out slightly, and grabbing my cock with one hand, I spread her arousal through her folds, up to her clit. She bucks again.

"Do you like my tongue fucking your pussy?"

She gasps at my dirty words. Then she nods, her cheeks flushing.

I grunt, pushing back in again. I pull out, then repeat, nice and slow, so she can get used to me.

She feels so goddamn good. So fucking perfect.

"Say it," I growl.

She hesitates.

"Say it!"

"I like your tongue fucking my pussy," she whispers.

I push inside again and start to fuck her a bit quicker.

"Your tight little pussy's strangling my cock, baby. Do you like how I feel inside you?"

She grips my ass, trying to meet my thrusts. "Yes… Adam…Nitro…God, yes!"

I chuckle. Running my hands up her body, I hold her wrists with one hand above her head, loving how her tits jiggle as I fuck her. I move my hips faster, grinding into her as her bed begins to squeak. I'm so fucking close.

"Didn't wanna come so fast," I growl. "But you cock teased me into submission."

She gasps as I quicken even more. Letting go of her hands, I push up onto my palms, giving it to her as she groans, her legs wrapped around me even tighter. I wish I could fuckin' last longer.

"Oh, God!" she screams as she finds her release, coming all over my cock as I watch her face morph into a picture of bliss.

I shoot my cum hard, stilling as I empty myself on a groan that doesn't even sound human.

I immediately collapse as we both pant for breath.

"That. Was. So. Good," she says, each word emphasized with her breathing.

"Babe, that's just me gettin' started. I did try to warn you." I roll off her, pull off the rubber, tie it up, then lean over and drop it on the bedside table.

And in the next second, I'm back, hovering over her and taking her mouth.

We just fucked and I haven't even kissed her.

I don't kiss. Ever.

But with Frankie, I want all of her.

She gasps as our lips and tongues meet. Fuck me if she hasn't got the sweetest lips in the world. I could kiss her for days.

When we pull apart, I know I have to fuck her again before she changes her mind, realizes who I am, and kicks me the hell out of here.

As I grab another rubber, her eyes go wide.

I smirk. "You didn't think we were done here, did you, Doc?"

She blinks in rapid succession as I go up to my knees and place the foil packet in her hand.

"Roll it on me."

Her eyes go wide. "Does that thing ever go down?"

I chuckle. "Not with you around."

She sits up as I kneel between her legs, and it's the hottest thing I've ever seen.

As she rolls it on me, I revel in her touch, needing to be so close to her.

When she's done, I pull her up to her knees, cupping her face and kissing her hard.

She's all about my cock; her hand reaching to stroke me as I move my mouth to her neck and suck and nip her skin. One hand snakes down her body, cupping one breast on the way down before I reach between her legs. Feeling how wet and swollen she is makes me want to go down on her all over again, but my cock's got other ideas. I rub her slickness around, coating her clit as she whimpers at my touch. Inserting two fingers, I start to fuck her tight pussy, marking her skin as I suck her neck harder.

I want to mark her.

I want to make sure she knows who she belongs to.

She tips her head back, inviting me in as I pump my

fingers faster, and she climaxes, clinging to me, her nails digging into my back. I pull my fingers out and bring them to my mouth, sucking them as she stares at me.

Then I put my fingers near her mouth and say, "Suck. Taste yourself, baby."

She looks shocked as I insert my fingers into her mouth, and she does as she's told.

I don't think she knows how good she looks; wide eyed and just fucked. I could do this all night.

I cup her breast and lean down to suck her nipple again as she moans at my touch.

"Call in sick tomorrow," I grunt against her flesh. "I want to discover this body all fuckin' night long."

"Nitro!"

"Bet I could make you come just by playin' with your titties. Couldn't I, babe?"

She groans as I pull my fingers from her mouth, trying to rub herself on my knee as I chuckle darkly.

Rolling over onto my back, I take her with me.

"Dreamed of this ever since you rode me the first time," I say, pulling her body over mine as she settles on my lap. "Ride me hard, Frankie."

She looks so fuckin' wild. Her hair hangs over her shoulders, almost covering her plump, beautiful tits. She grabs my dick and lines herself up, then slowly slides down on me.

"Jesus," she cries.

I chuckle, sitting up on my elbows, spreading my legs wider. "I was just inside you, Frankie. That little pussy just swallowed this big cock. Breathe, baby..."

She gasps at my words, and I pull her head toward me and kiss her roughly, pushing her down onto me as she gasps into my mouth. I hold her hips as we kiss, moving her back and forth until she shifts her hips to brush her clit against me.

Her strangled cries tell me she's close…again, and I watch as she spirals, moving my hands to cup her tits. I pull on her nipples hard as she climaxes.

It's not enough, though. I need more of her. I flop down as she begins to ride me, her hands pushing on my chest as I grip her hips, and this time, I help her move.

She bounces on my cock as I bury every fat inch inside her tight cunt. And it's so fucking sweet. So perfect. Made for me.

I don't think I've ever been this cock teased and ready to fuck all night in forever.

"That's it, Frankie, give yourself to me. Tell me how good it feels."

"It feels so good!" she cries.

"Talk dirty to me, let it out, baby…"

The way her tits move with her bouncing taunts me, so I sit up and suck a nipple into my mouth, still holding her hips as she fucks me harder.

"Fuck me, Nitro," she whispers.

"More," I demand, licking her other nipple with small flicks.

"Fuck me with that hard cock."

I slap her ass cheek. "Dirtier."

"Fuck my tight pussy with your fat cock, Nitro…"

I grin into her skin and move one hand between us to rub her clit. The second I touch it; she loses control and pulses around my cock. I let go too, coming violently with a roar against her, only wishing I was spurting inside her and not into fuckin' wrap. That's gonna change real quick.

We slow as I empty myself, and she slumps against me.

I fall back to the pillows, bringing her with me.

She's spent and tired, her head resting on my chest.

My heart beats like a runaway freight train.

I know I've never felt this way before.

I know that coming here wasn't a good idea because I can never have her like that. I can never take her to the club…that's just not the way this works.

Now I find myself thinking about how she'd see my life and how I live it. And I shouldn't be thinking like that. Men in my club don't think like this and they certainly don't act like it.

You'd be pussy-whipped to even admit it.

The club comes before anything else. Women don't

matter; they're there for one reason and one reason only. But it ain't like that with Frankie.

She's the fuckin' sun on a cloudy day.

I don't even want to move, but I'm still in her and she falls asleep in my arms.

I quickly discard the rubber and wrap my arms around her.

I don't know if she'll ever believe a word of it, but I never came here to seduce her.

I didn't even have the balls to knock on her door, or better still, barge my way in.

Still, I fall asleep soundly, and when I wake up, she's still wrapped around me.

I would never have known Frankie to be such a deep sleeper, but she sleeps like the dead. Me? Not so much, especially when I've got a shit ton going on in my head with how much I want her but don't want to involve her.

How can I, when I don't want her coming to the club? I don't want anyone to know about what we have going on, not until I've figured it out myself.

My heart palpitates at the thought that she'd take one look at church and run a mile. I don't know why, but it's inevitable. She doesn't know club life, and I'll bet that she won't want to know.

All I know is we have tonight, nothing more.

The sooner I get that into my head, the better.

I slide out of her bed in the early hours of morning. She stirs and I dress quietly, slipping into my jeans and tugging my boots on. I could watch her all morning, but I've got to get back to the club. We have a deal going down and this is one meeting I can't miss.

I slept soundly, for the most part, something I haven't done in years. Having a woman in my bed is something new for me since I usually sleep alone. The women that share my bed are just there for sex, not cuddling and shit.

I run a hand over my face. I know I'm getting in too deep.

My feelings for her run like fire through my veins.

I'll do anything to keep her safe, to make her smile.

Seeing her so upset about her father has me fucked up inside. I want to take that pain away and I can't.

I don't know how.

But I do know I can hold her. When she needs it, if she needs it.

That's if this whole thing wasn't just a one-off. She might wake up this morning and decide this was a huge mistake. And I wouldn't blame her. Being involved with me won't go down well in her circle. But I'm done worrying about all that shit.

I lock the door behind me as I jump on my sled and

head off back to church.

I should've known the minute I left her warm bed.
I should've known that it was all too good to be true.
I should've been fuckin' smarter.
But I wasn't and shit caught up with me.

BRACKEN RIDGE
REBELS
ARIZONA
M · C

CHAPTER 12

FRANKIE

One week.

One week.

Two weeks.

Three weeks go by.

There is no word from Nitro.

I stare at the clubhouse gates, wondering what the hell I'm even doing here.

It's not a place for a girl like me. It's not a place for any law-abiding citizen to be, yet here I sit. In my car, like a loser, wondering what will happen when I set foot through those doors.

He never called me like he promised. He never even texted me.

To say I feel like he used me just to sleep with me is an understatement. It makes me feel like the world's biggest fool.

Yet, I can't help but think his actions, that night we slept together, said otherwise.

He was kind. Caring. Considerate. And so damn sexy. The way he held me.

The way he cradled me in his arms afterward and held me tight. Those aren't the actions of a man who is set out to hurt me, to take what he wanted and then be gone forever.

He admitted he's been following me. I know we have a connection. What I can't work out is how we got to this; him completely ghosting me.

I feel wretched. Like he's got a piece of my soul and I can't function without not knowing what happened or what I did.

Things have been bad these past few weeks. I've only just returned back to work, but the halls are filled with sad faces, people avoiding me because they don't know what to say.

Trent Samuels is still on sick leave after Nitro beat him up, and I'm glad for it. I didn't want to face him or have his sympathy. I'd rather die.

Remembering him banging Carly in his bathroom turns my stomach.

Mom and I haven't been in a good place; she's been cold and distant. I know this is a big shock to all of us, but I thought that it would bring us closer. Only it has affectively driven us apart even further.

My brother is lost, and I don't know how to help him when I'm suffering myself.

And I've been offered a transfer, which came out of the blue. I've decided I want to be an obstetrician, specializing in childbirth and women's reproductive health when I start my residency.

It's not what my father would have wanted, but it's what I want. It's where my true passion is leading me.

The truth is, I have nothing holding me here. Most of my friends moved away after college, and though I have become close with Adele, she won't be staying in Phoenix either for her residency.

So, why am I thinking about Nitro and what this means? It's stupid. It was a one-night stand, nothing more.

I just can't seem to get him out of my thoughts. He haunts me night and day.

Screw it.

I take a deep breath and climb out of my car before I can stop myself.

I stare at the metal gates, feeling a little out of my depth. I can't see over them, but I can hear music blasting.

This isn't a great part of town. In fact, it's an old industrial area that most people have forgotten about. Weird to think a biker clubhouse actually tidied the place up a bit.

I press the buzzer.

A few moments later, a voice barks down the speaker, asking what I want.

"I'm a friend of Nitro's," I start. "I…uh, need to see

him. I'm his…doctor."

I palm my forehead, why did I say that?

"He's not here," the male voice says.

A few more seconds pass.

I clear my throat and press the button again. "Do you know where I can find him?" I frown as I say it, not quite sure if I want to know.

The speaker crackles again. "He's in county."

Shocked, I stare at the box on the gate like an idiot. "County?"

"Yeah, you know…jail."

Nitro is in jail?

I guess that explains his absence.

I press the intercom again. "What did he do?"

"You ask a lot of fuckin' questions."

My eyes go wide as I step back. A second later, the gate starts to open.

Do I really want to do this?

Nitro isn't even here.

I turn to leave when I hear… "Hey!"

I look over my shoulder as a tall, broad, long-haired man stands at the gate, hands on hips.

He doesn't look very friendly.

"I…I'm just leaving," I stammer, stumbling back and almost tripping.

He watches me, amusement crossing his face as he

comes closer. "Don't break your neck, sweetheart, we're all good here." He gives me a chin lift. "I'm Smokey, the V.P."

V.P.? What the heck does that mean?

"Uh, I'm Frankie."

"Right, Nitro's doctor?"

Okay, so I may have stretched the truth a little there, but I don't correct myself.

I nod. "Yeah…"

"The one who saved his life, right?"

"No, that was my f–" I stop.

He doesn't need to know my life story. Or maybe he already knows. The entire city is still talking about my father's untimely death. All of it hurts. Seeing it everywhere. Hearing it.

Having people whisper as I pass in the hall. Don't they know that's rude?

Feeling his loss is the hardest thing I've ever had to endure.

He cocks a brow, waiting.

"I had a hand in it," I admit.

He snorts. "Right."

"I was just…"

He sweeps his hand to the clubhouse. "Coming inside?"

My eyes go wide, and my feet stay put.

He smirks. "What's the matter, Doc. We don't bite."

"Nitro's in jail," I reaffirm.

He nods. "Unfortunate, but true."

I straighten my spine. Showing weakness won't help here, Frankie. Be strong.

"What did he do?"

He clears his throat. "Club business."

I frown. "Which translates to…you're not going to tell me, are you?"

"Let's just say, he was at the wrong place at the wrong time."

"How long…when will he be out?"

"Ninety days," he says.

Shit.

I'll be in New Jersey by then. If I decide I'm really going.

I take a long breath.

I need to talk to him, and I know that I should not be feeling relieved that he's locked up and that's the reason he hasn't contacted me. That would be a sick thing to think…

"You gonna wait for him?" he muses. "It ain't that long."

My eyes snap to his. "It's not like that…we're… friends."

He snorts again. Leaning lazily against the side of the gate, he's in no hurry to leave. There is no way I'm going inside that place. I was stupid to come here.

"Nitro isn't friends with women."

I don't want to hear this.

"Well, he's friends with me."

He looks at me curiously. "I can see why he kept you a secret, I would too."

I open my mouth and close it again. "Can you give him a message?"

He does that one eyebrow quirk thing. "What am I, a fuckin' errand boy?"

"No, but I'm going to be moving…I won't see him when he gets out. I wanted to let him know in person, that's all. But that's a little difficult being he's in jail."

"You could always visit, if you care so much."

I stare at him for a few moments. "Visit?"

"Yeah, you know, you sign in and they let you see him through a glass partition."

I have no words.

"Then again, he's in low security, so I doubt there'd be a barrier," he goes on. "Don't think they allow conjugal visits, assholes."

I narrow my eyes. "Like I said, it's not like that."

He stares at me. "You wanna know something?"

I don't answer, but I also don't reach for my car door.

"I've never seen Nitro happy, in the coupla years I've known him, except since he got shot and met you."

Why is he telling me this?

"That can't be true," I say quietly.

He folds his arms over his chest. "It's the truth. You can believe whatever you want, but that's what I know."

I swallow hard. "This sucks."

"Can say that again, he's a good guy." Our eyes meet. "Wrong place at the wrong time, darlin', don't overthink it. He's had a shit life, but unlike a lot of us, he's good underneath. He's not rotten to the core."

I close my eyes momentarily. "I shouldn't be here."

His lips twitch. "That's probably true, but at least you know now that he wasn't an asshole. That's what you were thinkin', right?"

I look to the ground. "I don't know what I was thinking, to be perfectly honest."

For some odd reason, I think he feels sorry for me.

"I have to go," I say, waving to the car.

He nods like he understands, then he says, "What about that message? That all you got, Doc?"

I open my car door, shaking my head. "Don't tell him I was here."

He watches me as I drive away, crying all the way home.

NITRO

Four weeks into my sentence.

"How the fuck did I get locked up with you?" I complain to Hoax as we play some ball.

"I don't know, but I haven't gone without pussy this long. Gonna fuckin' kill me."

I shake my head. "Bullshit is what it is."

Unfortunately, when we raided the frat house that night on the stakeout, courtesy of Tex's orders, the place also got raided by the pigs, and we were caught in the middle.

Not a good place to be, considering the amount of drugs these dudes had on them.

Tex has some pigs on his payroll, so Hoax and I only got done for possession, even though neither of us had drugs on us, and got a reduced sentence of ninety days instead of twelve months.

Sometimes I can't believe my fuckin' luck.

I think about my baby girl, and I get even more agitated.

I wonder what she's been doing this whole time. Plus, she now thinks I'm a fuckin' asshole for sleeping with her and then ghosting her.

She needed me, or at least my body, whatever. We were just getting closer and bam, like everything in my life, it got ruined before it even begun.

She's hurting because of her father's death, and I should

be there for her, to lean on, to look out for her. To hold her.

Instead, I got sloppy. I got too cocky. Now look at me.

I'm locked up in here and can't do jack shit about it. Can't even get word to her that I'm in here. Even if I did get a message to my brothers to give to her, it'd mean she's on the radar.

That's not keeping her safe, not when assholes like Tex or Rachet would be interested to know why I kept her away from the club. I don't need them sniffing around.

I don't trust them.

She's too pure for club life; I always knew this, but a part of me thought I could get away with it if she were just on the side. Selfish of me, but I'm an asshole, what can I say.

My main intention, aside from wanting to be with her, has always been to keep her safe.

I vowed that to myself when I was on death's door, and unlike most people, I keep my promises.

The only thing I really have left is my integrity, and even that is hanging on by a thread.

"Least the food isn't too bad," Hoax goes on.

I snort. Fuck's sake. Food and pussy, it's all this man thinks about.

"Jesus fuckin' Christ, Hoax."

"What?" He shrugs, throwing me the ball as I make a basket.

"Nobody likes fuckin' prison food."

"Let's just be thankful Tex has friends in low places."

That I've got to agree on. I've been in and out of county my whole life, and my track record with the law is shady as fuck as a juvenile, but I can hold my own. I'm lucky I'm bigger than most and for some reason, unless they're bigger than me, they don't pick a fight. I wouldn't want to put that theory to the test in here, though.

I pass him the ball as the whistle tells us the outdoor recreation time is over.

As we head back indoors, one of the guards stops me. "You got a visitor."

I frown.

Hoax side-eyes me. "Don't fuckin' believe it. If it's fuckin' Candy, you're gonna feel my fist down your throat."

He tries to shove me, but I dodge him and follow the guard instead.

I didn't think anybody was gonna miss my presence, but maybe I'm short-changing myself.

I walk into the visiting room, which is just a large, open space filled with tables and chairs.

I glance around as he leads me to a table by the window.

I can't believe my eyes when I see Frankie sitting there. She's in her hospital scrubs.

The guard eyes me as he presses himself against the wall not too far away.

"Frankie?" I never would have thought I'd feel embarrassed to be wearing my prison jumpsuit, but here we are. I feel like a total fuckin' loser.

She blinks a couple of times as she takes me in. I take the seat opposite.

"How did you know I was here?"

"Smokey," she whispers.

My eyes go wide as I run a hand through my hair. "Don't tell me you went to the clubhouse."

She nods. "I did, but I didn't go inside. He came to the gate…I was…I was worried about you, Nitro."

I swallow hard. She's so goddamn beautiful. Too good for me. It swims between us like an obvious truth, one that neither of us will admit to but we both know it.

I'm a thorn in her side. I always will be.

"You shouldn't have come." I glance around. "This isn't the place for a lady."

Her hands are clasped together, and I've never seen her look more uncomfortable.

"What happened?"

I don't want to lie to her, but club business is club business, so I simply say, "Drug bust gone wrong, babe."

She blinks rapidly again. I wish I knew what she was thinking.

"Smokey said you were at the wrong place at the wrong time."

I shrug. "Something like that." I lean closer to her. "I never wanted you to see me like this."

She shakes her head. "It doesn't matter."

I snort. "It matters, babe, it really does fuckin' matter." I'm annoyed with myself that she's sunk to these levels to be here. I'm leading her down a dark road, and I know it.

"I…I got offered a transfer," she blurts out as our eyes meet again. "New Jersey."

Holy shit.

She's leaving.

I nod. Even though I don't believe a word that's about to come out of my mouth, I say, "It might be good for you, a fresh start."

She frowns. "Is that all you have to say?"

"What do you want me to say, Frankie? We were never gonna be anything more than what we were that night I came to your door."

Lies. Lies. Lies.

"How could you say that?"

I know now what I have to do. If she's out of the state, I can't follow her. I can't be around her. I can't stalk her to make sure she's safe. But that'll mean she'll be unprotected…still, she'll have a good life. One without me in it, but that's the whole point.

I'm not good enough.

I don't want to be an asshole, but it feels like if I tell her to stay, then she might just do that.

Tell her to stay.

"It's never gonna work between us." The words feel like poison.

She looks shocked, even though I know she knows what has to happen here.

"Was it all just to get in my pants?" she whispers.

I shake my head. "No. It was never about that. I told you, I'd never lie to you, not about that."

"Then why?"

I throw my hands down body. "Look at me!" I growl. "In this fuckin' jumpsuit. It's not the first time, and it sure as shit won't be the last. You deserve better than this. You want a walk on the wild side, Frankie, but you don't want this, not really. A life with me would never be any kinda fairy tale, not one where you get all the things you want."

She looks so fuckin' sad that I have to look away. "That's for me to decide."

Shut her down.

"Is this what you want? Transferring?"

"Jersey?"

I nod.

"I did at one point, but it came out of the blue. Things at home are…strained, to say the least, ever since my dad…" she trails off. Tears form in her eyes as I flick my gaze back to her.

She wipes her eyes with the back of her hands. "I thought I could do it, but I have to walk those halls every single day, Nitro, and it's killing me. I don't know how much longer I can do it."

"Then you have to go," I say simply. "Start fresh somewhere, make new friends, find a place where you feel most like yourself. I know it isn't here."

She stares at me. "But we have a connection. You feel it…don't you?"

My lips twitch.

I'll never forget you. I'll die with you on my mind, Frankie.

"Sometimes you have to learn to love what's good for you, babe, and we both know I ain't good for you."

More tears fall, rapidly this time.

"But, we can write?" My attempt at a joke falls on deaf ears as she shrugs her jacket back on.

"I'll never forget you, Nitro." She echoes my thoughts as a lump forms in my throat. "You were kind to me. You can't even be an asshole, because when you're saying one thing, your face says another."

She's a special woman, one that I have no business pursuing.

It's better this way, so much better. She'll be okay; she's so much stronger than she thinks.

I fight every instinct I have to not reach over there and

pull her across the table, kiss her, and tell her not to go. That we can work it out. That somehow, I'll think of something.

But that voice in the back of my head tells me no.

Leave her the fuck alone.

Don't fuck up her life.

She's still young, she's got her whole life ahead of her. If she stays here, she'll get roped into club life, and she'll never do anything, never get out of this godforsaken place.

And Frankie Stevens is going places.

She stands. I stay seated, looking up at her.

She looks to the guard. "Am I allowed to hug you?"

I shake my head.

I go to stand too and before I know it, she's in my arms, holding me so tight that I'm surprised by her strength. I kiss the top of her head as the guard marches to us and breaks us apart.

"I'll never forget you," she whispers, tears falling down her face as she backs off.

I smile. "Make sure you do everything you can, Frankie. Life's short, baby girl. Live every minute of it."

She walks away, her head hung low as my heart breaks into a million pieces.

This is it. The last time I will ever see her.

She turns at the door and gives me a wave.

I give her a chin lift in return. And then she's gone.

"I love you," I whisper.

I know that there will never be another woman who will ever claim my heart like Frankie Stevens.

And now she's gone.

BRACKEN RIDGE
REBELS
ARIZONA
M · C

CHAPTER 13

NITRO
PRESENT DAY - 18 YEARS LATER
BRACKEN RIDGE

I throw back the shot Hutch shoves my way down the bar. The Stone Crow isn't the place we usually meet. Hutch likes to keep a low profile, being the newly refurbished bar and restaurant caters for families now, and he doesn't want all of us fuckturds scaring the customers away.

Since he put me in charge of the used car yard, I've been in my element fixing shit and sorting the yard out, so the used cars are in one section and the scrap metal and parts are in another.

I never planned on being in Bracken Ridge. But when I reunited with my sister, Lucy, things changed. I wanted to be a family again.

Then one night I saw a girl I thought I recognized at the bar. I didn't dare to dream it was Frankie; so much time had passed and while she looked very similar, she had also changed so much. It had been so long, that I honestly thought my mind was playing tricks on me.

Then I realized it was her.

Then, when I found out Frankie was actually living here, everything changed once more.

I watched her for a while, since she didn't know I was in town at first. I've changed a lot over the ten years since she's seen me last. I doubt she'd even recognize me. In fact, I passed her a couple of times by accident—it's a small town after all—and she wasn't any the wiser.

Amusement crosses my lips as I remember how I used to stalk her.

Then, when she did find out I was back, we had an awkward first meeting and then I haven't seen her since. I can't say that it was the joyful reunion I once dreamed of.

If I had to guess, I'd say she's mad at me. Fuck knows why. I did her a favor, and she can't say otherwise.

After I shot Tex when he tried to kill my sister, and Bones, the Road Captain of the Rebels here in Bracken Ridge, I finally put the past behind me.

Or so I thought.

I'm still good friends with Smokey. He's resurrecting the old club, and they're now known at the Sons of Phoenix Fury. Hoax is still around; he inherited a house in his grandma's will, and they're making that into their new clubhouse.

I opted to start fresh in Bracken Ridge. More than

anything, I wanted to get to know Lucy, and now she's married to my old buddy, Rubble, and has a baby. I wanted to put some roots down here. After the life I've lived, I needed the stability.

Then I saw Frankie.

Just like that, all the memories came flooding back.

I've never settled down. There's never been anyone special. I don't meet women like that, not any that I'd want to settle down with or have kids, God forbid.

I'm twenty-nine now.

Frankie is thirty-five, and my, hasn't she grown into the most beautiful woman I've ever laid eyes on.

She's filled out, got some curves, her hair still hangs in long, auburn waves down her back. She has this confidence about her that I never saw when I knew her at twenty-five.

She's an Obstetrician now. She did it.

The only reason I knew she was here was because Brock, the clubs V.P., mentioned she was his wife, Angel's, doctor.

Then I had to see for myself.

I could never be so lucky to imagine that she's single, but I've never seen her with a man. She doesn't appear to have kids.

There is absolutely nothing in this world stopping me now from going to her and rekindling what we once had, or what I thought we had. Except I'm chicken shit.

I've got her on a pedestal so high that it's hardly fair on her, but I can't help it.

If she rejected me now, I'd probably wanna slit my wrists again. I did some bad shit when I ran away from home, that point was the lowest I've ever gone.

So in typical coward fashion, I've kept my distance.

Just lately, though, I've been seeing her everywhere.

Like here, I know she has dinner with her work colleagues every Thursday night.

I guess some habits die hard.

"You gonna fuckin' make a move, or do we have to sit here listenin' to your brain tick over like a Milli Vanilli record on repeat?" Hutch always has a way with words.

I turn to him. "What are you talkin' about?"

He shakes his head. "What do you think I am? I might be old, but I'm not fuckin' dead."

I sigh. I guess I have moped around here for a fair bit lately, and I continue to punish myself by continuing to watch her from a distance. I guess I really am just piss weak after all.

"It's complicated."

"You get your dick wet since you've been here?"

I frown.

Obviously, I've got my dick wet a lot in the last ten years, but since I got to Bracken Ridge and joined the club, I haven't sunk into any pussy. It seems even my dick knows who it really wants.

"Just as I thought," he snickers.

"Like I said, it's complicated."

"Show me a woman who isn't." 3, 2, 1… "When Kirsty and I got together, it wasn't a picnic, son. Women are hard work, but it's even harder when you sit back like a pussy and let a fine woman like Frankie Stevens get snapped up by any of the bachelors in town. You know it's gonna happen sooner or later."

Hutch loves nothing more than telling the same ol' story about him and Kirsty getting together. She's his ol' lady and has been since they were in their late teens.

Forty years or thereabouts.

They don't make them like they used to.

"She's a workaholic," I say, trying not to sound pleased about it. Working means she's less likely to find any of those bachelors. I see the logic.

"You think you're not good enough, is that it?"

"Somethin' like that."

"Got news for you. I know you think you're bein' all noble and shit, but there ain't nothing to be proud of lettin' this woman who's right under your nose get away. No logic in that."

He doesn't know our history.

I vowed a long time ago that my heart was never going to be held to ransom like that ever again.

Letting her go almost destroyed me.

When I got out of jail, shit went from bad to worse. I don't know how any of the Fury survived it, and a lot didn't.

I shot Tex last year. Hutch, Bones, and Steel, the club's Enforcer and the Sergeant at Arms, helped bury the body out in the desert. The one great thing about Arizona is there's a shit ton of dirt.

"Too much time's passed," I say, like that's any excuse. "We're different people now."

He just shakes his head, not even looking pitiful for me. It's more like a look of complete pathetic-ness.

I know.

Trust me, I know.

No one feels more of a loser than I am.

He slaps me on the back as he gets up to leave. "You hear from Smokey?"

I nod. "He's gonna let me know if he hears anything more. So far, he's tracked down the few loose cannons askin' around about Tex."

He nods as his phone rings. "Better take this."

"Have a good night," I say, as he heads out.

Yeah, the thing about being part of a 1% club like the Phoenix Fury, even though the club has since fallen apart, is that you never really escape it.

Some brothers from the club have been sniffing around the Sons and Smokey is keeping a close eye on things. Of course he, Hoax, and Griller, who's still knocking around, all know that Tex is six feet under. And not before time.

The Sons and the Rebels joined forces and snuffed Tex out. Rachet died a few months before in a shootout. The other brothers scattered right after shit went down a few years before that.

Tex was trying every trick in the book he could to get the club back together, but at the same time, Smokey was resurrecting his old club, so that was never gonna happen.

Tex had burned too many bridges, and those that were still loyal, like Popeye, Ratchet, and Snake are all six feet under. Rumor has it, Tex had a brother, not that he was close to him, and he's been asking around about his whereabouts.

I signal to Axton, my friend and the bartender here, who's also prospecting for the club. He also happens to be Brock's brother.

"You drownin' your sorrows again, bro?" He smirks as he pours me another whiskey.

"Why is it when a man has a couple of drinks, everyone assumes I'm drownin' my fuckin' sorrows?"

He gives me a look. "Aren't you?"

I take the shot and knock it back. "No. I'm not."

He shakes his head, not satisfied with that answer.

Since he and his boss, Stevie, who runs the bar, got together, he's been like a lovesick puppy.

I need to get me a drinking buddy, that's what it is.

I go to stand. "I gotta go."

"By all means, get the fuck out of here before she sees you."

I give him a look.

"Whatever, dude. Later."

I throw some cash at him for the drink and make for the door.

I'm probably in no fit state to ride home, but I could always walk. Not like I've got anything better to do.

When I get to my sled, I light up a cigarette and take a long drag.

A few moments later, I watch the doors open, and the hospital crew all walk out.

I glance up as Frankie says goodnight to her colleagues.

As I blow the smoke out of my mouth, my eyes travel down her body.

She'd still look good in a paper bag.

I know that Hutch is right, he's always fuckin' right. I've been here a few months now and I'm too chicken shit to even talk to her. The one time we saw each other for real, we said hi, and she gave me an awkward hug and then made some excuse to leave and practically ran out of the place.

I can't say I blame her, really.

I did basically tell her to fuck off in a nice way, even if it was ten years ago. I guess some things just should be kept buried.

What do we even have in common anyway?

She's a high falutin' doctor, and I'm the same old shit kicker with nothing to show for the last ten years.

I'm starting again, for about the tenth time over. Nothing seems to ever stick with me, and I don't know why.

I can't even blame my shitty childhood, though that does equate to some of the instability I've felt over the years. But I'm a grown man now. I can't keep blaming my dead-beat dad for everything, or the fact my mom died so young when I needed her.

I watch her as she laughs at something someone says, and then she's standing there with just one of the other doctors. A male.

She tucks hair behind her ear as he says something, and she laughs.

Oh yeah, he's not just telling jokes, he's trying to wrangle his way into her pants.

If I were any kind of a man, I'd be doing the same thing.

She's a vision.

She's still lean, her hips curvy, breasts full with a small waist. That pretty skin and those eyes that could render any man powerless. She's in her prime.

And pretty boy knows it.

She shakes her head at something he says, then laughs again. What is he, some kind of fuckin' comedian?

Anger, that I've no right to feel, rises in me.

It hits me like a ton of bricks; the wasted time. The years that I let slip through my fingers all because of one mistake.

Like a siren's call, her head turns and suddenly, those hazel eyes are staring right into mine.

Her smile falters.

I never wanted to be the one who made her frown, but that's exactly what's happening.

She says something to the dude, and he nods, taking off in the other direction.

I'm stunned when she starts walking toward me.

I take another long drag, my eyes raking down her fine body as she adjusts her purse on her shoulder. It feels like an eternity as I watch every damn step she takes. Thinking she'll walk right past, I'm dumbfounded when she, all of a sudden, is steeling her shoulders back as she comes closer and confronts me.

"Adam."

I blow smoke out the side of my mouth so it doesn't go all over her.

"You know that's not my name."

I place the cigarette back in my mouth as I take another drag, like it's fuckin' oxygen instead of chemicals that will eventually kill me.

She places one hand on her hip, shaking her head. Then she reaches out, takes the cigarette from between my lip, and drops it on the ground, stubbing it out with her shoe.

"Didn't anyone ever tell you these will kill you?"

She also still has the ability to read my very thoughts. How fuckin' disturbing.

She's gotten a hell of a lot sassier. I like this confidence; it's so different to the Frankie I once knew. That Frankie was a girl, but this chick right here, she's all woman.

"Someone did, but then again, I don't really give a shit."

"Right, because you've got to die of something, right?"

I shake my head. "What's got your panties in a twist? I'm surprised you're even talking to me."

There she goes with that frown again. "It's not like you can blame me, Adam. I didn't even know you were in Bracken Ridge until recently."

Yeah, and when you did, there wasn't exactly fireworks going off.

"It's Nitro, sweet cheeks, and you don't owe me nothin'."

"Then why do you come here every Thursday night?"

"To drink."

"And Tuesday lunch?"

"To fuckin' eat."

"What about Sunday afternoon?"

"Someone's been noticin'."

She stares at me, defiant. "Just like old times, isn't it?"

I shake my head. "Nah, because if it really were like old

times, I'd be throwing you over my shoulder and takin' you home to bang that pussy I've been missin' for ten fuckin' years."

Her eyes go wide as I try, and fail, to hold back my smirk.

She always did get embarrassed by my dirty talk.

A flashback of me makin' her tell me what she wanted me to do to her has my dick leaking.

The truth is, I want to bang her so fuckin' bad it hurts.

I've not banged anyone since I got here. Some of the guys are gonna think somethin's up, but I don't give a shit. I blame work and lack of time. There are plenty of sweet butts and hang-arounds at the club; pussy is in no shortage even in this small town, but once again, it goes to show just what a fuckin' sap I am. All I want to do is fuck the living daylights out of Frankie Stevens to make up for lost time.

"You really haven't washed your mouth out after all these years."

"Didn't hear you complainin' back then, when I had my face buried in your pussy, babe." She rolls her lips, and I raise my eyebrows in question, then I spread my arms wide. "Just sayin' it like it is. I bet nobody has made you come like I did that night, have they?"

Clearly, I'm a little drunk, because she probably has had way better orgasms than the ones I gave her. It was one night; she probably doesn't even remember.

I was nineteen then. I knew a little bit about sex, but not a lot. I guess practice makes perfect. Knowing what I could do to her now, what I like to do in bed and what I like being done to me, things would definitely be interesting.

I have kinks that I know for a fact would shock the hell out of Little Miss Perfect over here. But, I'd pay anything to see her trussed and tied up. What a fuckin' sight that would be.

"It was so long ago, I barely remember," she says, echoing my thoughts again. "It wasn't like I had the opportunity to make it a second time round."

I lean toward her. "So, you are pissed at me?"

She laughs, but I don't like the sound.

It's one of those laughs that tells me I should start my sled and drive away quickly.

Stupid me, I stay put.

"Why would I be pissed at you?"

"Because I got put in jail."

"It was ten years ago, get over yourself."

"Then why did you stalk off when I saw you the first time."

She holds her own. "I think I was in shock," she admits. "I never thought I'd see you again."

I give her a chin lift. "You single?"

She stares at me, those depths of her eyes; I could swim in them forever. The way she makes me feel, even after all this time…

"That's none of your business."

I snort. "So, some of the old Frankie is still in there."

She narrows her eyes as I try a couple of times to put the keys in the ignition. "You're not driving," she says.

I fumble, missing the ignition, and the keys fall on the ground.

She swipes them up before I can reach and twirls them around one finger. "I'll drive you."

"Now, why would you wanna do that?"

"Because you're over the limit."

"Since when did you care?"

She ignores me and starts walking away.

"Hey!"

She struts those goddamn hips as I stare after her, heading over to a nice looking suburban SUV. I should be grateful she doesn't have a soccer mom van with a swag full of kids.

This woman is infuriating.

I swing my leg over my sled and take off after her. She's already in the car, starting the engine.

I tap on her window as she looks at me through the glass. "Keys."

She shakes her head. "It's a ride home or a long walk."

Do I really want to be stuck in a car with her, so I can hear all about what a fuckin' failure I am and what I'm doing here. I don't have many answers, that's the problem.

I glare at her.

I don't submit to women; if anything, they submit to me. So this new challenge not only excites me, but it also makes me mad at the same time. My dick, however, throbs in my pants, begging to be let out. I want her. I'll always fuckin' want her, no matter what.

"This isn't funny, Frankie," I bark, stalking around to the passenger side of the car as I climb in. Once I'm seated, I turn to her. "Keys."

She reverses the car, and once she's pulled out and puts it in drive, she turns to me. "Seat belt."

I roll my eyes, pull the belt over my shoulder, and strap myself in. Only then does she drop the keys into my palm.

We're moving through town in her quiet as fuck SUV. It smells like new.

"I'm only doing this so you don't wrap yourself around a tree."

"Right," I mutter, staring straight ahead.

We drive silently through town, and I wonder how she knows where I live. I've obviously never told her.

Right now, I'm fixing the place up at the small apartment above the office at the car yard. It's small but compact and neat enough, only needs a little updating. I got professional cleaners in once Jack, the old guy who used to run the place, sold the business to Hutch and the club.

Some nasty shit went down with him ripping off the Rebels, and Steel broke all his fingers one by one.

"How have you been?"

It's the most civil she's been.

"Cut the small talk, Frankie. Why have you been ignorin' me?"

"I haven't," she stammers.

I snort. "Right. First, the night I ran into you by accident. Then the night of the charity auction, when you realized who I was, and every other day in between."

She shrugs. "What do you want me to say, exactly?"

"I don't know. Tell me what a jerk I am. Anything would be better than the cold shoulder."

She keeps driving in silence as we hit the 101. "It was hard when I left for New Jersey. Everything changed. I was in a new city surrounded by strangers."

"I told you I'd write."

She side-eyes me.

I know I'm being an ass, but she's the one making this awkward.

"It was the best thing I probably ever did," she says finally.

Because it got me out of her life?

"You're makin' good coin now, babe. I knew you had it in you."

"I've been summoning the courage to talk to you, Ad–"

I glare at her. "Nitro."

"Why would you need to summon the courage?"

She shrugs. "Things are…different now."

"In what way?"

"We grew up."

Never a truer word spoken, I can't deny that.

Little does she know, what I still want is right in front of me. That hasn't changed.

I may be older now, but my stance is the same. If anything, it's only gotten stronger as the years have gone one.

And here we are.

The road led us back to each other. Only, she doesn't see it that way.

Maybe she never will.

BRACKEN RIDGE
REBELS
ARIZONA
M · C

CHAPTER 14

FRANKIE

I cannot believe he's sitting in my car.

All the old memories rush to the surface.

He still smells the same.

He kinda looks the same, but so different at the same time.

If anything, he's only gotten more handsome as the years have gone on.

He's bigger than I remember. His body has filled out, his shoulders and arms are huge, his hair is longer but cut in different lengths, and it's no longer black. It's a dark chestnut, and it almost hits his shoulders. He has this way about him, this arrogance that I don't remember. But it's there. Like a giant chip on his shoulder.

His face is chiseled with a strong jaw, dark brows, and a small amount of stubble around his face. To say he's sexy is an understatement.

His eyes are exactly the same. Green and so beautiful it shouldn't be legal.

I remember now why Adele kept saying he was "too pretty" to be a biker. He's certainly stepped out of the pretty stage and blossomed to a fully-fledged hottie.

Nitro shows everything on his face, despite the fact he thinks he's probably stealthy. I've always been able to read him.

He's larger than life, sitting in my SUV, and he's still able to stir things inside me that I thought I'd buried long ago.

When I made the move to the East Coast, it wasn't easy. Nothing in that time of my life was.

I was heartbroken and lonely. I wanted to throw myself into work so I couldn't feel the pain anymore, and that's exactly what I did.

I got a night job, not because I really needed the money because I had my trust fund, but I wanted something to keep my mind occupied. I waited tables at the local diner, nothing fancy, but it kept me busy. It kept all my carefully aligned goals in check. I never wanted to steer off course. Doing that would mean the end.

So many times I thought about what could have been. So often I thought about him and what he was doing. I sent him a text after he got out, but I never got a reply. He cut me out of his life and in return, I willingly left. A "walk on the wild side," as he so eloquently put it.

The fact remains that I was young and didn't really

know what I wanted, aside from finishing my internship and then my residency. I didn't know anything about relationships or how to be a girlfriend, or even who I was. I'd been sheltered so much growing up, always mixing in the same sorts of circles. Until I left for New Jersey, I'd never really lived. So much of the world opened up to me after that.

Ten years later, I'm still not sure I learned anything about men. I've had a string of failed relationships, and I've made bad decisions. My longest boyfriend was three years, but once we moved in together, things slowly went downhill.

I've just never met anyone I connected with, who really gets me. Who lets me be myself, flaws and all, and doesn't care. I've even begun to wonder, as time has ticked along, if he is even out there. The one.

I shift in my seat.

"Penny for your thoughts?" Nitro asks as I take the exit toward the car yard.

I know where he lives. I shouldn't, but word gets around fast here.

I know he's running Jack's Car Yard, which has now been renamed, Bracken Ridge Used Cars and Parts. And he's joined the Rebels without having to prospect.

I'm good friends with Angel, and with Lucy, his sister. They're also my patients. So, I do get tidbits of information from them, enough to keep up with what's going on.

"What is there to say?"

"You never answered my question."

"Which one was that?"

"About havin' a boyfriend."

He won't let up, and that's exactly how I remember him. Protective.

Possessive.

Downright infuriating.

But he had his sweet, tender moments, too. So many of them.

"What do you think?"

I feel his eyes on me in my periphery. "I think you're a busy woman."

"Well, you'd be right."

"You fuck that guy outside the Crow?"

I turn to him sharply. "That is none of your goddamn business!"

"Had his eyes all over you."

"So did you."

"Yeah, but at least I'm not pretending that I'm somethin' I'm not."

I snort. "Really, Nitro? Are we honestly going to go there?"

"What's that supposed to mean?"

"If you don't know, then there's no point in talking

about it."

"You mean, because I haven't come to you and banged your door down?"

I stiffen in my seat.

The thought of him doing just that sends tingles down my spine. His ability to read me is about as infuriating as his annoyance at me for talking to a colleague.

"You want me to do that, babe? It can be arranged."

"That isn't what I meant."

"Right, well, you've just got it all figured out, don't you, Doc."

The way he says my nickname has my heart hammering in my chest and my blood pounding in my ears.

He does so much to me with so little effort. Even now.

He should not have this effect, not after all this time.

I should never have given him a ride…

"Why didn't you, then?" I blurt out before I can stop myself. When he gives me a mystified look, I add, "Come to me and bang my door down."

"Is that what you really want?"

"No."

"Then why would you ask that?"

"Because you used to stalk me, Nitro, remember?"

I remember. He was everywhere.

He has no idea how that made me feel.

How sick it was for me to feel protected and loved by

this man who followed me and owed me nothing, yet gave me so much. Just by being in the shadows.

I never felt that when I left for New Jersey.

He took my independence away without even realizing it, like a weakness, and even after all these years, I haven't quite gotten it back.

No man I've ever been with has given me the same level of passion and possession that he did in that short space of time.

It's why he is my weakness and why I shouldn't have let him get in the car with me. But I know he would have driven home inebriated, and I didn't want that on my conscience.

"Stalking is a little harsh," he says. I glance down at his legs, his knees spread wide, and I have a flash back of him kneeling between my thighs while he fucked me into next week.

He's right; I've never been banged quite like that. I've never had a man talk dirty to me or even try to turn me on with words.

I've never enjoyed sex like I did with him, and that truly is pathetic.

I remember every single moment of that one night we spent together.

"Really, what would you call it, then?"

"You know why I did it, but then again, I wouldn't

expect you to remember."

"Are we really going to fight about this?"

"What would you prefer? A fuck for old time's sake?"

I would, actually, because every single one of my cells is on fire for him. My body has a mind of its own when it comes to what it wants.

I'm a grown woman and I can't seem to hold my emotions in check, nor control my hormones when he's around.

I can safely say that I'm shallow when it comes to the way he looks. Even when I want to knock that smirk right off his face.

"No, you'd prefer to watch me instead."

I do not need to look at him to know that I just ignited a fire.

His voice is low and lethal when he says, "I've made no secret of the fact I like watchin' you, Frankie, but I won't be watchin' anyone else fuck you."

"That's great, because I never asked you to."

He cracks his neck and mutters, "Unless it's me."

I let out a slow breath, my temper flaring. "That's awfully presumptuous, and it's also not going to happen."

"I bet your panties are wet right now, aren't they, babe?"

"Please tell me we're getting close to the car yard."

Panic sets in because he's absolutely right. My body aches for his touch.

"Didn't tell you where I lived, Doc."

I close my mouth. No, he didn't.

I can almost hear him chuckle.

"Kind of figured it out," I say, though it sounds lame.

"What else did you do, in Jersey?" he asks out of the blue.

Is he serious?

"I worked really damn hard. I figured out what field I wanted to specialize in and went for it. I settled in, left the past behind me…" I shift in my seat. "I didn't mean…"

"I wanted you to go, Frankie. Not because I didn't want to see you, but because I knew I wasn't good for you. I've been bad, since I saw you last, really fuckin' bad."

I take a few deep breaths. "Like, with the law?"

"With everything."

"You went back to jail." I already know he did.

"More times than I care to admit."

"What about drugs?"

"I'm clean now. Never touch the stuff."

"So your poison is alcohol now?"

He pinches the bridge of his nose. "I feel another lecture coming on."

"I just wondered how you spent the last ten years, that's all."

"I'm still here, ain't I?"

Touché.

I turn to him. "You look good, Nitro."

"Yeah? Then why you ghostin' me?"

I turn back to the road. I don't know why.

Seeing him again, being around him again, brings all those old feelings up. To a time in my life that was the hardest. A time when I didn't even know who I was or where I was going. Then my father died.

I shake it off. Going down that road only leads to more pain.

"You know we're not good together, you said it yourself. And too much time has passed." I know it sounds like an excuse. I'm still attracted to him, that much is certain, but getting involved with him could only lead to more heartbreak. I barely knew this man, yet he had an impact on me that I just can't shake. And that's the reason I've stayed away.

"Sounds like an excuse, but I can take a hint. May as well let me walk the rest of the way home because sittin' here listenin' to all the reasons why you're too good for me isn't exactly how I planned on spendin' the rest of my night. I already know them all."

I shake my head. "Is that what you think?"

"It's the truth, isn't it?"

I grip the steering wheel hard. "No, Nitro, that isn't it."

"You talk in riddles, Doc."

I pull onto his street and take it slow down the gravel

road. When I stop out front, the gate is locked.

We sit in silence, and he makes no attempt to get out of the car.

I turn to look at him. "I've never once thought that I was too good for you, just for the record, Nitro. When I left Phoenix, it was a really hard time in my life. Everything happened so fast."

"You don't owe me any explanation."

"But I think I should give you one."

"You did the right thing. You've thrived. That makes me happy."

I look down at my hands. "I thought about you often," I whisper. "When you didn't reply to my texts, I figured it was out of sight out of mind, but it wasn't like that for me."

The intensity coming off him is electric. His hands are balled into fists.

"It was for the best. You know I couldn't offer you anything, not the life you deserved."

"There you go making assumptions."

He turns to me. "What would you have done, if I'd have asked you to stay?"

I shake my head. "You wouldn't have."

"Don't bullshit me, answer the question."

"I was young," I say honestly. "Naive. I think that I would have been too scared to be a sweet butt, or whatever you guys call the women who hang around the clubhouse."

"For one, you'll never, ever be a fuckin' sweet butt," he growls. "I kept you away because I didn't want you seein' that life. I loved my club, but not all of the people in it. I didn't trust them with you, and you never would've let me claim you at the table."

"I don't even know what half of that means," I admit.

"It means, I'd let them know you're mine and off limits. That's how it works in most clubs. Women who live the life know what it entails. Choosin' pussy over your club isn't done, it's seen as weakness, and I was fallin' hard…"

I turn to him, and his eyes shine so bright in the darkness between us. He looks pained.

"Is that all I was to you? Just another vagina on a platter?"

He shakes his head. "You know the answer to that. How could you feel anythin' for me, you barely knew me."

"I know how I felt," I say. "I know that you made me feel things that I haven't felt before, and you gave me so much more than you'll ever realize, Nitro," I trail off, unable to continue.

That time in my life is simply a hard limit. I don't know what else to say.

"Trust me when I say that you're better off."

I look down, and he reaches two fingers to push my chin up so I'm looking at him again.

That simple touch brings back the memories. How it felt

the first time he touched me.

That night of passion and lust in my bed.

How much it hurt when I chose to leave.

He's right, though; it could never have worked then. I wouldn't want to be part of the Phoenix Fury's fender fluff, or whatever it is hang-arounds are referred to. Just talking with Smokey at the gate that night frightened the living daylights out of me.

I know that the Bracken Ridge Rebels aren't a 1% club, Angel explained it to me.

They have legit businesses and don't have a hand in organized crime or running drugs. But, admittedly, I know very little about the club itself. And I wonder why I even care now.

Nitro and I are still in two very different worlds, yet I feel that spark all over again, just like I did ten years ago.

"Tell me you haven't thought about it," I whisper, his hand still holding my chin.

"That would be a lie."

"Don't you think it's weird, that we both ended up in the same small town, after all these years?"

His eyebrow knit together. "Are you implying that I knew you were here already?"

The surprise on his face tells me he didn't, but I still want to hear him say it. "Didn't you?"

His eyes dance with amusement as he shakes his head

slowly. "Fate, baby girl, that's what it is."

My heart throbs in my chest.

I want him to kiss me.

It's absurd. I've been in close proximity with him for less than ten minutes and he's managed to unnerve me and get me practically panting for him.

"That could explain it, I guess…" I trail off, unsure what he's going to do.

Unfortunately, he doesn't kiss me. He leans back and says, "You should get home."

Disappointment floods me. "I guess I should."

The words hang between us.

I don't know, but it's almost like he's waiting for me to take the lead. We're not kids anymore, though, and he's man enough to go after what he wants. He obviously doesn't want me.

I push those old insecurities away. I've dealt with them, and I'm not that person anymore.

I'm a strong, confident woman who has the world at her feet.

Brushing the hair back off my face, he then kisses the top of my head. "Night, Doc, make sure you go straight home."

He reaches for the door handle and within a few moments, he's gone. Walking toward the gate, he punches in a code as it opens, and he disappears inside, only the headlights on my car lighting the way.

I guess old habits die hard after all.

Nitro is just as complicated as he ever was before. Or is it possible, he's even more so?

I put the car into reverse as I contemplate that, and the fact that the throb between my legs and the racing of my heart just won't go away.

I don't know what the hell I'm going to do with any of this, or how I will be able to run into him on the street and just be cool.

Some people you just never forget. And he's one of them.

He's left an imprint on my soul that I've no idea how to erase, and the scary part is, do I even want to?

CHAPTER 15

NITRO

I don't know what I expected, but that wasn't what I'd planned in my head.

Then again, we've been avoiding each other for months. She also spends one weekend a month going back to Phoenix; I need to find out what that's all about. She did just move here not long ago, so she could be still sorting shit out, but something's up.

I'm being stupid, but it's like she's holding something back. I don't know what and clearly my instincts when it comes to her are a little rusty, but I can't put my finger on it.

Does she just fucking hate my guts, and that's the end of it? If so, why did she give a shit about driving me home?

Even with no obstacles in our way, she's got better things in her future. I get it. I wouldn't date me either.

I'm a serial bachelor who never grew up. Being able to work out a washing machine isn't exactly screaming boyfriend of the year material. Not that I've ever been that.

The thing that strikes me the most is how much she's

changed. Don't get me wrong, she's even more beautiful than I remember. Thirty-five suits her all the way down to the fucking ground. I could get me some of that, but as usual, it isn't just her looks or her long legs that get me hard. It's how she holds herself.

Long gone is the shy, unsure girl that I fell for in a heartbeat, and in her place is a smart, successful, confident woman who did what she set out to do.

I'm just dumbfounded that she's acting this way. That she basically ran a mile the minute our paths crossed. And tonight, what was that all about? Fucked if I know.

Going down that road would be like going down a rabbit hole I'm not sure I'd come out of. One that, if we revisited, could end me for good.

I have a shitty sleep. My mind won't let up.

When I turn the television on in the morning and start making myself some breakfast, I see the headlines and do a double take at the screen.

Well known biker outlaw Brenton "Tex" Dottard's remains found in Arizona National Park.

I drop the carton of eggs and the packet of bacon on the counter and stare at the screen.

What the fuck?

I turn the television up as the reporter announces, "Homicide detectives swarmed the area of the National Park near Fort Ridge Canyon today when hikers found the remains of alleged drug cartel and registered sex offender Brenton Dottard, also known as 'Tex,' the former president of the notorious motorcycle gang, Phoenix Fury. In a statement from the Chief of Police today, they will be opening an investigation and combing the area, which has now been closed off to the general public so forensics can move in and try to piece together Mr. Dottard's final moments."

I run a hand through my hair.

Double fuck.

I reach for my phone, and just as I do, Rubble is calling me.

"You seen the news, bro?" he asks as I turn the TV down.

"Just turned it on."

"Hutch has called an emergency meeting. You're invited."

"Funny that," I say, unable to tear my eyes away from the screen. "Since I'm the person who shot the fucker."

"Yeah, well, this shit just got real."

"No kiddin'."

I'm not naive, but I never once considered this would come back to bite me.

I've been arrested more times than I care to admit, and I've spent a lot of time in jail, but going down for murder isn't in my future plans. Not happening.

The night I shot Tex was one of the greatest of my life. I don't regret it for a second.

The added incentive that he was going to kill my sister was just the icing on the cake. The truth is, I pretended to help him for months when he went rogue because I found out he had revenge on his mind when Rubble left the club and moved to Bracken Ridge with Lucy.

He wanted to kill her to hurt Rubble, to get payback for leaving the club.

I'll never forget the look on his face that night when he realized I was the one who betrayed him.

Too sweet for words.

I'm not one of these guys who feels guilty for killing someone. Frankly, it's an inconvenience, but necessary all the same. Some guys just have it coming and Tex was one of them. The world's a better place without him in it.

How he treated women, hurting and forcing himself on them, because he's a sick fuck, he deserved what he got. My only regret was that I didn't get to drag it out and watch him bleed. That would've been far more satisfying. Unfortunately, time didn't permit.

It can't make up for all the years I knew what a shady fuck he was, but I wouldn't go back and change a thing. That bastard is off the street, and he can't hurt anyone anymore.

This last six months or so, Smokey and I have gotten

quite close and I'm back in contact with Hoax. I know they'll give the new club everything they've got. Unlike Tex, he isn't a self-centered asshole and doesn't take the risks Tex took without a care in the world. To him, we're his brothers. To Tex, we were all expendable.

The two are like comparing chalk and cheese.

They may still be involved in running drugs and guns, something I gave up a long time ago, but they're good guys.

"Your silence is deafening," I add, when the line goes blank.

"Nothin's gonna happen, I'll make sure of it."

"Know it."

"You know I can never repay you for what you did…for what happened. I'll always be in your debt."

He's been saying this for the entire time since I got back into town. I know how much he loves Lucy and seeing her happy is all I need to know that she made a good choice by staying with Rubble.

She's helped him build his business and stuck by his side through the good times and the bad ones. I admire that. More than they'll ever know. But that's just Lucy, she's selfless.

"Well, technically, Bones is the one who got stabbed in the chest, and for the record, you don't owe me shit."

"She's my sister and the only person on earth I actually like."

He scoffs.

Bones literally dived in front of Lucy when Tex lunged at them with a knife; she was pregnant at the time with little Avery. I shudder at what could've happened. I'd never forgive myself if any harm had come to her or the baby. Rubble was out of town when all this went down.

That's the thing with this club; they look after their own. All of them would've done the same thing.

"And you shot Tex before he could hurt her."

I run a hand through my hair and turn the TV back on.

"And I'd do it again if I had to. Fucker had it comin'." The more I think about that night, the angrier I get. I had to fuckin' pretend that I had it in for Rubble too, just so I could stay close to Tex and keep up with his plans. Nobody knew I was Lucy's brother at the time.

He didn't suspect a thing. I'd always kept that part to myself. Not even Hoax knew and we shared a lot of shit over the years.

She's the one person I would never put in harm's way, inadvertently or not.

"I know you would, brother. Get your ass to church in half an hour."

"I'll be there." I hang up and stand, staring into space for a moment.

I've been jail free for five years. Granted, I've spent five of the last ten in and out of the joint. I've got a record as long as my dick. But I turned my life around in the years since leaving the Fury.

I did not count on this resurfacing, though.

When I shot Tex, Steel, Brock, and Hutch took care of it.

I knew he was buried out in the desert, but I never expected he'd be unearthed.

In a fucking National Park?

Lucy's one of their own, so there isn't anything they wouldn't do for her and for Rubble. Now I'm part of the MC, I know that I'm family too. I just don't know what the fuck is going to happen next. What I'm expected to do…I guess I'm about to find out.

He's been buried for over a year.

I discard my breakfast and jump in the shower for a quick wash. I dress in a fresh shirt, shrugging on my jeans and my cut, I'm out the door fifteen minutes later.

Then I realize I don't have a fuckin' sled.

I take the pickup instead. I should've shot Axton a text last night to let him know my sled was out back, but it's not like it's going anywhere.

I get to the clubhouse in about ten minutes.

When I park the pickup and make my way inside, the meeting room doors are open and I head over there, hearing raised voices across the threshold.

Never having been in this room before, I hesitate as I

loom in the doorway.

Sitting at the helm is Hutch, and clockwise around the table are Brock, Gunner, Colt, Bones, Rubble, and Steel.

Hutch waves me inside.

"Feel like I need a stiff drink for this," I mutter as Bones kicks out the chair next to him for me.

I give the others a chin lift around the table as Hutch's eyes land on me.

"Fuckin' shitty news to wake up to," he says as I feel the urge to light a cigarette. Nobody else is smoking in here, though, so I refrain.

"Can say that again," I reply. "I was under the impression the coyotes finished Tex off and he was buried in the middle of nowhere."

"He fuckin' was," Brock interjects. "He was found miles from the place we buried him. My guess is a mountain lion or a coyote found him. That'd explain why he wasn't where we left him. He was located just off a trail in some scrub."

"So they found fuckin' bones?"

"Yup," Rubble confirms. "DNA results came back as the announcement was made a coupla hours later. They've shut the whole fuckin' park down."

"This ain't fuckin' good," Hutch goes on. "Should've known this fucker would come back to haunt us. I had that feelin' in my bones that somethin' wasn't sittin' right."

"What could they know?" Steel asks. "Forensics can find whatever they're gonna uncover, but nothin' is leadin' any of this shit back to us."

"What if it does? What if we got sloppy?" I begin.

Steel holds up a hand. "Weren't sloppy, don't even know the meanin' of the word. What we need to make sure of is that no footage of him in Bracken Ridge surfaces. I'll get Linc to check the surveillance on Main Street, gas stations and such. It'll eliminate the fact that he was here at all. It won't take anyone with half a sack of shit for brains to figure out that a rival MC had somethin' to do with it."

Linc is the guy on the end of the phone who can do anything with IT and tracing shit. A lot like Snitch used to do. I often wonder what happened to him after the club disbanded.

I feel uneasy, no matter what color Steel's painting it.

Frowning, I feel like we should be doing more. "So we're just sitting tight?"

"What do you suggest?" Brock asks. "Ain't shit we can do about it anyway. If Linc eliminates any evidence of him bein' down here, then there will be nothin' linkin' him to us, you or the club. Not rocket science. The less we do or say, the better. If cops come sniffin' around, then we'll be ready."

Not for him, or any of them. They weren't the ones who shot him. The gun was stolen anyway and destroyed at the junkyard, where Bones had it melted down. At least the weapon isn't around to incriminate me. I should be thankful for that, at least.

Still, Brock and Steel are right, there's nothing linking the club to Tex. The fact remains, though, that Rubble used to be part of the Fury, and I was his right-hand man.

There is one thing they didn't count on, however.

"They'd have surveillance on me," I say, as they all turn to look at me. "I was with him, pretending to be his loyal subject, keepin' tabs on what he was plannin'. They'll wanna know where we were on the day he went missing."

I try not to let it get to me, but I know that as good as Linc may be, he can't erase every fuckin' camera in Arizona.

"You weren't together every second," Rubble reminds me. "In fact, he was keepin' a low profile for months. Like the brothers said, Linc will get rid of any evidence you were together when you arrived in Bracken Ridge."

"Fuck." This shit is heavy.

"Meanin', you also gotta have a story and stick to it," Hutch counters. "The Vipers ended up takin' the club down when that drug bust got turned upside down. Can always turn the tables on them, point in their direction, would make a perfect cover story."

When the Rebels came to help Smokey and Griller with a takedown with a rival club, they put Tex and the disbanded Fury members in the firing line. Somehow, Tex got away and went after Rubble. He blamed him for the club going into disarray.

The rest is history.

"Which means I'll probably need to explain why we were tight. Or at least that's how it looked."

"So you point in the direction of the Vipers and wash your hands of it," Brock says, like it's a done deal. "Nothin' to be worried about. The more you overthink it, the more guilty you're gonna seem. Far as we're concerned, you came to Bracken Ridge to be closer to your sister and start a new job, putting the past behind you."

"Got it." I look at him. "That part won't be hard, considering it's the truth."

He nods. "We got your back, Nitro." He motions around the table. "We all do."

"Appreciate it. I've done this shit before, brother," I say. "First time I actually killed somebody, though."

Something passes in the room. If I didn't know any better, I'd say it was respect.

"Turnin' that gun on Tex saved Lucy, and Bones," Hutch says after a moment. "This club is gonna stand by you no matter what happens. Don't forget, we're implicated too. As much as we like to believe we're not linked, we were there." He turns to Steel. "Call Linc as soon as we adjourn; I need him on this pronto. The first thing the cops are gonna look at is surveillance on the days before he went missing, if they haven't started already."

Steel nods, deep in thought.

"Who the fuck would miss him?" Colt wonders.

"His brother." I shrug. "Or so Smokey said. He could start to make things difficult for us if he knew Tex was comin' down here."

"Let him make it difficult," Rubble says. "Don't forget we were all out of town the night he broke into my house. That can only play in our favor. We each can have an alibi. Got motel room receipts to prove it."

Hutch nods. "Agreed. They don't know shit. They've just got a pile of bones and a DNA test."

"Enough to bring a whole forensic team and close the National Park," Gunner says. "Let's face it, they're not messin' around."

"What always gets me is the fact they should be grateful a man like that is gone, off the streets, unable to hurt anyone again," Bones says. "Instead, they want to try to put an innocent man in jail, and for what? A drug dealer, a crime boss, and a fuckin' rapist? They should be thankin' you."

"I'm not so innocent," I remind him. "I did shoot him."

"In self defense," he maintains. "They need to let sleepin' dogs lie."

"While that's true, for the most part, some asshole will think it's his duty to come down hard on motorcycle clubs and underworld crime syndicates," Brock says. "The Chief of Police looks like a hero and gets a big fat bonus for keepin' more scum off the streets. That's how it works."

I pinch the bridge of my nose. I know I can do this.

I'm not scared of the law; I just don't want to be on their radar after being clean so long.

A cell ain't for me. I've got too much to live for. I used to not give a shit about anything, always thinking I'd probably die young, but since reuniting with Lucy and Rubble and being accepted into their little family, along with the MC, I've found my purpose.

The club gave me a chance with running the car yard. I'm grateful for everything they've done. It's the brotherhood I always wanted.

"In any case," Rubble says. "If and when the cops come sniffin' around, we'll be ready. That's the main thing."

"Famous last words," I mutter. I don't want to be Negative Nancy, but I don't get how any of this can be good.

"So our story is, what exactly?" Colt rubs his chin.

"The boys were out of town on business, Bones, Nitro, and me were here," Hutch says. "Nitro left the Fury some time back, cuttin' ties with the club, and he hasn't seen Tex or any of the club members since. Don't forget, Nitro isn't the only ex-club member they could potentially be talkin' to. How many were at that club?"

"Around sixty," I say.

Brock whistles between his teeth.

"And he made a lot of enemies," Rubble says. "All of the members who were still hangin' off him like leeches are all dead. The other members left of their own accord to other clubs out of state. The Sons of Fury ain't gonna say shit. If anything, Smokey is the one takin' the heat bein' he was the V.P."

Steel nods to confirm it. "Griller and I keep in contact. The shootout at the raid, that night we were in Phoenix, had the Vipers takin' most of the trash out. I don't foresee any major problems. I'll check in with him after Linc, see if the pigs been sniffin' around there yet."

"It's only a matter of time," Brock says gravely.

Hutch looks to me again. "In the meantime, if you get anyone tryin' to question you, then you tell them you want your lawyer present. That's where Kennedy comes in."

Bones gives me a chin lift. "She's the best in the business, not that you're gonna need it."

I wish I had their air of confidence. I need a stiff drink.

Trouble is, I've been here before. Maybe not for murder, but definitely for some serious shit.

I don't know how good a lawyer Kennedy is, but I'm just hopin' I won't need to find out.

"Anythin' happens in the meantime," Hutch says. "I want to know about it."

Aye's ring around the table as he bangs the gavel down.

I go to stand, and Bones slaps me on the back. "Don't look so worried."

"It's a little hard not to," I reply. "But you're right. As long as we stick to the plan, I'll hopefully fly under the radar."

We head toward the bar.

"Once Steel talks to Linc and he checks out the surveillance, we'll know more. He can tap into anything."

"I'm countin' on it," I reply.

Lord knows, now I've got Frankie back in my sights again, there is no way I'm going back in a concrete box.

BRACKEN RIDGE
REBELS
ARIZONA
M · C

CHAPTER 16

FRANKIE

I see patients all day, and it's only when I take a very late lunch break that I get to think about the events that took place last night.

I can't stop thinking about him.

Guilt riddles through me, but then again, I've lived with it this for so long that it feels second nature to me. All of the emotions come naturally whenever I picture his face and think about him being locked up all those years.

Would things have been different if I'd have stayed and we got together?

Who am I kidding?

I did what was best for me at the time.

We had a one-night stand. Nothing more.

Except it was a whole lot more.

I put my head in my hands.

I don't know what to do.

There's a knock at my door.

I glance up and see Gerard in the doorway.

"Hey," I say as he leans against the doorjamb with a smile on his face.

"Hey, yourself." He gives me a chin lift. "A little birdie told me you haven't had a proper break today."

I motion to my half-eaten sandwich, and he gives me an eye roll.

"Fancy getting a coffee?"

"As in, leave the hospital?" I laugh.

He feigns shock horror. "I know, sacrilege, right?"

"Could we sneak away?"

"I think if I guarded the door and you made a run for it, then yes."

I laugh and ditch the rest of my awful cafeteria sandwich in the bin. "Maybe I might find something decent to eat while we're at it."

"When's your next appointment?" he asks as I grab my purse.

"Not for a half hour."

"Better make the most of it, then." He gives me a wink and presses a hand to the small of my back.

I like Gerard. A lot.

He's the epitome of tall, dark, and handsome. Plus, he's a doctor too. He ticks all the boxes.

It's a pity he favors the company of other men, otherwise we might've shared something important, but we've grown pretty close in the last few months.

When we can, we sneak away and indulge in coffee and chocolate cake, though admittedly we've both been so busy we barely get time to do that anymore.

Whoever said moving to a small town would be easy, clearly hasn't worked in a busy hospital before.

I love my job, more than life. The dynamics here are fast-paced, but more personal than that of the city.

I love getting to know my clients, being on the journey with them, sometimes with difficult and complex pregnancies, but the satisfaction I get from helping my patients and their babies is why I became a doctor in the first place.

When I started my residency, I knew I wanted to move into this field, and though I've had some very large hurdles along the way, I always had the end goal in sight.

We head down the elevator, and once outside, we walk around the corner to the small cafe that serves the best chocolate fudge cake this side of Arizona.

Sitting at a small table by the window, it is nice being away from the hospital, even if it's for just a quick break.

Gerard babbles about the date he had a few nights ago. Bracken Ridge is slowly expanding, but it's still very much a small place compared to Phoenix. Eligible bachelors can be hard to come by.

I laugh as he tells me the story about how bad it was, and how the guy looked nothing like his Tinder profile.

When I glance up, looking across the street, I see Nitro sitting on his motorcycle across the lot, staring right at me.

My eyes go wide momentarily, and I wonder how long he's been sitting there.

It's a little sadistic that a thrill runs through me, just like it used to do when I found out he was watching me, or as he told me multiple times, "keeping me safe."

He was a man of his word back then and he was really just a kid.

So much has changed, yet last night, those feelings resurfaced.

I know I owe him an explanation…about a lot of things.

I wish I'd persisted in trying to contact him. When I went back home, I went by the clubhouse again and some biker told me he was back in jail. For three years, this time.

I saw it as a sign to stay away. Then another time he'd apparently left the club.

The things I had to tell him were too big and too grave to give a man behind a glass wall in a prison cell. It wouldn't have been fair.

I stare back, tuning out Gerard as I wonder why he's here.

Back to his old tricks? But what for? It wasn't like he was all over me last night or even trying to hit on me. He was intense, sure, but that's Nitro.

He's a man of few words and even fewer emotions.

I wish I could tell him all the things I want to say…
but I'm terrified that when he learns the truth, he'll hate me forever.

I watch as he starts his motorcycle, revs the engine very loudly, and with one last throttle, he takes off from the lot and spins his tires as he drives in the other direction.

I know that was a warning.

The squealing of his tires could wake the dead.

He won't like me having coffee with Gerard. He'll see it as a threat.

The look on his face said it all.

The fact I'm even making excuses for his behavior says more about me than it does him, though. I internally face palm myself.

I should not be so stupid. I'm not the same girl I was ten years ago.

And if that's the case, why does he make me feel like I'm twenty-five again, with my head in the clouds?

I take another mouthful of cake.

Gerard is none the wiser. Luckily, he likes to talk a lot and doesn't come up for air.

I feel like a bad friend because all I've done for almost half an hour is think about Nitro instead of listening to Gerard's man woes. Maybe we should start a bowling team.

When we pay the check and leave, I feel something wash over me. I know it's that old feeling, when Nitro used to follow me. It wasn't like I didn't know, not after he told me he checked on me. It sounds weird in my own head, but it wasn't creepy. On anyone else, I'd say yeah, it's pretty screwed up, but nothing with Nitro is ordinary.

"So are you up for salsa night if I can get a few people over?" Gerard asks me as we get in the elevator.

"Of course," I reply. "That sounds fun."

He glanced at me. "What's going on, Stevens?"

I shake my head. "Nothing."

He turns to me. "You think you can lie to me? You've barely said three words the entire time. It's the last time I take you out for cake, by the way."

I swat his arm. "Sorry, G, I've got a lot on my mind."

He smokes kindly. "Well, if you need a drinking buddy, a karaoke partner, or just a shoulder to cry on, you know where I am."

I give his forearm a squeeze. "That's kind of you, G. I'm just still trying to figure my life out. Sorry that I'm a complete stick in the mud."

"It'd be nice if you were getting some stick." He dodges a punch to the arm this time.

"Very funny."

"Who's the lucky guy?"

I sigh. "Someone from my past, it's complicated."

"Isn't anything when it comes to men?"

I laugh. "You said a mouthful there."

"Well, if he's worth that dreamy look in your eyes, he must be okay."

"Dreamy look?" I splutter.

He grins. "Well, that may be a little far-fetched, but please tell me you're at least getting some action."

I shake my head. "Sadly, I'm not. I don't know if you've realized that there's a shortage of men in Bracken Ridge."

"I have indeed noticed that small detail."

"I seem to repel men lately. It's like I have a neon sign on my head, saying complete loser and complicated wreck."

"It could be worse." He laughs. "You could be a gay man living in a small town with ZERO other gay men."

"True. We so need to do something about that."

"Maybe a bar hop in the city?" He looks hopeful.

I only have one thing in the city I'm going back for, and it sure as shit isn't going to bars.

I don't want to hurt his feelings, though.

"Right, and when you do you plan on getting a weekend off?"

He makes a face. "You got me there."

"We can live in hope, though."

"Totally," he begins, but then his beeper goes off, and he adds, "Gotta run, sweet cheeks. Rain check on the bar hop?"

"Or I could help you update your Tinder profile?" I suggest as the elevator doors open, and he takes off. "You're too cute to not have them lining up from here to Phoenix."

Jogging backwards as he heads in the opposite direction, he points at me with a giant smile on his face. "This is exactly why we're friends."

I head back to my side of the building. The practice where I work has a separate medical center, but it adjoins the hospital. Very handy.

I've still got five minutes to spare. I take out my phone and check my messages, since I always have it on silent at work.

My heart jolts when I see a message from an unknown number.

Straight away, I know it's Nitro.

Who's the guy?

I stare at my phone and shake my head at the same time. Who the hell does he think he is?

I see red.

I may have been thrilled by the idea of him watching me like he used to when I was an intern; hell, I maybe even liked it, but is this the shit he's going to pull every time I have coffee with a man who he doesn't know? Where does he get off?

Fury blazes through me at his audacity.

So he doesn't want me, but nobody else can have me? What a goddamn joke.

I've got news for him, and it's all bad.

I don't bother responding.

If he thinks he can just waltz back into my life after ten years, not to mention be a bit of an ass last night, and then watch me from across the street just now…he's got some nerve.

I can't wait to give him a piece of my mind because that's exactly what he's going to get.

I don't give a shit who he is within the Bracken Ridge Rebels, I knew him as Adam first, long before he was Nitro to me.

Unfortunately, I don't get my chance to confront him because I have an emergency C-section the next day and I stay to monitor the baby and my patient. It was a complicated birth and I like to be close by in the aftercare. I have slept at the hospital before, and lucky for me, my condo is literally around the block.

When I get in my car, I feel more tired now that I've physically stopped.

As soon as I get home, the first thing I do is pour myself a glass of wine.

I check my phone, and I almost choke when I see another message from Nitro.

You think ignoring me is gonna work? We know how well that worked last time.

I take a big gulp of my wine and decide to reply.

Me: Stop following me.

Nitro: Answer my question then.

Me: I don't have to answer anything. You've no right to question me.

A few moments go by.

Nitro: I want to see you.

My pulse quickens.

I chastise myself out loud because I am being ridiculous.

I take another long drink from my glass.

Me: That is not a good idea.
Nitro: Why?

I sigh. Why am I even having this conversation?

Me: Because I'm tired. I had an eighteen-hour day. I need to sleep.
Nitro: Tomorrow then. We need to talk.

I kick my shoes off, take my phone and my wine to my bedroom, and I pull the duvet aside. Old habits die hard, though, and as much as I want to just dive in and forget about everything tonight, I drag my carcass to the shower.

I spend an indulging amount of time in there, enjoying the hot water as the spray pulses against my back and my sore, aching muscles.

I know I can't deal with Nitro tonight. I'm past the point of being coherent.

I crawl to bed and turn the lamp off.

A second later, I hear the loud roar of a motorcycle engine starting up and I know it's him.

He's here.

Waiting for me to turn out the light.

I wish I could feel mad at him, have any kind of emotion, really, aside from how I feel and how I've held the biggest secret from him for ten years.

I close my eyes and try to tell myself that I did the right thing. That all of this will blow over tomorrow and none of it will seem so bad. It's always better in the morning, right?

It's funny how one part of your life starts to go exactly how you planned, then another falls spectacularly apart. It's like the minute anything good happens, something bad has to counter it, to keep the balance.

And here we are, both in Bracken Ridge.

There's unfinished business between us.

And it has me questioning everything.

I don't see Nitro at all the next day and I'm almost relieved, to some degree. That is, until the following day when I grab a bite to eat with Gerard and a couple of work colleagues at the Stone Crow.

They have the best burgers in town, not that I should be surprised since Roxy is a magnificent chef and can keep a busy kitchen running under pressure. I've met her a couple of times in passing on a rare night out, usually when Lucy invites me for drinks and I need to let off some steam.

I go up to the bar to order a round of club sodas when I see him sitting at the end of it, deep in discussion with Axton. He hasn't even noticed me standing there.

I decide to play him at his own game. Marching up to him, I stand with my hands on my hips.

His head turns to me at the same time Axton looks up.

"Hey, Frankie, what can I get you?"

I shift my eyes to him momentarily. "Five club sodas for table six, please."

He gives me a chin lift and pushes off the bar.

Nitro avoids my gaze, but says, "Hello, Frankie, long time no see."

"Cut the crap," I say, my tone curt. "I know you've been outside my condo. They could hear your motorcycle in Canada."

"Was there a question in there somewhere?"

"I'm getting to it."

He smirks, turning to look at me.

His eyes are so damn bright that I'm momentarily caught off guard. He's a badass biker; he can't have such pretty eyes.

I don't miss his broad shoulders and thick biceps as he rests his elbows on the bar. It makes me wonder what they were both talking about before I interrupted.

"Really? Or did you just want any excuse to come over here and talk to me."

Infuriating ass! "I thought we could be friends, but clearly that isn't in your vocabulary," I spout at him, crossing my arms over my chest.

"Friends?" He scoffs. "Doc, you and I could never be friends, may as well stop deluding yourself."

"Why not? People who are the opposite sex can be friends, I do it all the time."

His eyes narrow. "With that guy from the hospital?"

"Aha!" I cry, triumphant. "So that's what this is really about."

"Not all of it."

"But some of it?"

His eyebrows knit together. "What do you expect me to say?"

"Nothing," I fire back. "But I thought we could be civil, being we both live in the same small town. I don't need you…checking up on me."

He bites down on his bottom lip with his teeth as if he's considering my words. "Yeah, that's just the thing, Doc, no can do on the checking up on you thing."

"Nitro, what is this all about?"

He shrugs. "I told you before that I'd always look out for you, that I'd keep you safe, and this is me keeping that promise."

"I'm a grown ass woman, I don't need you to do that for me."

He looks completely undeterred.

"Well, if you minded, you should've said something when you saw me outside the cafe and I would've told you that it's a free fuckin' country."

"Like I had time, Nitro, you took off like a bat out of hell."

"Are we fighting?" His lips twitch.

I roll my eyes. "No, you're being a pain in the ass."

"Do I have to explain what I was doin' there?"

"Not much as I do having coffee with a friend."

"Are you fuckin' him?"

I try not to snort with laughter, knowing what I know about Gerard. The nerve of this man is second to none.

"Like I said the other day about being presumptuous."

"So you're not denying it, then?"

My temper flares. "What gives you the right to be so obnoxious?"

He shrugs. "I was born that way, babe. Can't help it."

"Keep your nose out of my business."

"It didn't have to be this way."

I prod him in the chest. "You made it this way."

He looks down at my finger, but when his eyes meet mine again, they're stormy, I'm not afraid of him. I never have been, even when I learned he was stalking me.

"I'm just bein' honest, Frankie, maybe you should do the same. I want what I want."

Not done I move closer to him. "Fine, you want honesty? I resent you, okay? I texted you and called so many times, and you never replied."

"I was in jail for quite a few of those years, remember."

I snort. "I had important things to say, things that couldn't be done over the phone, things that I needed you to know."

"Why didn't you say this the other night?"

"Because you were drunk. You can't reason with drunk people."

He looks affronted. "Well, what is it that couldn't wait? I'm dying to hear."

Panic runs through my body. Do I really want to do this right here?

I swallow hard.

Telling him what I have to tell him in a bar for anyone to hear is not how I want to break the news.

"You know what, Adam, the moment's gone."

I turn to leave, and he reaches for my wrist, dragging me back to him, pulling me closer.

"Get your hands off me," I whisper-shout.

He snickers. "Your mouth says one thing, but you're forgettin' I know you, Frankie. I know every little detail about your face, your body, your eyes…you can't lie to me."

"You're deranged."

He smirks, his hand still snaked around my wrist.

He's right. The asshole.

I'd never let anyone man-handle me, and I can't let him see how much he affects me. How much my heart is broken. How much he hurt me and how much I will eventually hurt him.

When he finds out the truth, he'll never forgive me.

Best off he hates me already; it'll save the heartbreak later on.

"You'll come round." He lets me go.

"You're dreaming." I stalk off angrily, unsure why I'm acting this way.

I am supposed to be an adult, but then again, so is he. He just knows how to wind me up.

This is who he is. I'm fully aware of it. He's never been anything else; the years haven't changed him in that regard.

Sure, anyone else in my position would probably report

him to the police. I mean, stalking?

He made a living out of it.

But, I've seen a different side to him. The side, when he's not being a possessive asshole, that's kind, generous, tender, and loving.

The way he held me…I feel like bursting into tears.

Why am I such a sap? It was ten damn years ago.

I head to the ladies' room before I either go apeshit or start crying, I haven't decided which yet.

I'm more mad at myself. Did I really think that I could outrun time?

It's come full circle.

Oh, the hatred will come. That I know.

And I brought every last moment of it on myself.

Chapter 17 - Nitro

I stare after her, watching her hips sway as she disappears back into the restaurant, willing myself not to go after her.

What the fuck was she insinuating?

It makes me check myself…I'm not a drunk. I'm not like…him.

I'll kill myself before I'm ever like that man I call my father.

I close my eyes as Axton rounds the bar on my side, collecting glasses.

"What the fuck did you do to Frankie? She looks like you just stabbed her with a pencil."

"Don't ask, brother."

He shakes his head. "I may not have had much experience with women…"

I give him a pointed look. "I sense a lecture comin' on."

He ploughs on regardless. "But I think the general idea is to compliment a woman and be…nice, not a dick. That's if you want to get lucky. Maybe you just want a woman to smack you out, 'cause it's gonna happen, bro."

I shake my head. "You've been with Stevie all of five minutes. I think I'll take my chances."

"She's a good woman, Nitro, and you're fuckin' it up."

He's heard many nights of my re-telling of our story,

minus the parts where I did indeed act like a dick. He also knows I haven't touched her since I've been in Bracken Ridge.

Ten years of hell waiting for her. Of making bad choices and always wondering. And yeah, he's right, I'm fuckin' it up big time.

Like I fuck up everything.

I've always been socially awkward, and I always get into trouble for being truthful. I haven't quite mastered the art of being polite to not hurt someone's feelings. Not someone you care about. To me that's the same as lying.

I run a hand through my hair. "No shit. And I'd like to point out, she came and took a jibe at me first. She's not as nice as she appears."

He frowns like he doesn't believe me. "Poor baby, did she hurt your feelin's?" He squeezes my shoulder.

"Fuck off," I growl, shoving him off.

"Well, just keep doin' what you're doin', dude. She'll be sure to stay fifty miles away, and you'll have no chance of gettin' anywhere near her, or her bed."

He laughs and walks off.

If only he knew this isn't just about me being in her bed. It's so much more than that.

I finish my soda. Yeah, I don't drink during the day and never have, despite the fact Frankie apparently thinks I'm a drunk. I still have to get back to the car yard and finish the day.

I chuck some cash on the bar and shoot Axton the two-finger salute as I head out.

I have to get out of here before I go and do something I'll regret.

Accosting her in front of everyone won't go down well.

She just doesn't understand. She's mine. She's fuckin' mine.

And it doesn't matter what she says or does, I will always look out for her.

If she doesn't want me, then I suppose I'll have to live with that, but I don't believe what she's spouting. I think she's all talk. If she tells me to fuck off like she actually means it, then I'll have no choice. I can't make her want me.

In the ten years since I saw her, I've never had a committed relationship. There's been other women, but nothing stuck.

I'm not in a good mood as it is.

I got off the phone with Smokey, who was brought in for questioning, since he was the Fury's V.P. during Tex's reign. They wanted to know all the juice about what was going on around that time. Since the club had broken up some months before, it wasn't hard for Smokey to tell them Tex went AWOL and the club disbanded, everyone going their separate ways. All of that is true.

But that gives the pigs even more reason to suspect

Smokey or someone else from the old club because of the
bad blood spilled. I guess Smokey building his own MC
doesn't exactly scream innocent. Plus, all they have to do is
question any of the legit members who left when Tex almost
killed everyone in it with his bad decisions, and they'll tell
you the same.

That club was fucked for so long.

How I stuck it out, considering shit was turning south
years ago, I don't know. I guess we all just hoped that things
would get better.

Tex had that way of screwing up, then redeeming
himself. It was rinse and repeat. One good drug run and
everyone got paid handsomely; how quickly one forgets
all the shit when you've suddenly got thousands of dollars
waving you in the face.

The flip side also being, Tex had a lot of enemies, far
more than those who were loyal.

As I say, the loyal ones were few and far between, and
all of them are six feet under.

They also have no weapon, so without any evidence, it's
a guessing game. Too many men. Too many enemies. Too
many clubs who wanted him dead.

Just look at the Vipers; big fuckin' club, but at least
Smokey wasn't on their bad side anymore. There had been
a truce of sorts once he'd given Tex's drug shipment in
payment of a deal gone south years before; it created a huge

rift between the clubs. It was all Tex's doing, but the Vipers didn't see it that way.

Once they got the score, which was millions of dollars, they called a ceasefire.

Smokey was no fuckin' angel, but with him starting up the Sons of Phoenix Fury, you have to have some allies.

With the Vipers off his back, the man was leading the charge in resurrecting the club, but only with men that were like himself, Griller, and Hoax.

It had been a deliberation whether to join them at the helm. Fuck knows, I'd wanted to, even if they were still one percenters, but that chapter of my life had come to an end.

I was at a crossroads.

Smokey may have the smarts to stay out of jail; the man was a fuckin' saint on paper, but the law just seemed to swarm to me like flies on shit. If I kept going how I was going, I would've been the next to be six feet under.

Since reconnecting with Lucy and Rubble, and now being an uncle to their baby, Avery, nothing could sway me to go back.

Call me a sap, but I wanted out of the life.

Did I want to try being good for a while? Not exactly. I know that I will never be any kind of angel, a dirty angel maybe, but no fuckin' saint. And that's okay.

But the law would catch up with me, as it has almost done now. Which is why, for the first time in years, I actually care about being locked up.

I've got my family, and I've got my girl.

Well, the latter is still debatable. But if I stay out of jail and keep my nose clean, then my theory is that at least I get to see her. Even if she hates me.

Even if she wishes I'd never met her.

Sure, I was an ass, but it was for the best.

I still maintain that back then, I was no good to anyone. We could never have shared anything important because I was too wrapped up in my club and trying to get everyone's approval. Back then, I lived for that shit.

In some sick way, I first saw Tex as a father figure, but that quickly waned into something I hated, not admired.

Smokey, while not old enough to be my pop, was more of a mentor that Tex ever was.

He saw the potential in me, and in all fairness, he saved my life.

I owe him.

Letting him down when I decided to join Bracken Ridge Rebels was a hard decision, but he understood. And I'm grateful for that.

Between him and Hutch, well, they're just two of most influential men I've ever met. Proving to my tortured soul that not all men are like my father, or like Tex. Hutch believed in me too, because he believed in Rubble, who got me the job.

That's how an MC works. You trust one another, implicitly. I see that in this club.

Every single one of those men at the table would take a bullet for the other, and for their bitches.

I saw it with my own eyes when Bones dived in front of Lucy, to take a knife that could've killed him. He took a fuckin' knife for an ol' lady. For my sister.

In any other club, I seriously doubt any brother would put his life on the line for anyone's ol' lady, and definitely not for any sweet butt or hang-around.

Back at the yard, I call Gears. He's the prospect that's been helping me run the place.

He's worked here for years, and though he's barely twenty years old and has a huge chip on his shoulder, he knows the place inside out. He knows where everything is in this place, and there's a lot of scrap metal and used car parts. Somehow, this huge car graveyard is very organized. Inventory is kept up to date by one of the sweet butts, Chelsea, as she's been helping out until we can get a full-time office girl in here to keep on top of everything. Lucy was doing it in the beginning, but she also has Rubble's towing business to manage, as well as helping Sienna, Steel's ol' lady, when she's swamped at Steel's garage. When I find him, he's sitting at the desk inside the office, a big fuckin' grin on his face as a chick bends over the desk and tells a joke that has him laughing, her laughing, and his eyes dipping down to her chest as she animates with her hands.

I feel like giving Chelsea a smack on the ass, wearing a short skirt like that and distracting him with her tits when he's supposed to be working, but when I lean on the doorjamb and clear my throat, I'm surprised when I see it's not Chelsea at all, it's Amelia, Axton and Brock's sister, who turns her head to look at me.

I look down at her long legs, fuck me boots, and the tight blouse she has on. She's older than Gears, by quite a bit.

"You lost, sweetheart?"

She stands quickly, her cheeks flushing as Gears' eyes narrow, clearly not impressed with the intrusion.

This is interesting.

I don't know yet if they're fuckin', but I'll know by the time she steps on outta here.

"No," she says as Gears, the little fucker, doesn't even attempt to get out of my chair and scurry back to work like a good prospect should. "I was looking for…a part."

Looking for a dick, more like.

"Really?" I frown. "What kinda part, maybe I can help you find it."

I shoot a look at Gears, his eyes back on Amelia. Okay, he's got it bad.

This ain't good. If Brock and Axton find out, he'll be

joining Tex out in the National Park. Though maybe with a slightly better hiding place for his body.

One thing the brothers are around here is protective of their siblings.

Holy crap, I can't even imagine the shitstorm that's gonna rain down if Gears has had his dick in Amelia. He's cocky enough to pull it off; all the chicks at the club like him because he's got a baby face and has that whole feed me a bowl of soup and put me to bed kinda vibe going on. I know, I've been there myself. Women in my old club always wanted to take care of me. It pissed the other brothers off big time, especially when I was a prospect.

I had no business going there, but half the time, it wasn't always my fault.

"That's okay," she goes on, crossing her arms over her chest. "Gears is going to order it for me."

I give him a look. "Is that right?"

He has the good grace to look a little sheepish.

"We don't have it, I checked."

"Right," I say, then look back at Amelia. "Will that be all?"

She narrows her eyes. Okay, so she has a temperament very similar to Brock. I've never seen Axton mad unless it's a patron in the bar who goes a little too far with the chicks, harassing them and shit, but other than that, he's placid. But Brock. Brock is his own kettle of fish.

Just like Amelia.

"Don't go giving me orders like I'm one of your club bitches," she has the nerve to say.

"That's no way to talk about your fellow club sisters, Amelia."

The ol' ladies are the women claimed at the table and belong to you, like Lucy is to Rubble. Club sisters are the girls of the club like Amelia, Summer; Gunner's sister and Deanna; Hutch's daughter, who are all a part of the club but who the brothers don't fuck with.

Bitches are women around the club who hang around or are sweet butts, the women there to please the other members who don't have ol' ladies.

"I wasn't talking about them." She rolls her eyes. Her sass has a smile on my lips. She's very fuckin' brave.

"I wouldn't piss Chelsea off when she gets here. She's the only one keepin' up with the book work and makin' sure the stains stay off the furniture." I give her a wink.

She shakes her head, and I can feel the annoyance coming off Gears. He may have worked here longer than me, but he's being an ass on work time, and he's playing with fire.

If she's wet between the legs for Gears, she'd better think twice about going there, if she knows what's good for her.

"I've offered to give Gears a hand," she goes on as my

eyebrows knot together.

"A hand?"

He runs a hand through his wayward hair.

"And here I was thinkin' I was runnin' this place," I go on, pushing off the door frame as I step inside. "Stupid me, huh?"

"What she meant was, givin' us both a hand…" He stops as I roll my lips inwards, these two are fuckin' hopeless. "In a total, non-sexual way…"

Amelia looks a little embarrassed, like I've caught her sucking his dick or something.

"Listen," I say, stopping short of the desk. "I don't give a shit what the two of you do when you're not on this property. Go at it like fuckin' rabbits for all I care, but don't make me an accessory to Gear's murder."

"We're not fucking!" they say the same time.

I pinch the bridge of my nose. "Jesus fuckin' Christ."

Do I actually believe them? Yes. At this moment in time. Do I think it'll stay that way? Hell no.

Pretty sure Gears has a death wish that would rival mine when I was his age. I thought I could walk on water too because I had a pretty face and got a lot of chicks. It all catches up with you, though.

"Just because you have a one-track mind," she sasses, poking me in the chest as she begins to walk toward the door. Brave little thing. "Doesn't mean everyone does."

"Got it," I say, purposefully looking down at her fuck me boots. "Nice office attire, by the way."

"It's called fashion. You might like to try it sometime."

I put my hands on my hips. "Nice mouth you got there, princess. Good thing we're not in church."

She gives me another eye roll. Clearly, she's from the school of Deanna Hutchinson. These girls get away with a little too much back-talk. Still, it's funny to see her trying her hardest to be badass and pretend she doesn't have a thing for the resident prospect and a man at least seven years her junior.

"I'll call you when the part arrives," Gears calls after her.

"Thank you, Gears." I'm sure she emphasizes his name just for my benefit, since I'm off the team.

When she's gone, I turn to Gears. "What the fuck, dude?"

He shrugs. "Nothin' goin' on, before you slug me. I need this face for Saturday night. If Hutch thinks I've worked hard enough, I might get a hang-around."

I shake my head. "You know, he only knows if you've worked hard if I tell him you have."

I let that sink in for a moment before he says, "Oh."

"Yeah, oh." I shove him from behind my desk as I sit, and he loiters around like there's more to say. I'd quit while we're ahead if I were him. "I meant what I said. Do what you want off the property; I just don't wanna know about it."

"It's not like that. We're…friends," he says it like he's trying out the words, so much so, I look up at him from the stack of papers on my desk. He's being truthful.

"Since when are you friends with a chick?"

"Since now, I guess." He runs another hand through his hair, fucker needs a haircut.

"Yeah, well, I'd pick another friend, bro. You don't wanna be sippin' through a straw for the rest of your life. Brock and Axton are very protective of Amelia. She's been a wild child in the past, which I'm sure is what attracts you to her, but if you've got any sense in that thick skull of yours, I'd say back off while you've still got a life ahead of you."

He rubs his chin. Like he even needs to think about it. That tells me everything.

He likes her, as more than a friend. Maybe more than a fuck.

"What's a man gotta do around here to catch a break?" he mutters, sauntering off toward the door.

I'm pretty lenient with him. Being a patched member means I obviously rank higher than him, and he shouldn't be back-talking, but we get along. He has my back. I guess when it comes to women, we can't help who we're attracted to.

I snort at the irony.

Thinking about Frankie.

How she's pissed at me, and me at her.

I don't know how to fix this, or if we even can.

Is my fault I'm a dick? Yes, but she caught me on a bad day. I didn't mean to be an ass, but I also don't appreciate being poked at. Not by anyone, but especially not her. Not when I can't have her the way I want her.

The one woman I want keeps slipping through my fingers, like only she knows how.

Ten fuckin' years.

Not on my watch.

I'm gonna go to her.

She can tell me to fuck off again, I don't care. She needs to hear me out, hear my side of the story. I did her a fuckin' favor, and I'm gonna make her see that.

She can be mad at me all she wants, but honestly, was she ever really intending on making a life with me? It was one night broiled in passion and sorrow. She was in mourning, so pained and full of sadness. Is it sick to say it was the best night of my life? Not because of all that sadness, obviously, but because of how we connected and how it has stayed with me all these years. For me, it was never just about the sex. It was great, don't get me wrong, but it was the closeness I felt. The way we were two shredded souls coming together, loving one another, taking what we wanted…all night long.

Maybe that's all we really had? That one night.

If that's the case, then why do I refuse to believe it? Why do I keep torturing myself that this is the girl for me? That the connection we had wasn't just all in my head, that we shared something really important. I'll give it a few days, let her cool off, but after that, I'm going to confront her. Lay it all out on the table, the good, the bad, the ugly.

If she rejects me, then that's a bridge I'll have to cross. Seeing her around town and potentially in the arms of another man will make me want to commit murder, but that's the price I'll have to pay. That or I could start day drinking.

One reminder of my father and his drunken rants is enough to put me off that thought immediately.

She's gonna hear me out, sober. She had shit she has to tell me, too, and I need to at least listen to what she has to say. Even if whatever it is probably isn't groundbreaking.

It's probably how much of an asshole she thinks I am, and I already got the memo on that one.

Whatever it is, it can't be that bad.

There is nothing that Frankie could tell me that changes the way I feel about her.

Nothing can.

But I'm tired of waiting.

Her time to decide about me is up.

BRACKEN RIDGE
REBELS
ARIZONA
M · C

CHAPTER 10

NITRO

The party is in full swing at the club.

It's Angel's birthday and Brock organized a band. Being summer, they set up in the outdoor pavilion with loudspeakers that could wake the dead, but luckily, we're out in the sticks.

The woodfire pizza guy, Rusty, is serving up piping hot pies like nobody's business.

Hutch has his arm wrapped around Kirsty as they sway to the music.

What I'd give to have a love like that. After forty odd years together, they're still crazy about each other.

It hits me suddenly that maybe that's all I've ever wanted. To love and be loved, not that I'd ever admit that to anybody.

I'm still sticking to soda. I don't want to be inebriated when I see Frankie. Angel said she was coming tonight. They've grown close since Frankie was the one who helped her through a difficult pregnancy with Ethan Wolf.

Even Axton and Stevie are here, though Stevie can't

help herself and is helping Ginger and Summer pour drinks behind the bar.

I've had my eyes everywhere tonight, and I still haven't caught sight of Frankie.

Maybe she had to work late?

She better be here because if I have to go to her place, shit might just hit the fan.

Just as I'm thinking it, Steel slaps me on the back.

"You look like you just sucked on a bag of lemons," he says, then nods to my soda. "You on the hard stuff, brother?"

I give him a chin lift as he takes the seat next to me at the bar. "Nah, man, got a headache."

"PMS?"

"Funny," I mutter. "Had a little bit goin' on this past week. Potentially being wanted for murder is up there on the stress level scale."

"Yeah, heard from Griller, said the cops are asking around but nothin' concrete has surfaced. If they're tryin' to find a link with his murder, they'll be lookin' a long time. He had more enemies than I've had hot dinners. Nobody is gonna vouch for that fucker. The only ally he had was Rachet, and he's six feet under."

"That could play in our favor."

"The authorities are lookin' for witnesses around his last known whereabouts; the old clubhouse before it burned to the ground."

"Convenient," I mutter.

"Guess they can't charge him with arson, then." Steel always has a way with words.

"I guess not."

"Things are gonna be fine," he assures me. "Ain't nothin' they got on you. Linc wiped everything he could get his hands on with surveillance cameras. At the very least, they can't link Tex bein' here, or you, for that matter. You're in the clear, so don't look so fuckin' worried. My man always comes through, he's the best."

I wish I could be as confident. "Thanks, brother, appreciate it."

"Where's Frankie?"

I give him the side-eye. "Good news travels fast."

"Ain't no news about it. It's my job to know everythin' about this club."

"Right, includin' who I'm not fuckin'?"

"Question is, why aren't you? She's a damn fine woman, smarter than you, so that could be a problem, but you got history, right? What's the problem?"

"The problem is she's too damn stubborn to see reason."

He gives me a pointed look. "What did you do?"

I shrug. "I kinda…followed her."

His lips twitch ever so slightly. "Right, 'cause chicks really dig that in this day and age."

"Trust me, she used to be grateful when I kept her safe ten years ago."

"So I take it you're fallin' back into your old habits, and she's all grown up now and doesn't need your help?"

I shoot him a glance. "What are you, a fuckin' therapist?"

He shrugs. "I know women. Practically raised my sister, plus all the other women in this club who give me nothin' but trouble and lip. It ain't that hard to figure out."

"Touche. Good to know you're not growin' a pair of tits."

He downs his whiskey. "The ones hardest to tame are the ones worth fightin' for. Must be why my ol' lady's sendin' me gray."

"When did you get so philosophical?" I laugh.

"Somewhere between bein' shot in Afghanistan and gettin' divorced from my cheatin' wife."

I stare at him, stunned. Steel never usually discloses much information about himself, and he never brings up the military, even though I know he served.

"That'll do it."

He taps his glass on the edge of the bar for a refill. Then I see his ol' lady behind the bar.

She also jumped in to help with the crowd. The place is absolutely packed inside and out.

Sienna struts over and gives him a devilish grin.

"This reminds me of how we first met," she says, giving me a smile as she takes his glass from him.

"Got that wrong, princess. We first met at church."

"Right, but remind me again how long you followed me around before we met in person."

I give him a side-eye, then slap him on the back. "Not sure we're all that different, really, bro."

He shakes his head as she struts off to get him a fresh drink.

"That was different," he begins. "She was our new landlord at one point."

I chuckle. "That I cannot imagine."

"Threw the contract in my face, literally."

"Seems it didn't deter you."

"She had just the right amount of sass. Didn't know club life at all, wasn't sure she would get used to it, but she surprised me."

"You plannin' on kids?"

"Nah." He shakes his head. "I don't do cryin' babies and dirty diapers. That shit's not for us. We've got dogs, Lola and Rocky, both rescues. Lola's my baby; she's a pit bull, a survivor. Rocky's more timid, but he's gettin' used to people now. Took a while because he was abandoned and neglected. Smart to never trust people."

His love for dogs, or any animals, is legendary around Bracken Ridge. Steel has done a lot for animal rescue, even setting up the local shelter, Faux Paws, and shutting down an illegal dog fighting ring and a shonky dog breeding operation. If there's anything that gets the big man riled up, it's animals being mistreated.

Each to their own on the kid front. I respect it. There was a time when the only woman I could ever see being the mother to my kids was Frankie. Now I don't know if that window is closed for good. I've no idea what kind of father I'd make. Not a very good one, probably.

Sienna comes back, places Steel's drink down in front of him, and leans over. He meets her halfway, planting a kiss on her lips.

"That was hardly a kiss, Steel," she chastises.

"Sittin' with my brother. Not like I wanna get hard while we're talkin' about difficult chicks and how to tame them."

She bites her lip as her gaze flicks to me. "Don't worry about him, he's always this jovial."

"He's all yours," I reply, and just as I do, something catches my attention in my periphery.

It's like Frankie calls to me on another level, one even I don't understand.

I turn my head and see her weaving through a crowd of people, Deanna dragging her toward the bar, and they're both laughing.

Deanna is the wildest out of the girls. Rumor has it Hutch thinks she's some kinda angel, but that couldn't be further from the truth.

I don't take my eyes from her as they approach, and when her gaze finally lands on mine, she looks momentarily surprised to see me.

This is my fuckin' clubhouse after all.

If she were my ol' lady, I'd be spankin' that little ass of hers for looking at me with such defiance. I know she thinks she won, but she's got no idea what a persistent asshole I can be when I set my mind on something.

She looks away first, and I take a glance down her body.

She's wearing tight-ass, leather-looking black jeans and an even tighter silver tank. It makes her tits look huge.

Every man in this place will be doing a double take at her body, and that lights a fire inside me that makes me want to punch every last one of them in the throat.

If anyone so much as looks her way, I will go fucking apeshit.

She leans against the bar on the other side of Steel as Sienna moves off to go serve them.

Deanna orders their drinks and Steel, unceremoniously, moves off the stool so there's no distance between us.

He goes behind the bar and manhandles Sienna while I feel Frankie's eyes on me.

I turn toward her. "Evenin', Frankie."

She gives me a tight smile. "Hey."

Deanna begins talking to the chick on the other side

of her, so I take it upon myself to take the stool Steel just vacated.

"Still mad at me?"

She stares straight ahead. "I don't know. Are you still being an ass?"

That was fair, I suppose. I didn't tell her any lies. She is mine, and I will not sit by and watch another man slide in; she just didn't wanna hear it.

"I think we need to call a ceasefire." My hand meets the back of her stool, but I don't touch her. The tank is low at the back, showing off far more skin that I'd allow if she was my ol' lady. Her ass is damn fine in those pants. I want to peel them off her and fuck her in every hole. Jesus Christ.

She turns to me again. Her makeup is heavier too, and as pretty as it is, I don't like it. I like her fresh faced and natural. She doesn't need makeup.

"Oh, and why do you think we need to do that?"

I lean toward her and whisper, "Because you comin' in here, lookin' like that, makes me wanna take you out back and fuck you against the wall. That'd shut that pretty mouth up."

She takes in a long breath.

Satisfied I'm getting to her, I move my hand to the small of her back, caressing her flesh.

She opens her mouth, then closes it again. I like the idea that I can still shock her.

"What's the matter, Doc? Cat got your tongue? Or haven't you been fucked thoroughly for a while?"

She swallows hard, avoiding looking at me and says, "You always did have a way with words."

I snort. "Nah, babe, but we both know I've got a way with my hands, my tongue, and my cock. You should know, you begged me for it."

"I don't beg for anything," she says shakily.

I move my fingers ever so slowly against her, seeing little goosebumps rise on her skin at my touch.

Licking my lips, my cock could burn a hole in my pants. I want her so bad, like nothing I've ever wanted before.

"Really? I seem to remember differently."

"That was a long time ago, things have…changed."

I move my hand lower, down her back, taking a gamble as I slip lower and run my palm over her ass. She still doesn't stop me.

"Things definitely have," I whisper. "You've filled out nicely. This ass…I wanna take a bite, and those tits, so fuckin' perfect." I move my other hand to her stomach, trailing upward, but she smacks it away.

"Nitro!" she whisper-shouts.

The lights go dim and the party starts to crank up. Perfect timing.

She reaches for her drink as I move closer so she's standing between my legs.

She takes a long sip as I grip her ass tighter and she closes her eyes. "You want my touch, don't you, Frankie?"

I move my hand to her stomach again as she clutches onto the bar like that'll save her. My hand moves north, sliding over one of her tits as I cup it and she groans. The hand gripping her ass pulls her closer, so she's pressed up sideways against me.

I know for a fact she wouldn't be letting me do this if those lights hadn't dimmed.

If she touches my cock, I'll fuck her on this bar, and I don't care who watches.

"Nitro," I hear her whisper as my thumb flicks her hardened nipple back and forth.

"Yeah, babe?"

I want to suck her tits so bad, that my dick just about explodes at the thought.

"I can't...I can't let you..."

"Can't let me what?"

"Fuck me."

I move my lips to her shoulder and kiss it lightly. "Yes, you can, you'll like it. Ridin' my cock, squeezing that tight pussy around me as I make you beg me to let you come."

I see her bite her lip as I pinch her nipple. She practically melts into my touch.

"Jesus," I hear her mutter.

Biting her shoulder gently, I begin to fondle the other

nipple, cupping her breast, feeling every fuckin' inch of these beauties while I keep my other hand on her ass.

"Nah, just me, babe, but if you don't want it…" I take my hands off her, and I know I'm not playing fair. I just fine-tuned her body like a guitar. I can't see her face properly in this light, but I'll bet she's flushed.

She grabs my hand and pulls me off the stool with a rough tug. I follow her gladly, rounding the corner of the bar toward the restrooms. Beyond that there's a room where they store the kegs.

We head there without one word, my eyes on her ass the whole time. My cock barely contained it's so hard. We don't make it; I pull her to me and cup her face. Ready to do what I've waited a long ten years for. I need her lips on mine, now.

"This is for defyin' me the first time." I kiss her roughly, my tongue meeting hers as I walk her into the wall, and she moans, wrapping her arms around my waist.

She gasps as I push my cock into her stomach. "Feel that, Doc?"

She nods.

"That's what you do to me in this slutty little outfit, comin' in here with your ass and your tits on display." I cup her breasts with both hands. "These are mine."

She bites my bottom lip as our kiss intensifies. I reach down and pull her tank out of her pants and shove it up. Her lacy black bra coming into view as her tits heave with her racing heart.

I cup them, pushing them up as she watches me. I'm about to rip the thing down when I hear someone in the keg room.

I check myself and push off her, reaching out my hand as she takes it. I would go upstairs, but I don't know what atrocities await us up there. The only option is…my truck. Thank fuck I drove that here and not my sled.

I keep pulling her along as we take the back door out to the deserted parking lot.

Pulling her to me, I spin her around so her back is against my truck door, her top still shoved up against her armpits. I slide the tank over her head and discard it, cupping the back of her head as our lips meet again.

We're both urgent, her hands gripping my ass as I move one hand to her bra and pull it down. One of her tits pops out, and I quickly move my mouth to suck her nipple like I'm a starving man. Tugging down the other side, I pinch that nipple as I nudge my knee between her legs. She rubs against it eagerly, her hands reaching into my hair as she gasps and pants. I'm rough with her, but fuck me if it isn't the sweetest thing I've done in a very long time. We're like angry animals, acting on instinct. Our bodies pent up and needy. She rides my knee, and I know she's fuckin' close.

I move my mouth to the other nipple and pay that the

same attention, my hand trailing south to unbutton her pants, zipper, and then I'm sliding my hand into the front of her panties.

She's drenched.

I groan, sucking harder, my cum threatening to explode if I keep this up, but I can't fuckin' stop. She's like a drug.

She just about convulses at my touch as I run my fingers through her wet heat.

"I wanna fuck you with my tongue," I whisper, kissing her all the way up to her mouth. "But I won't last. Need to be in you. Now."

"I need it," she cries. "Nitro, I need you inside me."

I swirl my fingers around her clit as she lets go, crying out as I rub her through her pleasure, inserting two fingers and thrusting them until she's grabbing at my belt buckle, trying to get my pants off.

I pull my fingers out of her, very deliberately putting one hand around her throat as I suck them into my mouth, closing my eyes as I taste her.

She watches me in awe, panting, flushed, her tits heaving and my, my, is she a sight.

Placing those fingers to her mouth next, I make her suck, just like old times.

"See how good you still taste?" I whisper as I kiss her pulse point. "Do you see what I can do to you?"

"Nitro," she begs, and her hand begins to stroke my

cock through my jeans.

I look down as I watch her hand. "Undo my pants," I say, letting go of her neck as I shrug out of my cut and discard my t-shirt. "Get my cock out."

She fumbles as I take delight in watching the great Frankie Stevens come undone.

Eventually, she unzips me and tugs my jeans and boxer briefs down, my cock finally springing free as she fists me, her hot little fingers barely fitting around my girth.

"I need to make sure you're wet enough for this," I say.

"I am," she counters.

I smirk, then reach around and open my backseat door.

She climbs in and I waste no time in tugging my boots off, followed by my pants as I follow her inside. She's pulling at her jeans, trying to get them down as I fumble with the foil packet I just took out of my wallet.

Once her jeans are off and I've rolled the rubber on, I move on top of her, her arms around my neck as I hold my dick at the base and tease her with it, moving the head through her crease and nudging her clit. I keep circling, watching her big, hazel eyes take me in as she breathes heavily, squeezing shut as she climaxes again. This time, I don't wait, I move to her entrance and shove inside her full tilt, making her gasp. I'm big, but man, is she so damn tight. Her sweet cunt is exactly how I remember it; strangling my cock as I settle deep inside her, one hand planted against the leather seat at her head, the other holding on to the passenger seat so I don't crush her.

"Fuck yeah," I groan, sliding out and then back in again. "So tight, babe."

I can't go slow; I need to feel every inch of her. This isn't gonna last long, no matter how slow or hard I do it.

I start to fuck her with abandon as she grips my ass, our eyes meeting as I take in this beautiful, complex, and adorable woman beneath me.

"Nitro!" she cries. It only encourages me as I pound into her, her tits jiggling as I rock back and forth.

"Gonna be quick this time," I grunt. "Then you're gonna ride me nice and slow."

She tips her head back as I grip her hip with one hand, her legs wrapped around my waist, as she screams out and comes all over my dick. I groan my release, coming violently as the earth feels like it's splitting in two at the intensity.

Nah, it's even better than I remembered it.

BRACKEN RIDGE
REBELS
ARIZONA
M · C

CHAPTER 19

FRANKIE

Nitro stills as he grunts his release, and I'm panting hard. I cannot believe I was only at the party for like ten minutes, had one sip of my drink, and ended up being fucked in the back of his truck.

I should be thoroughly ashamed of myself. Instead, I reach for him as he brings his lips down to caress mine softly.

"Fuck, that was so good, babe," he mutters against my lips.

Discarding the condom, he tells me to crawl through to the front seat. He gets out of the backseat, then he sits in the front, sliding his seat all the way back as I climb over him. I guess he wasn't kidding about me riding him.

My body is on fire, craving his touch, already craving him inside me again.

I cup his face as I straddle his lap. His cock ready again, and I slide my pussy along his hard shaft without him penetrating.

He watches me, his hands gripping my ass.

"I forgot how good you were at this," I whisper, our lips

more tender this time, touching gently as he encourages me to hold him at the base while I tease myself.

"Use me, babe," he whispers back. "Use my cock however you want it."

I do just that, rubbing the head through my folds. I'm so wet it's ridiculous, and he's just loving every single second of my submission. His eyes glisten in the dark as I take charge.

Suddenly, I'm careening toward him as he lets the seat go backward farther. He spreads his knees as I fondle his cock and cup his balls, hissing at my touch, his head dips down to suck my nipple. My hand moves to hold my breast to his mouth as he suckles, his eyes on me the whole time. It's so erotic. So damn hot that I feel another climax building.

His hands cup my ass tighter as he sucks on my tits, and I rub against his cock with quicker movements. I begin to build, climbing higher, cupping the back of his head I straighten my back, my tits pressed against his face as I hold on for dear life and my orgasm rips through me once more. Panting, I lose myself, so high from what he does to me so easily.

As I'm coming down, I'm aware he's rolling another rubber on, and I waste no time in spreading my knees as wide as they can go, holding him at the base, and sinking down onto his fat cock. Jesus, he fills me so damn full. I can feel every inch of him.

"I love your cock," I whisper, unable to help myself.

He grunts with satisfaction, his hands gripping my hips as I move back and forth. Reaching between my legs, he gathers some slickness on his fingers and watches me intently. Soon, it's not enough. I need to ride him harder.

He moves the chair back some more so we're almost horizontal, my hands pressing against his chest as he uses one hand to grip my hip and helps slide me up and down. The other hand reaches around to press a finger against my back hole.

Rubbing his fingers against my bud slowly, he's testing if I'll let him go there. I've never let anyone give me anal before, but with Nitro, nothing is off limits.

He works his tip into my ass as I close my eyes, and with each thrust of my hips, he gets a little deeper. It feels… different, but not in a bad way. I can barely breathe, it's so hot.

All the while, he lies back and watches me taking him, while his finger fucks my ass.

"You look so good takin' me," he growls. "Gonna claim this ass with my cock sometime soon, babe. We'll work up to that."

I throw my head back and clench down on him harder. His dirty words send me into a spiral. His finger works in and out until he's all the way in and I'm groaning and whimpering recklessly.

"God, Nitro."

"Fuck yeah…let go, ride me, baby, that tight little cunt is chokin' my cock so damn good."

I begin to climb higher and higher, and when he reaches his other hand between my legs and rubs my clit, I explode with such an urgency, with him fucking me in two holes at once, I feel like I might lift off. I come harder than I ever have before, crying out as he pumps into me furiously, meeting my thrusts before he stills and groans my name over and over as he comes hard. I flop down on his chest, heaving and panting as our slick bodies try to come down.

"That was…"

He strokes my hair with one hand. "A five out of ten?"

I smack him on the arm as he chuckles. "I'm still mad at you."

He's panting just as hard as me.

He kisses my head. "I just had my finger in your ass. I'm pretty sure you're not still mad at me."

"Just so you know, I don't usually do…the anal thing."

He chuckles again, and I like the sound. It's so…unlike him. "Is that right?"

"Yes, especially with that huge thing."

He cradles me, holding me as I let him, in no hurry to go. I should be. We just fucked twice in his car, where anybody could be outside watching. Though, I noted the windows are darkly tinted and so steamed up, I doubt anyone could. Hearing us is another story, though.

"You'll take it." He kisses my hair again. "So fuckin' beautiful, Frankie. Need to get you home."

I shake my head. "You just fucked me twice," I remind him. "My bones feel like they may shatter."

"Sleep with me, then. I'll wake you up with a good morning kiss."

"Which isn't really a kiss, is it?"

I feel his chest rumble. "You know how much I like eatin' your pussy. It's only fair you let me after all the sass you've been givin' me lately."

Guilt threatens to hit me from all sides, but I push it away.

Not tonight. Just let me have tonight.

Imagining him waking me up with his head between my legs almost has me forgetting the reasons we need to talk.

Tomorrow. I tell myself. One more day won't hurt.

I selfishly want this to last, so I can have the memory of him at least. So when this all comes crashing down, I can remember his touch.

I didn't come here planning on sleeping with him. Of course, I knew he'd be here, watching me. Now this complicates things even more.

I get dressed awkwardly in his truck and then he tells me he's driving me to his place. To go back to the party now would be slightly awkward, given my current state.

We're both silent most of the way, though it's not unpleasant or uncomfortable.

Finally, he says, "You didn't see much of the party."

I can't help but notice the irony in his tone. "Was that your plan all along?"

"Would you believe me if I said that it wasn't?"

"I suppose next you're going to say it's my fault."

"It is. If you were my ol' lady, I wouldn't let you anywhere near the club lookin' like that."

I turn to him. "Lucky I'm not your ol' lady, then, huh?"

"Damn straight."

"I forgot how direct you are."

He snorts. "Really? I thought you'd come to that conclusion the last time we spoke."

"When you were being an ass, you mean?"

"I never agreed to be a boy scout, but I did agree that I'd always be honest with you."

I guess I can't fault him for that, even though he really was being an ass.

"You never were one to sugar coat things," I mutter.

Out of nowhere, he suddenly asks, "Who's the guy? From the hospital."

I try not to laugh. He's still going on about Gerard.

"You really are something else, Nitro."

"Answer the goddamn question."

I throw my hands in the air. "He's a friend. Last time I checked, men and women can be friends. It's not that uncommon."

"Not where I come from."

"His names Gerard, if you must know. He's sweet, funny, very clever, and he's one hundred percent into other men."

He glances at me to see if I'm joking, and when he sees I'm serious, he cracks his neck.

"Good. I'm likin' Gerard a whole lot more now I know he's not into you."

"He is into me, just not in that way."

"Lucky for his neck, then, isn't it?"

I stare out at the darkness ahead of us. There's nothing on the road around here this time of night.

"Do you like being here?" I ask after a while. "In Bracken Ridge?"

He drives carefully, not at all like I expected.

"Yeah, I like it."

"I came here about six months ago, for three weeks' relief. That's when I met Angel for the first time," I say, the time still vivid in my head. "I remember thinking how nice it was. It still had the feel of a small town, but with all the modern conveniences. Somewhere I could plant some roots, settle down…"

"I can imagine your life has been pretty crazy, bein' a

high falutin' doctor."

"It wouldn't have pleased my father, he always had high hopes of me being a real doctor. I don't know why he felt that way. But I had to be true to myself when I knew what I finally wanted to do."

"How's your mom?"

I'm surprised by the question, and my spine straightens. It'll be ten years this year since I've seen her properly.

"I don't know, honestly. We lost touch after I moved to New Jersey."

"I'm sorry to hear that."

"Don't be," I retort. "Trust me when I say, she isn't a nice person. After Dad's funeral, we grew even further apart. My brother, Chris, defied everyone and went to college on a football scholarship."

He turns to me, surprised. "Did he do any good?"

"Clearly, you don't follow football." I laugh. "He renewed his contract with the Miami Dolphins just a few months ago; he's an offensive lineman. I wish I got to see him more, though. Miami is pretty cool when I get time to visit."

"Not much of a sports fan," he admits. "But that is pretty cool."

We pull up to the gates, and Nitro puts in a code at the pin pad and they slide open.

"I'm not sure this is a good idea," I say softly.

He chuckles. "You said that right before I took you on the backseat."

"I can assure you I've never done anything like that in my life." Color floods my cheeks. I feel like I'm in high school all over again.

"Glad to hear it."

"I'm sure."

"I meant what I said."

I frown as we drive through the entry. "About what?"

"Us."

I wait for him to elaborate. He doesn't.

"Nitro, you're talking in riddles."

He waves a hand between us. "This thing between us, it isn't done."

I swallow hard. I know he means every word.

I go to open my mouth, and Nitro's phone rings.

I need to tell him…

He answers it, sounding annoyed, pulling up to the back of the building. Jumping out of his truck, he stays on the phone, and he's around to my side before I even get the door open.

He holds out his hand as I look up at him.

Has too much time passed?

I just don't know.

I don't know what the hell I'm even doing, and I can't even blame alcohol.

I'm fully sober and so is he.

"Fuck that," he says, his eyes still on me. "I'll call you tomorrow about it, kinda in the middle of somethin'."

I take his hand and jump out. His eyes graze down my body as I adjust my heels, slamming the door closed.

Hanging up, he tugs me along with him and unlocks the back door.

Once we're inside, he doesn't turn any lights on, and we meander through the small apartment. Even though it's dark, it looks surprisingly neat.

We reach what appears to be his bedroom as he turns to face me.

"What, no grand tour?" I whisper as he stares at me.

"This is my place, that's the bed."

I roll my lips inwards. "You brought me here just to fuck?"

His face softens. "No, babe, not just to fuck. We can cuddle afterwards."

I don't mean to reach up to cup his face, but that's what I do. His stubble is soft under my fingers.

"I've missed you, Nitro," I say, even though my head screams at me to stop.

"I've missed you too, babe."

"But we have to talk."

"Tomorrow," he says. "Let's have tonight. I need to be inside you again. I need to feel your body wrapped around me."

I try not to let tears glisten in my eyes. I look down, trying to avoid him. He's so intense.

It's honestly like we're on the same wavelength, like he can read my very thoughts.

Sometimes it scares me how well he knows me, yet he barely knows who I am these days.

He lifts my chin with two fingers. "Don't hide from me, Frankie," he says softly. "You never have to hide, not with me."

If only it were that easy.

Tomorrow.

Tomorrow I'll tell him everything.

He starts to lift my shirt out of my jeans.

He's a magnet. He's always been my magnet.

Someone I can't stay away from. I know that the feeling's mutual.

I study his face. His eyes. His hands. His body.

I will remember this moment forever.

Us. Like this.

It's what I will hold on to when the waters get stormy, and he never looks at me the same way again.

Tonight.

Then it's over.

BRACKEN RIDGE
REBELS
ARIZONA
M · C

CHAPTER 20

NITRO

I wake early to my phone ringing.

Club business doesn't stop on Sundays, but I'm surprised to see Smokey's name appear on the screen.

"Gonna have to learn to switch the damn thing off," I grumble as I rub my eyes.

He chuckles. "No rest for the wicked, brother."

"You can say that again." I glance across at Frankie. Her long hair splayed out on my pillows like a goddamn angel.

I fucked her long and hard. Being with her, being inside her, it's like nothing else. It makes me forget what it's like without her or why I waited so long to seek her out.

I know now that was a mistake.

It's not like I couldn't have; I just thought she was better off without me. That she'd be settled down already. And that I'd be able to forget her.

One look at her when our paths crossed dispelled that myth.

There ain't no getting over Frankie Stevens.

I haven't asked about previous relationships because, quite frankly, I don't want to know. It would make me sick thinking about another man sharing her life for all the years I missed. There's no point in torturing myself unnecessarily. It's in the past.

"Some mighty fine fluff at that club," he goes on. "Do the chicks still flock to you like they used to?"

"You know it," I say. "Fightin' 'em off with a stick."

"The way I hear it, some fuckin' chick has you all messed up."

"Where do you hear that?"

"So it's true?"

"It's complicated. Like most things when it comes to women."

I step out of bed and pull my crumpled jeans on and head toward the kitchen. I need coffee for this conversation.

"Don't tell me it's that fuckin' doc you were chasin' all those years ago? Rubble mentioned she was livin' there now?"

I yawn. "Did you call me to discuss pussy?"

He's snorts. "You're right, but I always did wonder about you two. She came around here a few times when you were locked up, lookin' for you."

I frown. A few times?

"News to me," I grumble. It doesn't matter now anyway. She's here, in my bed, and nothing's gonna get in the way of me being with her.

I didn't think she'd let me fuck her in my truck, but fuck me if it wasn't the best night of my life. Being with her again, feeling her body, smelling her scent, hearing her moan my name…

To say I'm besotted is an understatement.

"Some shit just doesn't go away, it comes full circle. I just hope this time you don't fuck it up."

"Tryin' hard," I say, switching the kettle on, "but it ain't easy with the shit going on with Tex. Brings all the past back up again, and I wanna forget it ever happened. I've moved on. Want to start a life here, and God willin', someday a family." I hope Tex isn't the reason he's calling me, but my gut tells me it's got everything to do with it. He doesn't just call to chat.

"Pigs questioned me, for the second time."

"Knew they would."

"They're not gonna get shit and they know it. Trouble is, back when Tex was Prez, he had a lot of cops in his pocket. Some of them are in with Tex's brother, and they're fuckin' nosy pricks."

"Don't remind me. Any of them been droppin' by?"

"Fuckers won't find the clubhouse. Hoax still has it registered in his grandma's name, until things settle down here. There's no reason to give anyone ammunition to come sniffin' around where they're not wanted. The old club was burned down years ago; it's wrecked."

"You got any pigs in your pocket yet?"

"Workin' on it. Club's comin' together nicely," he says. "Been a long time comin', but we're slowly gettin' the numbers. Also had the Chiefs part ways, big club fallout, so might be gettin' some of their brothers to join the ranks. Griller's workin' on gettin' Snitch back."

I know he'll get there. I've never met a more determined man.

"Snitch still knockin' around?"

"You bet. Can't keep him down for long."

I chuckle. "So, you call me just to fuckin' chat?"

"Be good if you could come up. Need to get some shit straightened out. Make sure we're all on the same page and we've all got the same story, just in case."

This doesn't sound good.

"What sort of shit, exactly?"

"You've got no alibi, for one, if the pigs knock on your door. We need to rectify that and be clear on a cover story that fits. Don't wanna do this shit over the phone for obvious reasons. Plus, Hoax wants to show off the clubhouse."

He's got a point, not that I want to hear it.

"You offerin' to be an alibi?"

"What are brothers for?"

Like I say, he's been good to me.

I make myself a mug of coffee. I wonder if I should make one for Frankie, or if she even still drinks coffee. I don't even know simple shit like that. I pour her one anyway, but don't sugar it.

I take a well needed sip and lean my ass against the kitchen bench.

"Not really the best timin', brother. I got shit to do."

"Cleared it with Steel already. He'll keep things covered at the yard."

"How thoughtful of you both."

If I go to the city, it means more time away from Frankie, and I don't want to be away from her for any length of time. Not when we still have so much to catch up on.

I haven't even touched the surface of what I want to say and do to her.

Ten fuckin' years. It's a lot of time to make up for.

"Like I said when you were just a kid, I'd always look out for you, Nitro. I may be an asshole, but I keep my promises."

I swallow hard. Everything he said is the truth. I know it. "You saved my life. Did I ever tell you that?"

He snorts. "Don't go makin' me out to be any kind of goddamn saint. I sure as hell beat you up enough times over the years for you to know that I'm not."

"Still, you didn't have to take me in. I was a lost cause.

Shoulda kicked my ass to the curb, but you didn't. You took a chance on me, won't forget it."

"Good, that means you can get your ass up here so we can sort this shit out. It's not a cause for alarm, but I get that feelin' this shit isn't over with. The tighter our story is, the better."

"I get it," I say, running a hand through my hair. "I'll be there in a couple hours."

"You got pussy in your bed, don't ya?"

I snort. "Worse, I got the woman I always wanted. Just gotta work out what to do with her."

"Well, don't wait too long, brother, you know how fucked up shit gets if you let it fester. You know the way to the clubhouse?"

"Yeah, I got the address."

"Later."

We hang up and I take another mouthful of coffee. Then I'm wandering back to the bedroom with the mug I poured for Frankie. She hasn't moved.

I place her cup down, staring down at her, contemplating if I wake her to fuck her. I decide to let her sleep. I know how tired she's been lately and how much she works.

I opt for a quick shower, not that I want to wash her scent off me, but I can make up for it when I get back.

After drying myself off, I pull on a fresh Henley and

jeans and run a brush through my hair.

When I get back to the bedroom, she's stirring.

My baby likes to sleep.

Here I thought I wasn't a morning person. Huh.

I sit on the edge of the bed on her side and look down at her.

"What time is it?" she croaks.

I stifle a grin. "Still early, go back to sleep. I've got some club business to get to. Gotta run up to Phoenix. I'll be back tomorrow."

She opens one eye, then closes it again. "Why?"

I bend down and kiss her hair. "Club business, babe, nothin' to worry about. I'll leave my truck keys on the kitchen table so you can get home."

She mumbles something incoherent.

Leaving her when we just found some common ground, even if it is between the sheets, tugs at my heart. I don't want to leave. But this is too important.

I take one long last look and push off the bed, leaving my keys where I told her they'd be.

Heading outside to the garage, I fire up my sled.

Sooner I'm gone, the sooner I'll be back, and we can straighten us out.

That's the plan.

Putting this to bed will be a welcome relief. Even if I am confident that I won't be questioned, it's always better to be forearmed.

Nothing can be better than having a plan in place and a story to go with it.

If I get implicated in this, my life is over.

I'll do down for murder.

A tightening in my chest threatens to erupt, but I push it down.

I've got everything to live for. And I need to keep telling myself that, just as Smokey did all those years ago.

One day, I may actually start to believe it.

"Vipers ain't sayin' shit," Griller says, looking bored. "We may not be besties, but we've got an alliance. After the drop they got on Tex's stash, they ain't gonna be bothered with rattin' us out about shit. They never know when their next pay dirt's gonna come. Least this way, we can ensure there's no war between the clubs."

Griller's right. When Smokey gave the Vipers the heads up about the deal Tex had going down and they stormed the warehouse, it was a peace offering for how shitty Tex had conducted himself over the years. And it never hurts to have one of the biggest clubs in Phoenix on your side should shit ever go down again.

Smokey is no dumb fuck.

"Two million dollars should set them right for a while," Smokey says. "Fuck knows what we could've done with it; our cut was only twenty percent, but it was enough to cover set up costs and get some renovations happenin' around here."

I whistle through my teeth as he looks at me, then adds, "Tex and the old club had a lot to make up for."

"What you sayin'?" Hoax pipes up. "Renovations? You don't like my grandma's wallpaper?"

We all chuckle as we look around. Yeah, the blue and white flowers don't exactly sing badass motorcycle club, but this place is huge.

And it's perfect since it's in the middle of nowhere. They can make as much noise as they like and not be heard. Perfect for parties and for doing club business without watchful eyes.

"Got an idea about the bunker," Dice, the club's Enforcer, pipes up. "Like we used to have at the old club. Think it'd be a good idea to keep the guns where we can keep an eye on them. I don't trust the dipshits at the warehouse as far as I could throw them."

The warehouse is fairly obscure and is in the middle of a minefield of shipping containers. That's where they keep most of the drugs until they're able to be moved.

"Plenty of land out here," Hoax replies. "But Tex wasn't exactly the sharpest tool when it came to keepin' shit on site, it gives me a bad vibe. Just another thing the pigs can ping us for if they ever do a raid."

"It'd be a bunker, stupid," Dice continues. "Hidden underground, covered in moss and shit. Fuck's sake."

Grunts of laughter go around the room.

Dice is a man of choice words and always has been. Smokey re-recruited him back from when he was the Fury's Enforcer. So being back here with only a couple dozen club members is like having a fuckin' long vacation.

I couldn't get too used to it, though.

I know that Smokey, Hoax, and Griller are all pushing hard to get this club going, to get some weight behind them so they can even out the playing field within the club ranks.

Smokey has too many contacts and deals to just piss it into the wind.

While I have no inclination to go back to my old life, I know how hard it's gonna be over the next year or so, trying to get shit up and running.

Helps when he's got a friend on the other side of the border, looking to do a huge trade.

He just needs the numbers.

The brothers respect him. That's the first order of business and he has it.

"Just sayin', didn't turn out too good for Tex." He gives me a chin lift. "Thanks to you, we're all free of the asshole."

I shrug. "Did what I had to do. Couldn't let anythin'

happen to my sister, or to Rubble. Minute I knew what he was up to, and was only out for revenge, I only had one job left to do."

Hoax frowns. "Sounds like you were willin' to go down with him."

I glance at him. "By that point, it didn't matter. Just bein' around him, pretendin' to be his right-hand man was so fucked up. Havin' to put up with his shit just about did my head in. So many times, I wanted to put a bullet in his brain, but without the intel on the warehouse drop or the location, none of what went down with the Vipers would've been possible until he gave up the address. And by then, we were already in Bracken Ridge, and as you know, Ratchet had gone bad long before."

Good old Rachet. Never been so glad to hear of a brother being six feet under. He was always a piece of work.

"Owe you one, brother," Smokey confirms as our eyes meet.

He gave me a cut. Enough to start up someplace else. That place is now Bracken Ridge.

I got myself a good set up, so I can't complain. Beautiful sled, my truck, and free rent at the yard with a job to go with it.

And my girl.

There ain't no ifs about that one.

Life is looking up, and I'm not gonna do anything to

jeopardize that.

"Was a lot of bad apples back then," Griller says, rubbing his chin, deep in thought. "Dumb fucks didn't realize when it was time to get out before the whole club broke away. I could never understand how Tex had so many alliances when he crossed so many people."

"Payin' the pigs behind closed doors helps," I say. "The Police Chief for one, various police officers and other officials to name a few, there's corrupt cops in every corner of the globe. Money talks, always has, always will."

"Which is why we need to stick to the story," Smokey reiterates. "To ensure we can't be linked to the Vipers or to Tex, it's best to make sure we weren't anywhere in Phoenix the night the warehouse bust went down, or anywhere near Tex. And we know he was in Bracken Ridge the week leadin' up to his death."

"Where the fuck were we supposed to be?" Griller grunts.

"Up at the lake house," Smokey says. "Lake Canyon."

I frown. "You still got that place?"

It was Smokey's mom's place before she died.

"Course I still have it, doin' it up in my own time. When I need to clear my head, that's where I go."

"I'll be damned," I mutter.

Some things really never change.

"What the fuck were we all doin' at the lake?" Hoax

asks, clearly as perplexed as we are.

"Havin' a boys' weekend?" Dice grumbles, sarcasm rolling off him.

"Not illegal to vacation at your own cabin. Plus, I got neighbors that owe me one," he goes on.

"Jesus Christ," Griller says, shaking his head. Between him and Dice, I don't know who's worse.

"Don't tell me your lakeside neighbors are payin' for protection?" Dice pinches the bridge of his nose.

Smokey rolls his eyes. "Fuck's sake, give me some credit. It's a semi respectable neighborhood."

Another thing the Fury will get back into once Smokey has the numbers is club protection.

The club used to do all right getting paid from businesses and influential people to keep them and their property safe.

That kinda shit's gone by the wayside since most of the MCs now only run drugs and guns. It's almost an untapped market and it's one way to cash in. Sure, the money may be a lot slower than the illegal shit, but it's a start.

Hoax snorts. "Semi respectable my ass. What did you do, bone the chick next door just to get back at her daddy?"

Smokey grunts. "If only. My neighbors are all old people, but they got my back. Trust me."

"That's why we're all here, ain't it?" Griller says, like it's obvious. "'Cause we got your back, too."

"I fuckin' hope so," he replies.

"So it was the weekend of the twenty-fifth," Hoax clarifies. "What did we do, go fly fishin'?"

I roll my lips to save from laughing. I forgot what a bunch of fuckin' clowns these guys are, especially Hoax. All those times he kept me awake on a stake-out, in the van, or out on the front gates of the clubhouse, and he never shut the fuck up. He talks more than any woman I've ever met, but the one-liners are still pretty fuckin' funny.

"Fly fishin'?" Smokey repeats, like he's hard of hearing. "Jesus Christ, I'm cursed in this life, I swear to God."

I know he didn't just call me up here to make up an alibi story. In truth, it's good to catch up with the boys. They're a big part of my life. While I may not be part of the club anymore, they're still my brothers.

Listening to them squabbling like little girls reminds me of old times. Not all of it was bad, only the last few years, courtesy of Tex.

"Better than them thinkin' we all holiday together," Hoax continues. "It's a one-bedroom cabin."

"With a foldout couch," Smokey adds like that solves everything.

Griller huffs a laugh and even Dice can't keep a straight face.

"Fuck's sake," Dice mutters.

"I've missed this." I laugh. "The old fuckin' banter."

"More like talkin' trash with you dipshits." Smokey shakes his head.

"Least it's never dull." Hoax shrugs. "Not much pussy around here to be had, though. First order of the day is to get that rectified."

"The first meet for new members is in a few weeks," Smokey says. "Got a couple of the old guns interested in patching back in, then the Chiefs' old crew. The pussy will follow."

"Not now pretty boy's gone." Hoax throws his screwed-up burger wrapper at my head and it bounces off.

"That's why it's good," Griller counters. "Means there'll be more pussy for the rest of us."

I roll my eyes.

I think back, and it almost feels like another parallel universe.

There's only one woman that holds my attention, though, and she's back in Bracken Ridge.

Maybe I'm pussy-whipped. I don't actually care. But it's her that holds my heart.

She's my Queen.

The only woman I want. There is absolutely no question.

And there is nothing that's going to stop me from claiming her at the table.

I just have to get her to agree.

BRACKEN RIDGE
REBELS
ARIZONA
M · C

CHAPTER 27

FRANKIE

"I think it will really help," I say to Lucy. "Going down an alternative route is something I would consider before trying IVF. I know it's tough to hear, but you got pregnant the first time naturally. We could also try hormone shots or a number of other alternatives before we even consider going down the IVF route. It is your choice, though. I want to give you all the options to consider."

Lucy and Rubble are trying for another baby. Little Avery isn't even a year old yet, but since it took them so long to conceive with her, and Lucy has had several miscarriages, I want to make sure she knows she has options.

I understand her concerns. She's in her mid-thirties, and while it's clearly not impossible, it is harder to become pregnant naturally the older you get.

Lucy really wants this, so much so her eyes glass over when she talks about conceiving and adding to their growing family.

"I think the hormone shots would be good," she says,

nodding. "It'll give us the best possible chance before we consider IVF. I know Rubble isn't concerned about having more kids; he's happy with Avery, but deep down, we always wanted a big family, and you know, I'm not getting any younger."

I smile warmly. "The best medicine, in all honesty, is not to stress," I remind her. "I know you've got a lot on your plate with the baby, and you're doing an amazing job, but I don't want you to worry. Things will happen in good time when they're meant to."

She bites her lip. "I know. I'm also very grateful for being able to carry Avery to full term after taking so long to get pregnant after several miscarriages. But the clock is ticking, Frankie. We both know it."

I know her. I know as much as she says she's not stressed or tries to convince me otherwise, she is. She wants another baby badly.

She's a strong woman.

She always says what she thinks, but this is her Kryptonite.

We both know it.

But the worst thing a woman can do when trying to conceive, is have anxiety and stress. It won't help matters.

"Lucy, we have a plan in place. As we discussed, let's start to increase your daily intake of folic acid right away, firstly to ensure that you're ovulating as much as possible and secondly to assist in the early development should you become pregnant. It's very beneficial. We've tested for diabetes and any other medical conditions, and you're fit and healthy. You're also at a healthy weight and eat a good diet. You don't smoke or drink. What I am concerned about is your anxiety," I say. "I want to make sure that you are getting the proper rest you need and are looking after yourself."

"I'm fine," she insists. When I keep my gaze on her, she adds, "Really, I'm fine."

"I'll write you a prescription for a high dose of folic acid. I want you to take them twice daily, before any food."

"Okay, I can do that."

"Rubble can help too by staying away from alcohol, too much caffeine, saturated fats, and tobacco, assuming he doesn't do any illicit drugs. Any prescription drugs that he takes could be a factor in determining sperm count."

"He's fairly healthy, and he doesn't drink, he hasn't for years, and no drugs. He could lay off the saturated fats," she says. "Though he thinks I'm bossy enough as it is. If I take away his donuts, I'm not sure any of us are fully equipped for the aftermath."

I squeeze her hands, clasped together on my desk. "It's going to be okay, Lucy. We're going to do everything we can to help you conceive. We just have to trust in the process."

"Thanks, Frankie. I know I'm being impatient."

"You're not," I say. "You just want the healthiest baby possible, it's understandable."

Her phone goes off as she reads a text. "Sorry, hon, I've gotta go. I've got Angel watchin' Avery so I can get a little shopping done, then I have to go hunt down my husband and have sex with him."

I laugh out loud. I'm used to Lucy's famous, no holds barred biker-chick talk. She might be pint-sized, but she sure has a big personality.

I begin to write out her prescription.

"Speaking of which," she goes on as she gets up from the chair. "How are things with you and my brother?"

I look up from my pad and try not to show her my surprise. "Uh, I'm not sure what you mean, exactly."

Good news sure does travel fast. Though if Lucy was at the party on Saturday night, which she very well could have been, she might be fully aware of just how things are going with me and her brother.

Screwing in his truck?

While it was hot, there's no doubt about it, it was also extremely reckless.

I don't usually behave that way, and definitely not in public places.

That's what Nitro does to me. He makes me so goddamn crazy and hot for him, that I end up doing things I wouldn't do otherwise.

Of course, it isn't all him. I'm partly to blame because my ovaries explode whenever he's around. Just one look at his gorgeous face…his eyes are so soulful, like nothing I've ever seen before.

He has the power to undo me so effortlessly.

When he looks at me, it's like he really sees me. Which is ridiculous; we barely know one another. We're connected by sex…and our pasts. Forever entwined.

I run a hand over my hair and hold my ponytail.

"Oh, knock it off. Adam has had a major jones for you since forever. Don't tell me you're playing patty-cake back at church because I know that freshly fucked glow when I see it."

Shit. Maybe she did see us?

My eyes go wide. "Lucy!" I scold. "I'm not doing any such thing!"

I don't like lying to her, but I am at work after all, and I'm not discussing my sex life with Nitro's sister, of all people. She's part of the club and no doubt part of the gossip, too, but I know that Nitro hasn't told anyone about us. That isn't his style.

If anything, he's the opposite; wanting to keep me all to himself.

I try not to flick my mind back to Saturday night, not just to the hot, angry sex we had in his truck, twice, but also back at his house.

He likes it hard.

He whispered to me that if this wasn't our first night of being together again fucking, he'd tie me to his bed and not let me go.

My cheeks flush at the thought of him tying me up to his bed post while I lay beneath him, helpless.

No man can get me as hot as he does.

"Righhhhht," she says, giving me a not-so-subtle wink. "Just know that he's a very deeply-feeling person, honey. You gotta take a little time to warm up to him. He doesn't always know how to express how he feels…"

Oh, I'd say he expressed it enough when he ejaculated all over my tits and rubbed his cum all over me, telling me I'm his. I clench my pussy at his dirty, filthy words.

Each and every one of them sent heat to my core.

I swallow hard, signing the prescription and handing it to her. "Thanks for the tip, but we're just friends."

She taps her nose. "Okay, Doctor Stevens, I'll be seein' you." She gives me a very exaggerated finger wave as she disappears out the door.

I slump back in my seat, fill my cheeks up with air, then let out a long breath.

It's been two days since I saw him.

He texted me to say that he wouldn't be back from Phoenix for a few days due to club business. Then, as if to clarify he wasn't up to bad shit, he said Hutch sent Bones up with a truck to a deceased estate so he and Nitro could bring a haul of stuff back for the junkyard.

I shouldn't pine for him, but I do.

It also gives me a little time to get my shit sorted out and work out exactly what I need to say.

He thinks I'm up on some pedestal. If only he'd realize, I've made so many mistakes.

I'm not perfect, I'm not even halfway to being the kind of human being he thinks I am.

I close my eyes momentarily.

Thinking about him doesn't help.

I shouldn't have jumped into bed with him before we discussed things. I feel a wave of guilt wash over me of what's to come. Of how I've lied to him and how I know that he may never forgive me.

The next day, it gets worse.

My SUV breaks down and I have to call Lucy to get Rubble to come out and see what the hell's going on.

I could call my insurance, but I'm only a mile out of town.

He brings Steel with him.

I haven't had much to do with Jayson Steelman, but to say he's larger than life, and just a tad bit intimidating, is an understatement.

He gives me a chin lift when he hops out of the truck, but doesn't say anything.

"Hey, Frankie, what seems to be the problem?" Rubble asks, from the other side of the truck.

"Hey, Rubble, I don't know exactly. It started sputtering and then everything just went dead."

I have a brand-new Toyota Rav 4 Hybrid.

Steel lifts the hood, has a look around, then goes to the driver's seat, shoves the chair back a mile so he can fit, then tries the engine.

He does a couple of other things behind the wheel as we watch.

"Engine's as clean as a whistle, all the bolts are tight, and it's not overheating. It could be an electrical issue," Steel says. "Sometimes signals get crossed in these new hybrid pieces of shit, hence why it would suddenly stop."

I put my hands on my hips. "My car isn't a piece of shit, thank you very much. It's brand new with all the trimmings, and it's good for the environment."

He doesn't even spare me a look. "Well, not much good for the environment when we gotta tow it back to the yard, is it, Doc?"

Somehow him calling me that sounds very different than how Nitro says it.

Lucky for me, I'm actually on my way home and not going to work because I'd be late by now. I also missed a call from Adele as I was in the middle of trying to maneuver my car off the road when it stopped.

"Can hitch a ride, sweetheart," Rubble says as he starts getting the truck ready to tow.

I'm just a little bit miffed. I didn't exactly pay this amount of money for a brand-new car to have its wires get crossed and stop on me, or to have Steel call it a piece of shit.

At least I can be thankful that the road isn't busy and there was nobody in front or behind me at the time.

"Thanks," I say, though I contemplate walking the mile to town because being squashed in that cab with these two doesn't exactly scream fun.

It doesn't take long to get my car hooked up, though, and I climb into the cab. Rubble is driving and Steel is on the other side of me.

"What kind of mileage do you get out of one of those?" Steel asks me as Rubble pulls onto the road.

"Uh, around 45 miles per gallon. Less when I take longer drives to the city, but then the electricity gets a chance to kick in," I reply, surprised he's interested after he made fun of it.

He grunts a reply.

"How are things at the hospital?" Rubble asks.

"Good, I'm starting to get to know my patients and build a good rapport with them. It's why I ended up moving. I prefer small towns to big cities. City life isn't for me anymore. I spent too much time in them when I was younger."

"Well, Bracken Ridge is very lucky to have such a talented obstetrician," Rubble says.

I smile. "That's very kind of you to say."

"Probably a good thing," Steel mumbles. "With all the chicks around town gettin' knocked up. Somethin' in the water."

"Are you trying?" I ask.

He gives me a look, as if determining if I have two heads. "Nope."

Rubble chuckles. "Too bad, though I don't know about cuttin' down on carbs and saturated fats, Doc. Lucy said I can't have donuts anymore."

I roll my lips. Obviously, Lucy has had the conversation.

"What the fuck, bro?" Steel pipes up. "Why's she got you on another crazy fuckin' diet?"

"We're tryin' to get pregnant again," he says.

"Didn't you just have a kid?" Steel looks baffled.

"Yeah, but we want more."

I try not to laugh when Steel says, "Why the fuck do you want more?"

Rubble chuckles again. "Because we like them, and I gotta keep my sperm count good, right, Doc? So no bad shit, until I get a bun in the oven, then I'm gonna go into a food coma."

"That's disgustin'," Steel grunts.

"What, the sperm count or the food coma?" I laugh.

"Don't wanna be sittin' in this cab talking about sperm, that shit's just weird."

"Don't mind him," Rubble whispers loudly. "He kinda forgets where babies come from, and when he remembers, he gets weird about it."

"Don't wanna think about all that shit," he replies. "Was gonna go surprise my ol' lady after this, but now all I can think about is creamed rice fuckin' pudding." He shudders.

Rubble howls with laughter.

"I take it you're not baby orientated," I say, once I've stopped chuckling too.

"Got enough squawkin' babies around the club. I got dogs. Dogs are easy."

Ah yes, Steel is well known for what he's done in the town for dog rescue and it's admirable.

"Speaking of which, I was thinking about getting a dog, once I'm settled and I get my…"

I stop, almost smacking myself in the face.

I almost let it slip.

He frowns at me. "Once you get your?"

"Ducks in a row," I blurt out. "Maybe a little lap dog. I don't really relish the idea of a puppy, so an older dog would be good. I hear they're harder to rehome."

It's something I have thought about for a while, not that I'm home a lot, but the thought of rescuing an animal appeals to me.

"Got a couple of older, little dogs at Faux Paws. See what I can do. Can shoot you some photos."

"Don't get him started on dogs." Rubble smirks. "We'll never hear the end of it."

"'Bout time you got yourself one," he counters. "Instead of tryin' to make more babies. A family isn't really complete without a dog. Most of the bigger ones we get are great with kids."

He's a good salesperson, I'll give him that.

"It's great what you do, with Faux Paws," I say. "It really makes a difference to those poor little guys who nobody else will fight for."

He shrugs. "Ain't no reason for any dog to be on death row. It's a fuckin' crime. Plan on expandin' next year. Need a bigger premises so we can start takin' dogs from the city. Since more people are going back to work after the pandemic, a shit ton of dogs get dumped every day through no fault of their own. January is also bad; unwanted Christmas presents and assholes who think having a dog is like havin' a new purse."

"That's so sad," I say. "Some people just don't think."

By the time we get to Steel's Auto, I pretty much know about every dog in the rescue, courtesy of Steel. He knows all their names and where they came from.

For a big, tough guy, he certainly seems all heart underneath.

I texted Nitro on the way to say I had broken down, so I'm surprised when I see him jumping out of a truck parked in the lot out front.

He's wearing the same dark jeans he left in, with a short-sleeved gray Henley and his cut.

He hasn't shaved for a few days, and the dark stubble looks so sexy on him. His hair is loose as he runs one hand through it, his eyes on me when he crosses the lot.

He stalks toward me as I stop, and Rubble and Steel keep walking inside.

When he gets to me, he stands towering over me, he cups my face.

"Nitro…" I start, but his lips crash down on mine, and I can't do anything to stop it.

I want it too. So damn much.

My hands reach for his body where I place my hands, feeling his ripped muscles through his shirt.

This man.

He gets me so worked up, and it's only been TWO DAYS.

When we pull back, he nudges my nose with his. "Need to eat your pussy, babe."

My eyes go wide as someone clears their throat behind us.

Pretending he didn't hear that, Rubble says, "Steel's gonna get Dalton to work on your car since he's got more experience with hybrids and electricals. Might take a few hours."

"I'll take her home," Nitro replies. "Can pick it up tomorrow."

Rubble nods as he disappears back inside.

"You know, I am capable of answering for myself," I say.

His lips twitch. "Didn't like the idea of you wedged between the two of them in that cab," he mutters close to my ear.

"Would you prefer if I walked the rest of the way?" I fire back.

He doesn't answer. "Let's go."

He grabs me by the hand, and I don't even get chance to say thank you for the tow before I'm climbing into the truck. Nitro's hand on my ass as he helps me up.

"Any excuse to cop a feel," I say, shaking my head.

He chuckles as he jogs around the front of the truck and climbs up. "Like I need an excuse."

I smile.

Dread fills me instantly a second later.

I have to have the conversation I've been putting off when we get to my place. I can't do this anymore.

Nitro talks the whole way home about what he's been doing and the stuff they found at the estate. In fact, I've never seen him so verbose. He seems…happy.

I swallow hard.

Looking out of the window, I hide the tears that threaten to fall.

I am about to ruin his life.

When we pull up at my place, he parks in the visitor parking and turns the engine off.

I start to climb out. "Thanks for the ride."

Giving me a chin lift, he reaches for his door. "Anytime."

He meets me round the front of the truck where he stands, shoving his hands in his pockets, and it instantly reminds me of something he'd do back when he was nineteen. I look back up at him, his lips curling into a smile. "Can I come in?"

I nod. "Yes, we need to talk."

He frowns. "Don't look so worried, babe. I don't bite." He winks as I fish my keys out of my purse, trying to avoid looking at him, which is almost impossible.

I'm a jittery mess.

My hands start to shake.

We go through the front gate. My condo is two stories, with a small garden in the front and a patio in the rear. It may be only a two-bedroom, but it has lots of space and an office. I love it.

Just as I turn the key, I hear a commotion behind us. We both turn.

Horror floods me as I see Adele's car pull up into the parking bay out front.

I never got a chance to call her back.

What are they doing here?

My whole life flashes before my eyes as I play in slow motion what is about to happen.

A second later, I hear, "Mommy! Mommy!"

Raven jumps out of the car and flies through the gate and up the garden path as fast as her legs can carry her. She's in my embrace, squeezing me tight, as I wrap my arms around her.

"Surprise!" she cries, squishing into me as I hold her, my heart racing in my chest.

"Raven," I whisper. "I'm so happy to see you, baby."

My eyes slowly lift to meet Nitro's.

He's staring down at her.

His face white.

She looks up at me beaming, then to him. Her eyes, they're exactly like his.

She's the spitting image of him, actually.

And she should be. She's his daughter.

Green eyes. Dark hair. Olive skin. Cheekbones that go for days. Lanky legs.

Our daughter.

He stares down at me. "Frankie?" the words are barely audible.

"I can explain," I say, tears well in my eyes. "I'm…I'm sorry, Nitro."

And just like that, ten years catch up with me right before my very eyes, and I've nowhere left to run.

BRACKEN RIDGE
REBELS
ARIZONA
M · C

CHAPTER 22
NITRO

The little girl looks just like me, but also like Frankie. I swallow hard, stepping back.

Frankie's eyes plead with me as I hear Adele follow along the path with a smaller kid. She stops when she sees me, then gasps and puts both her hands over her mouth.

"Adele," I say curtly.

She muffles my name as she darts her eyes to Frankie, and they exchange the same horrified look.

The key is still in the door as Frankie pushes it open. She kisses the kid called Raven on the head, who's still looking up at me.

"Mom, who is this?"

Frankie looks like she's about to faint when she says, "This is my friend, Nitro."

She screws up her nose. "That's a weird name."

"Raven, don't be rude," she chastises as the little girl looks at me curiously.

I look back at Frankie. "We need to talk."

She nods. "Raven, go inside with Sammy, and I'll be up in a minute."

Adele comes toward us. "I'll get the bags," she whispers. "I'm sorry, Frankie. We thought it'd be a nice surprise."

Frankie nods and wipes her eyes, tears freely falling as I follow her inside.

She walks through a long corridor till we're standing in the kitchen, closing the door behind us.

"Is she mine?" I ask, though the words sound foreign.

She nods. "Y..yes."

I start to pace. "We have a kid?"

She nods again.

"How? We used condoms, lots of them."

"One didn't work, Nitro. It happens."

"You named her Raven?" I pat a hand over my chest. My beloved tattoo of my favorite bird.

Jesus H. Christ.

"I've always loved that name. When she was born she had a flock of dark hair…"

"We have a kid, and you never even fuckin' told me?" I feel a rage like nothing else I've ever felt before. "She's ten years old, Frankie?"

"I tried…" she begins, and I can't even look at her. "I came to the club when I found out I was pregnant, but you were in jail. I didn't want to burden you with it, and I planned on telling you when you got out."

"Burden me?" It's like she's slapped me.

"Then I went to the club again, after the baby was born," she sobs. "You were locked up for three years, Nitro, and I didn't know what to do. When you got out, I went to the club in the hopes I could see you and tell you about her; I had no way of contacting you, then they said you'd left the club."

I frown. "I never left the club."

"The guy with purple hair said you did, then he tried to get me to come inside with him to check the club out. I didn't like him. He scared me…"

"Ratchet," I mutter.

"I tried to find you. I went through your hospital records, but you gave a fake last name, Nitro. I tried everything…you'd fallen off the face of the earth."

"I went by my mom's surname," I say. "I changed it years ago. I didn't want the reminder of my dad…"

"I don't know what to say." Her bottom lip trembles. "Say something, Nitro."

I run a hand through my hair. "Say something? What do you want me to say? You should have told me, locked up or not, you should've tried harder. It could've changed everything."

She puts one hand over her mouth to cover her sobs.

"And you know what's worse?" I shout. "That you've

made literally no attempt to rectify that since you got to Bracken Ridge. You've had plenty of chances to throw this at me, so why, Frankie? Where has this kid been stashed this whole time?"

She shakes her head. "I was going to today; this is what I wanted to talk to you about. I wanted to sooner, I did. The night at the club after the party…"

"But you preferred to let me fuck you instead?"

She ignores me, answering my other question instead. "I was trying to find the right time…Raven has been staying with Adele until the end of the school year; I didn't want to pull her out mid-term. I wanted to get things settled here and make sure the job was what was best for the both of us before I moved her across the state, and she has to start a new school."

"You lied to me." I point in her face, anger bubbling up. It threatens to take me over. "The first words out of your mouth when we saw each other should have been to tell me I had a kid, Frankie. This is fuckin' bullshit!"

She wipes her eyes, trying to regain her composure.

I can't do this.

I stalk past her to leave, but she grabs onto my arm.

"Please don't go, Nitro. Please don't…"

I look down at her hand as she scrunches my t-shirt.

When our eyes meet, I can see how much she's hurting, how hard this is for her. But that's no excuse. She should've told me. She's had ample opportunity this entire time and she kept quiet.

I can't even look at her right now.

"The right time to talk about this shit was ten years ago. What did you expect? That we'd just play happy families? That I'd see you in the street and not question who this kid was who looks exactly like me?"

"Please," she stammers. "I know I don't deserve it. I know I've done a lousy job by keeping this from you. I'm so sorry, Nitro. I was scared. I always wanted you to know her, ever since I found out I was pregnant. There wasn't a day that went by that I didn't think about you…"

I shake my head. "You're unbelievable."

The door handle turns and then Raven appears. She looks up at me, then to her mom.

"Mom, why are you crying?" she frowns, looking at me once more.

"I'm okay, sweetie, you just help Adele with the bags. I'll be there in a moment."

She stands in the doorway unmoving, and it seems she's not impressed.

"Why is he making you cry?" she asks as I stare down at her.

She's exactly like me.

She looks the same. Her eyes are bright green. Her hair is the same goddamn shade.

I run a hand through my hair. She's even got the same bad fuckin' attitude and is clearly protective of her mom.

"He's not, honey, we're just talking."

She folds her arms over her chest. "Why are you making my mom upset?" she fires at me, her nostrils flaring.

"I'm not meanin' to," I manage to grunt. It's not the kids fault her mom's a liar. "Like your mom said, we're just talkin'."

I've also got no idea how to talk to a ten-year-old.

"She's crying," she says, like I'm dumb. "That isn't just talking."

"Raven, you've been told to go help Adele with the bags," Frankie says in a firmer tone. "Now, please, go do as I ask."

She gives me one more grimace as she turns to leave, then stomps off up the corridor. I watch her until she's out of sight. Even the way she walks is like me.

"I want a paternity test," I blurt out.

I don't know why that flies out of my mouth. To be an asshole, mainly.

Frankie baulks. "She's yours, Nitro, but if that's what you want, go for it. I wasn't sleeping with anyone else."

I turn back to her. Every word on my tongue feels like acid. "You should've told me. You should have written me in prison."

She steels her back, trying hard to keep it together.

"You'll never know how sorry I am, how much…how much I love you, Nitro, how much I wanted you all these years… how I thought about you every single moment and what could've been."

I stare at her, confused. She loves me?

I open my mouth and close it again.

She can say what she wants, but she's had time to tell me. Instead, she let me get invested, fall in love with her all over again, and then hit me with this bombshell. Was this her plan all along?

I don't know what's worse. Being lied to about my kid all these years, or listening to her pathetic excuses to why she can't be truthful.

"Is that how this works?" I bark. "You pledge your love to me, so I'll be okay with the fact you've hidden my daughter from me for ten years? Jesus Christ, Frankie. I might not be the sharpest tool in the shed, but I never thought you'd ever play me for a fool. I never thought you'd be capable of lying to my face."

She looks shocked at my words. Nothing comes out of her mouth as she stares at me.

I take one last look and storm out of the kitchen, slamming the door behind me.

I tear down the hallway, hoping I don't run into the kid, or anyone else, for that matter.

As I get to the front door, Raven is coming up the

walkway with a small pink suitcase she's clearly struggling with. As I get closer, I lean down to help her, her eyes flashing up at me as her eyebrows knit together.

She's a striking kid.

Beautiful like her momma.

Bile rises in my throat when I think about what I've missed out on.

"I've got it," she says rudely.

"Set it down and pull it along with the handle like this," I tell her. "It's got wheels."

She narrows her eyes, but does as I say, muttering a belligerent thanks under her breath as she trundles past me. Even when she's mad, she still remembers her manners.

I watch as she gets to the front door, then she shoots me a look over her shoulder which basically says fuck off, as she disappears inside.

Fuck's sake.

I don't need no paternity test. She's mine.

Everything about her fuckin' screams my genes.

I scratch my jaw, completely blindsided, as I make my way back to my truck.

I'm a father.

This day just got so much more complicated than I'd ever imagined possible.

I place a hand over my chest.

My raven tattoo that I've had since I was eighteen.

She called her Raven, after me.

I shake my head.

I can't.

I can't go there right now, if ever.

If anything, I need to go beat the shit out of something and fast.

I hit the bag for all I'm worth.

Thoughts, most of them angry, swirl around in my head while I beat the shit out of the damn thing.

I don't even know what to say, or do. I just keep punching because that's the only thing that's in my control right now.

Have I really misjudged this person that I thought I knew?

She says she came to the club, and I don't doubt for a second that Rachet told her some shit story to try to get her away from me. It seems it worked.

Imagining him leaning against the gates while Frankie stood there, asking about me, makes me want to go find the fucker, dig him up, and kill him again just for the fun of it.

"You look like you're on a mission," Axton says, stepping into the makeshift workout room we set up outside near the pavilion. "Who pissed in your cereal?"

"Nobody," I grunt. I go back to punching, ignoring him as he comes around the back to hold the bag.

"Doesn't look like it."

"Observant."

"Wanna talk about it?"

I glance at him. "Does it look like I wanna talk about it?"

He has the good grace to keep his trap shut for a moment.

A good few minutes pass as I pound the sandbag, then I stop to wipe my brow.

"How long have you been at it?" he questions as I take long guzzle from my water bottle.

"A while," I reply.

"Gotta be a woman."

"Doesn't it always?"

"What did she do this time?"

"Didn't I just say I don't wanna talk about it?"

Axton and I may share some common ground because we've both done hard time, and we've become good buddies, but I don't know how I can share this to anyone. Not that it'll take the club long to find out, or the rest of Bracken Ridge, for that matter.

The kid's here.

Raven.

"Somethin' tells me you should get it off your chest.

This shit ain't healthy, bro."

I swipe my brow once more and begin jabbing.

"Fine. Frankie's only just gone and gotten herself a kid."

He frowns. "Am I missin' something, bro?"

"But not just any kid, Ax, my kid. And she's ten years old. Turns out that Frankie lied to me about it, and I'm all kinds of fucked up."

"Holy shit."

"Can say that again."

"You've got a kid?"

"News to me too."

"What the fuck, bro?"

"Bitch lied to me. I don't know what else to tell you."

"Let me get this straight, you've had a kid for ten years, and she's only tellin' you now?"

I punch harder. "See, this is as fucked up as it gets."

"Start from the beginning."

I give him the basics, which is all I really have myself.

"She claims she came to my old clubhouse, but it was when I was locked up for three years. She could've come and told me; they allow visitors in jail, or picked up a pen and said, hey fuckface, I'm knocked up with your kid, Happy Father's Day."

"Dude, I'm sorry."

I stop again, panting as I take a quick breather. "Fucked

up thing is, she's just like me. Got the eyes, hair, fuckin' long legs, and an attitude that would rival my own at her age."

"So there's no doubt she's yours."

I shake my head. "She's mine."

"What are you gonna do?" he asks.

For the first time in a long time, I don't know what to do.

I feel like Frankie betrayed me. Despite what she thinks is best for me, which is obviously well away from her kid, she had no right to keep quiet when she knew I was in Bracken Ridge.

"Fucked if I know. This is all so fucked up."

He gives me a sympathetic look. "Do you love her?"

I glance at him sharply. He cuts to the heart of it. "I thought I did, now I'm not so sure. It's not like I can trust her ever again."

"Did she say why?"

"Yeah, but it was all a bunch of excuses. Granted, Ratchet - an old member of the club who hated me - told her I left. I had no ID when I was shot that night when she got my heart goin' again, so nobody really knew who I was. She says she couldn't find me."

"But she tried to."

"Not hard enough," I grumble. "I missed out on years with my kid."

I run a hand through my hair, pissed off.

"Yeah, that's gotta suck."

"What's the kid's name?"

"Raven."

He glances down at my bare chest. "Kinda fittin', bro."

I point at him. "Don't start. I'm not in the mood."

He holds up both hands. "Hey, I'm on your side. I don't agree with her not tellin' you the deal from the get-go, but on the other hand, you were locked up. What would you have done in any case?"

"Maybe stayed on the straight and narrow, for one."

He winces. "Why didn't she say somethin' when she got to Bracken Ridge and knew you were here? Where's the kid been?"

"All good questions. Raven's been stayin' with Frankie's best friend for a while until she got sorted and made sure the job worked out, or some shit. It's probably all a pack of lies."

"It is kinda fucked up," he agrees. "But really, what could you have done from prison?"

"That isn't the point, but I could've worked on bein' a better man sooner." It almost sounds like he's in her corner for a moment. That only makes me even more angry. I start hitting the bag again. "But I guess we'll never know now, will we?"

He keeps quiet, and I belt the bag for another five

minutes, fully exerting myself.

"For what it's worth," he adds when I pull the gloves off and rest one hand on the post of the pavilion, "I don't think she's a bad person. Not that I'm sayin' what she did wasn't wrong. But it might pay to hear her out. Not the kid's fault."

I shake my head. "It never is," I mutter.

I'm still reeling, and I will be for some time.

I tell Axton not to tell anyone anything for the moment. I need to get my head around this for a couple of days.

Later that night at church, I drown my sorrows at the bar.

Frankie tried to ring me about a dozen times, but I can't talk to her right now.

I feel a pair of hands run up my arms from behind and I turn to see Star behind me, pushing her tits into my back. "Hey, stranger."

We haven't fucked, but she's well known to do anybody in the club who's willing.

Right now, I'm nursing my wounds and the last thing I feel like doing is fucking. It would only be in anger and to get back at Frankie.

I don't answer her.

"You look so lonely sitting here all by yourself, sugar," she purrs.

"Who says I'm alone?" I bark at her.

She frowns. "Looks like it from where I'm standing."

I roll my eyes.

Nobody can take the pain away.

Sure, I could fuck this chick into next week, but it ain't gonna give me time back with my kid. Or with Frankie. It ain't gonna do shit except make me feel guilty.

Before I can answer, I see Frankie through the throng of people, heading toward me.

Fuck.

I do not want to see her, not tonight.

She shouldn't be here.

I sling an arm around Star just as Frankie spots me. She halts in her tracks. Her eyes dip to the woman beside me.

I very deliberately whisper in Star's ear that I want her to blow me. She giggles as her large tits almost pop out of her top, then her hand grabs my ass as she nods, all too willing.

Frankie stares at me as I grin down at Star.

I don't want her. But I don't want Frankie to know that. She's done enough damage.

She's taken what was left of my heart and mangled the fuck out of it.

Star makes the mistake of trying to kiss me, but I don't break that cardinal rule for nobody.

Nobody except my girl.

When I glance back up, Frankie's gone.

I untangle myself from Star the second I know Frankie's left.

"Hey, I want your cock," she complains as I down my drink and go take a piss, telling her I'll be back.

Instead of going to the men's room, I walk outside to get some air.

I'm more drunk than I thought.

The cool night air hits me from all sides and I stagger, and finally making it to the bushes, I hear a commotion at the gate.

I head over there, seeing Gears having some trouble with a cop car.

Fuckin' pigs going to do a raid on us or some shit. They won't find anything.

"What's up?" I ask Gears as he turns to face me.

"Just called Steel, these guys wanna talk to you."

"It's fine," I grunt. "Got nothin' to hide. What's it about?"

Two things should occur to me at once; one that it's a little late for cops to be calling, and two; it ain't Jenkins, the local P.D. Two cops I don't know stand there.

"Just get in the car, Nitro," the cop says as I turn to look at him.

How the fuck does he know me?

All of a sudden, I'm being hauled, and Gears is shouting. I swing and miss, and I feel something hard hit me on the back of the head. Then it happens again.

Then everything goes black.

BRACKEN RIDGE
REBELS
ARIZONA
M·C

CHAPTER 23

FRANKIE

I don't know why I came. I don't know why I thought any of this was a good idea, but I've been going out of my mind ever since Nitro walked out the door.

I know I've done so many things wrong. He has every right to be mad; he has every right to want to kick me out of his life. It's what I deserve. Maybe I should have tried harder. He had a right to know, and I took that right away.

I could've gotten in contact with Smokey; he was kind to me that time when I first went to the club.

A part of me wonders why Nitro didn't try to find me. Why he stayed away. I get jail took a lot of years away, and I still don't know exactly what he did, though I do know he's not a bad person.

It takes me back to when I first told my mom I was knocked up and she went ballistic.

Things were never good between us after my dad's funeral, and that information just tipped her over the edge.

She demanded to know who the father was, and though

I never told her, things were never the same. She never wanted any part of meeting Raven or giving a shit about her grandbaby.

Not even after she was born, and I kept up with my studies while raising a kid.

To say that part of my life still hurts is an understatement. Maybe it always will.

It kills me.

Adele became my rock. We kept in contact all these years, and when I moved back to Phoenix, we lived in the same neighborhood. She's Raven's godmother and I honestly don't know what I would've done without her.

As I sit in my car outside the club, I try to pull myself together.

I have to put myself in his shoes, and that's what kills me the most.

He needs time to digest it all.

Then I think about the woman all over him at the bar and him whispering in her ear. I'm not stupid; I know he was doing it on purpose, to make me jealous. Well, it worked.

The only thing is, I have no claim over him just because he's my child's father.

As much as it turns my stomach to think about, he's probably used to women throwing themselves at him.

If we weren't in the situation we're in now, I would've

gladly gone over there and slapped the bitch. I wonder what Nitro would have done if I did…

I'm about to start the engine to drive back home, when I see a commotion at the gates.

Two men are accosting Gears and, even though his back is to me, I can see from his silhouette that it's Nitro.

Arguing ensues, then I yelp as one of the men whacks Nitro on the head from behind with the butt of his gun. He does it again as Nitro falls to his knees.

My hand is on the door, but something tells me to stop, shock coursing through my body as I see him slumped on the ground.

Gears swings at the other guy, but they overpower him, and he goes down too. Shaking, I watch them drag Nitro and then Gears into an unmarked van and shove them in the back.

I duck down as they look around before getting inside and driving off.

Starting my car, I keep them in view, and with shaky hands, I follow them. I fumble around with my phone, wondering who the hell I call?

The cops! my brain screams at me.

Yes, I should dial 911, but instead, I rack my brain as I keep following, staying a safe distance away.

Angel is the first person in my address list. I dial her number and put her on speaker.

"Hey, babe," she says as soon as she picks up.

"Angel," I stammer.

"Frankie, are you all right?"

I grip the wheel as I fight hard not to lose it. "I'm outside the clubhouse, Gears and Nitro just got assaulted by two guys and shoved into a van, which is now speeding away, and I'm tailing behind them."

"Holy shit, I'll call Brock. Hold tight. I'll call you back."

I hang up. No more than thirty seconds later, my phone rings.

"Frankie?" Steel barks. "What the fuck's goin' on?"

I tell him what happened as I keep following.

"Gears called me a minute ago. I was headed out front. Which direction are you going?"

"South toward the 101," I reply. "I don't know what to do, Steel, what if I lose them? This is terrifying."

"I'm gonna get a trace on your and Nitro's phones, sit tight. Gonna be right behind you in a few minutes."

I don't even ask how it is possible to get my phone tracked, but now isn't the time or place.

"Shit," I say, looking in the rearview mirror.

"What?" he barks.

"Steel, I think I'm being followed. This car pulled right out behind me, and now it's sitting really close…I mean, I could just be being paranoid." I start to panic. I'm not cut out for this kind of drama.

"Don't panic. I'm not far behind you."

"Should I pull over? But then I'll lose the guys that have Nitro and Gears."

"Don't pull over," he says slowly. "Frankie, I need you to pull it together and just keep drivin', you got me? Do not, under any circumstances, pull over."

My heart feels like it's going to beat out of my chest.

"Okay," I whisper. "I can do this."

He hangs up, and I take a couple of deep breaths.

This is going to be okay.

Aside from the fact nobody knows where I am or why there's a car tailing me. I should've asked Steel what happens when the van comes to a stop.

I've watched too many late-night criminal murder shows to know that none of this is good.

And they've got Nitro

What if he's…no. I can't think like that.

Anxiety washes over me as I try not to lose it.

In the far-off distance, I hear the roar of motorcycles.

Help is coming. Hold on.

I keep following along the 101 until the van takes an exit. The car behind me follows, but then takes another turn.

My paranoia is obviously getting the better of me. I sigh a long breath of relief.

Breathe, Frankie. Don't be a hero.

I think about Nitro and all the things left unsaid. I never wanted it to be this way. I never even got to tell him exactly how I feel, not truly. How I've felt all this time, even in the years that passed. And now he's been kidnapped and could very well be dead.

Why did I not tell him that night we spent together? Why did I take so long to say those words?

My face burns remembering the passion we shared and how I reveled in his touch. Just being close to him, while it could never be enough, makes me weak at the knees.

He's always been my downfall, I know it, and if he looked hard enough, he'd know it too.

My heart has only ever been his, and now I've ruined it.

I've had ten years to try to make this right, and I didn't. That's on me.

We drive for about twenty minutes, and I'm breaking every speed limit in Arizona to keep as close as I can to the speeding van without it being obvious.

It's not like I've ever tailed anyone before, so I don't know if they're aware I'm right behind them or not. This whole scenario is about as extreme as it comes.

I don't hear the rumble of motorcycles behind me, and that makes me panic even more.

Who'd have ever thought I'd feel safer being tailed by Steel and the Bracken Ridge Rebels?

This shit just got so much more real than I ever

thought possible.

Breathe, Frankie, breathe.

The car turns left, and when I get to the turn, the sign reads: Shot Gun Canyon. I dip my lights.

Nothing good can come of this and that sinking feeling punches me in the gut.

I pull out my phone and realize I have no signal out here.

Shit.

The car pulls over about a mile down the turn off. Of course, at this time of night, the road is completely deserted. There's nothing out here except coyotes and cacti. And desert. Lots of it.

The feeling creeps over my skin again and gives me goosebumps. This is not how I expected tonight to go.

I pull over too and kill the engine. I tried to veer off the road into the shrub as quietly as possible. My pulse racing and my thoughts getting away from me.

It's pitch black out here. The only light is from the moon, and the van's headlights, which they've left on.

My hand is on the door handle as I take a deep breath. I don't even have a weapon…the car jack is in the trunk, and I can't exactly risk opening it, as much as I would like something in my hands to use if I need it. I don't carry a gun and never have. I've seen too many gunshot wounds in my time at the ER.

I still do not hear any sounds of motorcycles heading this way.

Maybe Steel lost the signal, or maybe he never had it to begin with.

Cold prickles my skin as I exit my car to get a little closer.

I have to do something. I can't just sit here and wait for these people to kill him, and there's also Gears to consider.

My plan is useless, but I'm not going to leave.

If they come back this way and spot my car, I'm done for anyway.

I climb out and stick to the underbrush, trying to get as close as I can without being seen or heard.

It's so quiet you'd hear a pin drop.

As I get closer, I can hear raised voices.

I crouch down, trying to stay low, not even sure of what I'm going to do.

Anything.

I'd do anything to make sure he's safe.

I think about Raven, how much she's missed out on, and I want to cry. I know he's been entangled in some bad shit, but he's not a bad person.

Raven knows all about her daddy; she knows him as Adam. And after our meeting the other day, I think she may have an idea of who Nitro really is. She's not asked me yet, but she's a smart kid. And she looks exactly like him. Sure, she may have inherited my long legs and straight nose, but the rest is all him. And I have to tell her the truth. I want her to get to know him. If that's still what he wants, after all this is over…

I put my head in my hands. I want to weep.

Stay strong. For Nitro. For Raven.

I can't just sit here and wait for backup, or wait for Gears and Nitro to get their heads blown off.

Moving closer, I try to see how many of them there are, all the while hoping the sound of motorcycle engines is going to sound any second.

Just as I get my footing, something in my periphery catches my attention, and before I can turn, an arm grabs me, holding one hand over my mouth, the other gripping around my waist as he overpowers me and pulls me to the ground. I fight back.

Kicking, I try to scream, then he whispers. "Calm the fuck down, sweetheart. It's me, Smokey."

I stop, turning over my shoulder to look at him.

Sure enough, his confused face stares back at me. He releases his hand from my mouth once he figures I won't scream.

"Smokey?" I whisper-shout. "You scared the shit out of me!"

"I scared the shit out of you?" he whisper-shouts back. "What the fuck are you doin' here?"

"I followed them."

"Fuck's sake, woman, you shouldn't be here."

I poke him in the chest. "What the hell are you doing here? Creeping up on people in the middle of nowhere." I glance around. "Where did you even come from?"

He nods behind him somewhere. "Long story, but you almost blew this whole thing."

"What whole thing? Jesus Christ, Smokey, what's going on?"

He frowns a whole lot more at my tone. "Snitch, he's undercover."

I wave a hand at him. "I've no idea what's going on, or who that is, or what any of us are doing here."

"Bad cops, one owes Tex's brother a favor."

"Tex, as in, your old club prez?"

"The very one."

"Smokey, what the hell is going on?"

He holds one finger over his lips to quieten me. "Just stay here, and keep your pretty mouth shut, got me? I don't need your lip while Snitch is workin', bad enough you're even here."

"Who the hell is Snitch?"

His brow furrows. "Fuck's sake," he mutters. "Nitro never told me what a pain in the ass you are."

My eyes go wide. "You scare the living shit out of me, attack me and then tell me I'm a pain in the ass?"

"Why don't you skywrite it? I don't think they heard you back in Phoenix."

We have a stare off and, when he finally lets go of me, I take a few calming breaths.

"I was out front of the clubhouse when Nitro and Gears got snatched, so I followed the van here," I say, by way of explanation.

"I know, so did we."

I frown some more.

He gives me a chin lift. "Snitch is part of the MC, he's working undercover. When we knew these crooked cops were sniffin' around, we were aware they knew Nitro was last seen with Tex, so it was only a matter of time before they paid him a visit."

"And Tex is?"

"Dead."

My eyes widen. I don't want to hear the answer, but I still ask anyways, "Did he do it?"

He looks at me levelly. "That's a question for Nitro, not me."

I have that sinking feeling I'm getting to know very well.

"But these cops think he did it?" I press.

He nods. "It's why they're here; an eye for an eye."

I swallow hard.

He continues. "You're brave for comin' out here,

Frankie, but this ain't no place for a lady."

I steel myself. "I'm no lady," I fire back. "Shouldn't we be trying to, like…stop them?"

He gives me a look that implies I'm simple. "My boys are surrounding them, ready to take the shot. And you're a distraction."

I stumble with my next words. "You're going to kill them?"

"They're going to kill Nitro and Gears."

I feel all the blood drain from my face, though it shouldn't be a surprise. What did I really think was going to happen here?

For the first time since Nitro got shot all those years ago, I feel truly afraid.

"But they're cops. Won't people come looking for them?"

He smirks. "Don't worry your pretty head about that, Doc, we've got this."

"I'm scared," I say out loud.

Him not being here isn't even an option.

I won't consider it, not even for a second.

He gives me a nod, like he understands. "The best thing you can do is stay put, you got me? Stay here and don't move your butt until I come back."

"Why can't I come?" I blurt out. "I don't want to stay here by myself. It's coyote country out here."

"If you risk bein' seen. It'll blow everything."

"But Nitro…" I trail off.

He places a hand on my shoulder. "We've got this. What kind of a Prez would I be if I let one of my own brothers down?"

I nod. There's nothing I can do, and it's so frustrating. Sitting here, useless, when I could be doing something, anything, to try to get him back. Deep down, I know the best thing I can do is listen to Smokey.

"What about Steel, I spoke to him, I heard the motorcycles…"

"He's already here," Smokey says. "They parked up a few miles back. One of my crew picked them up; they came on foot the last half a mile. You're lucky your car didn't get spotted, that's all I can say."

As concern crosses his face, I know that he might be a tough MC President, but he's worried.

"I'll stay here," I say, my voice almost cracking. "I won't move until you come back…you will come back, right?"

He gives me a half-smile. "Not gonna leave you out here with the coyotes. Nitro wouldn't be too happy with me."

If only he knew how much Nitro actually hates me right now.

I palm my head, not knowing how the hell I'm going

to get through the next few seconds, let alone minutes or hours.

Bang. Bang. Bang.

I jump in the air, scream, and cover my ears as gunshots ring out through the deserted plain. Smokey's hands are on me as we tumble sideways onto the ground.

Who got shot?

I cover my mouth with my hands, unable to move, unable to think.

"Fuck," I hear Smokey grind out as he pushes off me.

By the time I gather myself and sit up, Smokey's already gone, and all I'm left with is a ringing in my ears and the thought that I may have lost Nitro forever.

BRACKEN RIDGE
REBELS
ARIZONA
M·
·C
BRACKEN RIDGE
REBELS
ARIZONA

CHAPTER 24

NITRO

I should be used to getting shot, hell knows it's not the first time. But if I ever needed a reminder how much of a bitch it hurts, then this is it.

I tell myself it could be worse; I can't come back from a hole in the head.

Smokey looks down at me. "You alive, brother?"

I grunt. "What is it with me and gettin' shot?"

Before he can answer I hear, "Nitro?"

I must be hallucinating.

That sounds like Frankie.

I'm pretty sure I have broken ribs from the beating those fuckfaces gave me, and I hit my head when they shot me, and I fell backwards.

"Am I dead?" I ask Smokey.

He chuckles. "If you were, it wouldn't be my face you'd be seein', that's for fuckin' sure."

I feel hands on my chest, then Frankie's voice again. "It's a flesh wound; it hasn't penetrated his body."

"I thought I told you to stay out of sight," Smokey drawls.

"Looks like you could use my help," she says.

Then her face comes into view. She's looking down at me with concern, as she says something to Smokey about my vitals.

She's really here?

She shines a little torch in my eyes and then feels around the back of my head.

"He's still bleeding, and he may also have a concussion from the fall. We need to move him."

"You know I can actually hear you," I grunt.

"We need to get you to the hospital," she says, examining the wound on my shoulder. "We don't want an infection setting in, and that gash on the back of your head is deep." She presses my ribs, and I wince. "You've also got a possible cracked rib. You need medical attention, Nitro."

"That it?" Smokey asks.

"No doctors," I reply. "Don't have such a good track record in the medical field."

She ignores me and turns to Smokey. "If we can get him to my office, I can clean him up properly. He's going to need stitches in his shoulder, and I need to examine his ribs to be sure if it's a fracture or a break."

"Will you at least look at me?" I bark at her.

She drops her head, but her eyes don't meet mine.

"Nitro, we need to get you out of…"

"Look at me!"

She lets out a deep breath, then her eyes shift to mine. "Please," she whispers. "I need to check the wounds…"

"She's right, bigshot, stop bein' a dick and let the good doc clean you up," Smokey says. He looks over his shoulder and yells something at Griller, and I'm sure I also hear Steel cussing.

All the while, I stare at Frankie hovering above me, holding her hands over my wound to stop the bleeding, just like the first night I met her.

My angel.

"Just like old times?" I mutter.

She glances to Smokey. "Get him to my car now. I don't want to take any chances."

Before I know it, Griller and Hoax lift me upright as pain hits me from all sides. It feels like my head is about to explode.

Frankie walks ahead of us, her medical bag in one hand. Steel starts talking to her, but I can't make out what they're saying.

"Jesus, fuck," I moan as Hoax tells me to toughen up. "What happened to the fuckers who snatched us, and where the hell is Gears?"

"We shot them, and Gears is fine, aside from a broken nose and a split lip," Griller says, like we're discussing the weather. "He'll live."

"Fuckers jumped us," I go on. "Seems as though Tex's brother knew I was his sidekick and put two and two together. Corrupt fuckin' cops. These two were particularly rotten, old school, and not in a good way."

It hurts like a bitch.

"Banged you up pretty good," Hoax says.

"Dog move," I gruff, the pain searing through me. "Though I'm glad you were tailing them. Question is, how did she get here?" I nod toward Frankie as we make our way to her car.

"She followed you when you got snatched." Hoax shrugs. "Bitch got a damn death wish, Smokey had to restrain her; she almost blew the whole thing. Don't know what she thought she was gonna do. She doesn't even own a gun."

I stare at her back. A feeling washes over me, as it does every time I see her. Even when I'm mad at her.

"For your information," Frankie says, turning to glare at Hoax. "I don't have a death wish, nor did I mean to blow your stupid cover, much less this ridiculous plan that included killing two cops, and bitch? Really? Can't you come up with a better term for women, it's a little outdated."

Hoax looks back at her, astonished, and I can't help but chuckle. "Sorry, cupcake," he replies. "Is that better?"

I turn to look at him. "Guess she told you, huh, brother?"

"Jesus fuckin' Christ," Steel mutters. "We gonna get this show on the road, or stand here whining about it while Nitro bleeds everywhere?"

The boys lower me into the passenger's seat as I feel the pain searing through me.

Frankie climbs in the driver's seat, and once the doors are closed, I feel the sense of urgency to make things right with her, even though I'm hurting more from what she's kept from me than from actually being shot at.

Sure, I'm not dying, but if I had been shot for real, there would be things unsaid that I'd never get the chance to let her know. Things she needs to know.

She starts the car, does a U-turn, and heads back down the 101 to Bracken Ridge.

"Quite a brave thing you did," I say. "Though it wasn't the smartest move. Could've gotten yourself killed."

She stares straight ahead. "Why were those men after you, Nitro?"

I don't hesitate to tell her the truth. "I killed Tex."

She turns her head, and our eyes meet. "You…killed him?" She tries out the words like she doesn't want to believe it.

"He was going to shoot Lucy."

She turns back to the road. "And they wanted revenge?"

"Tex's brother was owed a favor. They're crooked cops. They have their own set of rules, and so do we."

"I saw it on the news," she says quietly. "I had no idea…"

"Yeah, well, he was supposed to stay dead and buried."

"Does that mean the cops will still be looking for his killer, though?" I hear the fear in her voice. "For you, Nitro?"

"I don't want to talk about that. I want to talk about Raven."

"Answer my question first."

"The cops are doing their usual investigation, but nothin' can lead back to me. First, they need a weapon, and they're never gonna find it."

"This is scary shit. You have to know how crazy this all sounds."

I glance at her. "Has anything since you met me been anything but complicated?"

She takes a long, hard breath. "What do you want to know?"

I snort, then wince because it hurts. "Everything, Frankie."

"I don't know where to begin," she says softly.

"How about with the truth?"

She glances my way again, then turns back to the road. "Please believe me when I say that I'm sorry, Nitro, that I tried. When I heard you'd gone to jail again, I panicked. What sort of life was our daughter going to have brought up in a motorcycle club like that? Not that I'd ever let that happen…"

"Neither would I," I say. "What kind of person do you think I am that I'd want my child raised by a pack of wolves…"

"When I moved, it was a fresh start. I was able to finish my internship, even though at times I wanted to throw in the towel; I'm not looking for sympathy, Nitro, but she's the best thing that ever happened to me. When it all got too much, when I wanted to quit, I couldn't, because I had her. She kept me going. She kept me strong."

I feel all the anger and resentment that's been coursing through my body melt away. I'd never want the Fury knowing about my kid, not back then. People like Ratchet, for example, would've only used it against me. I may be an asshole, and the club always came first, but I'd never put anything above my kid. Above her.

Even though I guess she doesn't see it that way. Maybe she never will. Fuck knows I've caused her enough pain and heartache just by existing.

The old me starts to resurface; the Adam that was never good enough, no good for anybody, even my drunk father.

At least I can be thankful that of all the things I could've done, I didn't turn out like him.

Miracles do happen.

"Does she know about me?"

"She knows about Adam."

"You make it sound like he's my alter ego."

"You won't believe me anyway, but she knows all about you, what a good man you are."

I stare straight ahead. "She's my kid, Frankie."

"I know that."

"Should've told me."

"I can never take that back. I know that."

I run a hand through my hair. "Where do we go from here?"

After a few moments of silence, she says, "I want you to know her."

I close my eyes briefly, imagining how that would go. Then I palm the back of my head, chuckling.

She glances at me. "What's so funny?"

I shake my head. "She doesn't even like me."

"You're talking about that day, when you first met her."

"Yep, chip off the old block."

"She's very protective."

"Just like I said."

The corners of her mouth turn up slightly. "She's a good kid, Nitro."

"You sure you want me to fuck it up? I've never been around kids before."

"It's not as scary as it sounds," she says.

I don't know how I feel, how we can just make up for

ten lost years with the switch of a button. "I don't know if it's as simple as that."

"Because you're pissed at me?"

"Not just that."

"Then enlighten me. Be pissed at me, but Raven's innocent in all of this. She's just a kid."

I never thought I'd be a father, not even in my wildest dreams, though I hoped one day it might happen.

I never thought I'd get to see twenty, now I'm almost thirty. And I have a kid.

"You did good," I say after a long while. "With her."

"How do you know?"

I glance at her as our eyes meet. "If she's protective, it means she loves you."

She looks back at the road, diverting her eyes. Her breathing becoming more rapid.

She's still affected by me.

"Let me ask you something, Nitro."

"This should be good," I mutter.

"Why don't you let people see the good in you?"

I shake my head. "You think I don't?"

"I know you don't, my question is why."

I shrug. "It's what I know."

"There's more to it than that," she presses. "It's like you stop yourself from showing that side of you."

"When I grew up, my father said it was a weakness.

Showing emotion wasn't being a man. I guess I can't shake everything that miserable bastard taught me."

"Nitro…"

"When people see good, they expect good, Doc, and we both know I can never live up to those expectations."

Silence passes once more.

"You scared me tonight," she whispers, emotion in her voice as I watch her curiously. "I was so afraid something would happen to you before I got to tell you…"

"Tell me what?"

"All of this, how badly I want you to be in Raven's life…"

"What about your life?" I let the words hang between us.

"I…I didn't think that was an option anymore."

"What if it was?"

"Nitro, I've done so much I'm not proud of…"

"So have I. You think I'm some kind of saint?" I scoff. "Come on, Frankie. We both know that you're you, and I'm, well, me."

"What is that supposed to mean?" She looks at me like I'm absurd.

"That you're in a different league than I am," I remind her. "It's all right, it's not like it's a big secret. Anyone can see it, and I ain't after no pity party, but we both know you can do better."

"I don't know why you've always had this low opinion of yourself," she says, sounding annoyed, then she softens.

"That night we spent together…it was the most passionate night of my life. Nobody has ever looked at me the way you do, or held me like you did. I could never forget you, Nitro, no matter how much I tried. When I found out I was pregnant, I was in shock. It had nothing to do with you not being good enough. I wasn't ever unhappy about it, and I think that's because it was with you."

I swallow hard. "I'm sure being in jail had a big influence on your decision, and for that, I don't blame you. Fuck knows what kind of father I would've made."

I feel her eyes on me as I watch the road. "It's not too late to find out, if you want to."

I glance at her. "I'd like that."

"Small steps?"

I nod. "Small steps."

We get to the hospital, and she leads me around to the staff entrance where she swipes her card and we're through the doors.

"This is kinda different than comin' through emergency," I note as she shakes her head.

"Yeah, this getting shot thing, it has to stop," she replies, looking far from impressed.

When we're safely in her office with the door closed, I pull her to me. She gasps as my hands grip her hips.

"You know I'd never put you in danger, or our kid. That's why I moved here, to make a fresh start, Frankie. Got tired of that old life a long time ago. Unfortunately, some people just don't wanna stay dead."

Her eyes are wide as she moves her hands up my arms, feeling my biceps and shoulders until she cups my face. "You're a good man. I've never once thought you weren't good enough, no matter what you think. My only regret is that I didn't tell you sooner, that I didn't try harder to find you."

I pull her closer, so our bodies are pressed together. "There's never been anyone else."

Her breathing increases as I revel in her closeness, her smell, everything about her.

"Please don't ever scare me like that again, like you did tonight," she whispers.

"Hey, I didn't plan on gettin' kidnapped. It was kinda out of my control."

"And that girl?" she says, averting her eyes. "The one at the bar."

I snort. "I was tryin' to make you jealous."

"Well, you succeeded," she mutters.

I know she's battling with what happened tonight and how that affects us, how it affects our child.

I tilt her chin up with one hand when her head drops slightly.

"I'll never let anything happen to either of you. Never. You have my word on that. This shit is over, Frankie."

"What about those cops?"

"Smokey will deal with it. They're crooks. They left the force years ago because they're corrupt. Nobody is gonna miss them."

"I need to clean you up," she says, but when she turns to leave, I hold on to her, wincing as pain shoots through me.

She leads me over to the gurney and makes me sit down on it as she begins rummaging around in the cupboard for supplies.

"Come here, Doc," I tell her.

She looks up from her task and suppresses a smile. "I know that look."

"What look?"

"That look. It's not happening here."

"At all, or just not here?"

Despite the fact we've got a lot of shit to sort out and I'm still raging with my feelings over all of this mess, I can't hide my body's reaction. I still want her in every way.

And I need to feel her soon.

"Nitro."

"Don't Nitro me. I'm pissed at you. If anything, you should be tryin' to make it up to me."

She comes back to me with a bowl of warm water, gauze, and some solution in a bottle. "By dropping to my knees while I play Nurse Nancy?"

My eyebrows pique. "Is that an option?"

She swats me on my good arm. "All this MC stuff is new to me. All I've seen is the bad shit going on with this club and your old club."

"The Rebels have done everything possible to help me, Frankie. They accepted me and gave me a job, helped me get back on my feet. The old club is gone. Smokey is settin' up his club like it should have been done years ago. But that part of my life is over, just like I told you."

She steps between my legs as she begins to clean me up. "You don't always know what's best for me," she says quietly.

I frown. "What do you mean?"

"Us. Whatever this is. I need you so much, Nitro. What's best for me is wherever you are."

I watch her carefully. "Staying away from you, it's been almost impossible," I admit.

She looks down, then back up again. "If we tried to make this work between us, would that mean I'd be your old lady?"

My lips twitch as I imagine Frankie wearing my cut. Then I imagine her wearing it with nothing else on, and it has me hard as a plank.

"Fuck," I mutter.

I don't want to lose her, not again. I never did, but she's right, this will take some time.

But it's all new territory with a kid…my daughter,

involved. Things are different.

"Nitro?" she questions.

"Bein' my ol' lady means you're mine."

"I get how it works; you bikers think you own women." She says it so casually.

"We don't just think it, babe, that's how it is. But you'd own me, too."

She keeps working, and I can almost hear her thoughts as she processes what I said.

"But we don't have to think about that right now," I go on. "That'll come."

Her eyes meet mine. "You seem so sure."

"I've always known you're mine," I say. "Since that first night when you saved my life."

She looks down again. "Even after I kept Raven from you?"

"We'll work through it."

"I'd like that. I just don't know where to begin."

"Let's just take it slow, see where all of this takes us." I palm the side of her face. "I never wanted all of this time and space between us, but that's how the cards got dealt. We can figure it out."

"You'd be willing to take things slow?" She sounds as surprised as I did the minute those words left my mouth.

"My cock may not agree, Frankie, but sex complicates everything."

I could be wrong, but it seems a tinge of disappointment touches her face. "That's for damn sure."

"You sure you're not just sayin' this shit because you thought I was gonna die?"

She shakes her head. "We both know that's not true. I was going out of mind when you got kidnapped. I had no idea what I was going to do if anything happened…"

"So it's a guilty conscience?" I press. "Is that it?"

She looks horrified. "No!" she snaps. "That isn't it. Don't be a dick."

I chuckle, then wince again.

"That'll serve you right," she goes on. "Now keep still, I'm trying to patch you up."

"Bossy," I mutter, revelling in the fact that she hasn't told me to get my hands off her.

I want my hands everywhere. I want this woman more than anything, I know it, I always have.

"Oh, and Nitro?" she adds, as I glance from my shoulder back to her face.

"Yeah, babe?"

"If you get locked up again," she warns, "I'm going to fucking kill you."

I grin and even though it hurts, I pull her to me, cupping her face.

Our lips touch, and I groan when her tongue meets mine. She feels so fuckin' right in my arms. Like she's always belonged.

We kiss slowly, passionately, like two people who lost each other, then found their way back.

We've got miles to go, but I know that there is no other woman on earth for me like her.

She makes me want to be good, even when we both know when I'm bad, I'm better.

"I like that dirty mouth," I mutter when we pull apart. "But you better fix me so we can get outta here, before I bend you over this gurney."

She rolls her eyes. "You won't be bending anything for a while with cracked ribs, sorry to break it to you."

I wince again as she feels my abs. That fuckin' hurts.

"Sure I can't call you Nurse Nancy? I've always had this nurse fantasy," I mumble.

"It's Doctor Stevens," she says, mocking me.

"Can't wait to call you that when I'm buried inside you."

"Baby steps," she reminds me, though I think we both know where this is headed. "We've got to do this right, for Raven's sake. She comes first."

I know she's right.

"Whatever it takes," I reply. "This is where I need to be."

With my family.

With my girls.

Always.

BRACKEN RIDGE
REBELS
ARIZONA
M · C

EPILOGUE
FRANKIE

Raven looks at me over her milkshake. I purposely took her to the Coffee Bean after school so we could talk, and maybe it was to butter her up just a little bit.

Nitro has been coming over a lot and spending more time with us. Well, mainly hanging out with Raven and playing video games with her, which she thinks is pretty cool. But we still haven't had that talk yet.

"Mom, you're hopeless at lying," she says, very matter-of-factly, as she takes a sip, giving me that look that tells me I'm in trouble.

"You think I'm lying?" I retort, a little shocked at her tone.

She gives me a deadpan look. "Mom, puh-lease. I know something's going on. I'm not stupid."

I swallow hard, knowing that this conversation was always going to be difficult, but it's one that we have to have. Now Nitro is in our lives for the long run, she needs to know the truth and he wanted me to tell her.

A part of me thinks that he won't do it because he's afraid she'll reject him. I know a little about his childhood and a big part of that was not being accepted by his father.

"I would never think you're stupid. Please don't ever say that."

She shakes her head. I should know by now that she's ten going on twenty-five. "Is this about Nitro?"

I meet her eyes. "There are things to say, some of them include Nitro, yes."

"Is he, like, your boyfriend now?"

I shake my head. "Would it be so bad if he was? You said you liked him and enjoy hanging out with him."

Sure, things may have been strained the very first time they met, but he's been trying hard, and in the subjects Raven enjoys, they've found some common ground.

"I do. He's pretty cool. But he definitely wants to be with you bad, Mom. It's obvious."

I stare at her. When did my baby girl grow up all of a sudden?

I snap my gaze back to hers. "Raven! I don't want to hear you talking like that."

She tuts. "Why? It's the truth. I see the way he looks at you, all warm and fuzzy." She emphasizes the warm and fuzzy part.

"He does not!" I scold, embarrassed. "We're getting to know one another, and a big part of that is getting along with you."

"Is that why you asked me here and bought me cake and my favorite milkshake? To ask if it's okay?"

I don't think I've ever felt more mortified in my entire life. "That isn't exactly what I had in mind. We never get to do girlie stuff anymore."

"Will Nitro be staying over?" she presses.

"No, Raven, he won't be staying over."

"I mean, it's okay if he does. As long as he brings pizza."

I want to slap my forehead.

"I'm glad you like him," I say.

She takes another big, noisy slurp of her milkshake, then asks, "Why do I look like him?"

There is no denying the fact that they're the spitting image of each other, and there is also no denying that she needs to know.

"Raven, remember what I told you about your father, and what a good man he was?"

She nods, her little nose wrinkling. "But you said his name was Adam."

I take a deep breath. Not knowing how she's going to react is the hardest part.

"I know I did…"

"Nitro's my dad, isn't he?" She says it so nonchalant. Like duh, Mom.

Her deep green eyes stare back at me. I should've guessed she'd have it all figured out.

I take a deep breath. "Yes, Raven, Nitro is Adam, sweetie, and he's your dad."

She looks down at her milkshake, processing what I said. "So, are you guys getting back together?"

"Like I said, we're taking things slow."

"Do you love each other?"

"I love Nitro very much," I say honestly. "I always have, but when we were younger, things didn't work out so well."

She's momentarily distracted by the giant piece of chocolate cake that arrives. After shoveling in a mouthful, she says, "I'm okay with it if he wants to date you."

I'm surprised by her admission, though they have been getting along well lately.

"Well, this is more about you and spending time with him, which he wants very much."

"Why wasn't he around, when I was small?" she asks so earnestly that I feel my throat thicken.

"He made some bad choices," I reply. "But he wants to make up for that now, if you'll let him."

She starts eating again. "I'd be cool with that."

This kid.

"And you're okay with the fact that he's your dad?"

She looks back up at me. "Mom, I kinda figured that out

a while back."

This time, I do face palm myself.

Then she adds, "Why didn't he want to tell me?"

I stir my coffee, unable to take a sip because of my nerves. "Because he was worried about your reaction," I say truthfully.

"Mom, sorry to say it, but I look more like him than I do you."

I can't help my smile. "You did get my long legs," I point out.

"And your stubbornness."

A frown. "I'm not stubborn!"

She laughs. "Nitro says you are."

I shake my head. "Is that right?"

"Yup, he also said you're the best person he's ever known."

There goes my throat thickening again.

"Have you guys been talking about me?"

She shrugs. "Sometimes, but mainly we talk about his motorcycle and all the states he's travelled to. Oh, and steak is our favorite food, and he likes strawberry milkshakes too."

I chuckle.

My baby has always been a tomboy and never a real girlie kinda girl. She's always had a streak of independence, which I kinda dig, but I also know how much trouble it's going to land me in when she gets older.

At least he's keeping it educational.

He's so good with her. He has so much patience and sometimes they'll just sit and play games with no words needed.

It's like she has been the missing link for him all along. There's something happening here that's so much bigger than the two of us.

We also still haven't slept together, as much as my body craves him. As much as I know he wants it too because when he pulls me close, I can feel how hard he is. I know he's a very sexual man; he likes rough, dirty sex, and abstaining probably isn't high on his list of things to not be doing. But, we had to get to know each other all over again, without sex getting in the way. We know we're compatible in the bedroom, but if we want to give us a chance, then this is how it has to be for now.

I want to really know him. What makes him tick. What his hopes and dreams are. What plans he has. These are things I want to get to the bottom of.

"How would you feel about us all having dinner sometime?"

"Can we try that new burger place?" she squeals with excitement.

The Rebels have a new venture, the Burger Joint, and it's just opened up. Roxy, the chef at the Stone Crow, has an award-winning sauce that's so good they're bottling it and selling it in swanky restaurants and shops.

There is clearly nothing these bikers can't do.

I've taken some time to observe the club. I know that they're nothing like the Fury. For one, they all act like brothers, brothers who would die for one another.

After that night where Nitro and Gears were kidnapped, I didn't know if I could see past the danger of the lifestyle he lives, but I also know that his club aren't one percenters who do anything illegal. Except shoot corrupt cops.

I try not to think about that too closely.

"Sounds like a plan." I smile as she finishes off her cake.

This really couldn't have gone any better.

I know how confusing this all is for her, but she's taking it all in her stride.

Baby steps.

"Oh, Mom?" she says, with her mouth full.

I look at her expectantly.

"Can we get a puppy?"

"Nice try," I reply, sitting back in my chair. "But gold stars for slipping that in and executing the art of bribery at the most opportune time."

Reminds me of someone.

She grins. "Love you, Mom."

"Right back at ya, kid."

FOUR WEEKS LATER

Nitro is pretty quiet over dinner on Friday night at my place.

When I told Nitro that Raven had asked why she looks like him and I'd told her he was her father, he was unusually quiet. It's hit him pretty hard, all of this.

Since that first meal at the Burger Joint, she insists on sitting next to him at dinner now, and he looks down at her like she's made of glass and may break any second.

He really doesn't understand how much like him she really is. She's tough.

"How's everything going at the yard?" I ask, since work is usually a safe subject.

He looks up at me. "Good." He nods. "Fixin' up my sled on the side."

Raven looks sideways. "Not that fender kit you showed me the other day?" she asks, looking horrified.

He looks back to her, his lips twitching in amusement. "You don't like the short ones?"

She screws her nose up. "I much prefer the benchmark fenders. The tire huggers don't really suit the soft-tail, it looks a little…silly."

My ten-year-old is giving advice on what looks good on a soft-tail Harley Davidson.

How did this happen?

Nitro bites his lip as his gaze lands back on me. "Chip off the old block."

"Yep."

"Mom said that she'd like to take a ride," Raven goes on as I shoot her a look.

"We both know that isn't true," I reply.

"Well, she's too much of a scaredy cat to try." She pokes her tongue out at me.

I know what's coming next…

"Nitro said one day I can go for a ride," she says excitedly.

"Right," I agree. "One day, when you're like forty-five."

"Hey, I drive safe," Nitro defends. "I think she'd look cute in a little motorcycle jacket and a brain bucket."

Raven giggles. "Brain bucket. That sounds so weird."

"Don't even think about it," I warn. "Not happening."

He smiles, then scruffs the top of her head.

She hasn't gotten to calling him dad yet, but I'm sure that will come.

They're getting closer the more time they spend together and seeing them like this is a dream come true.

"A puppy, then?" she fires back.

Here we go again.

"I wonder where she gets her negotiating skills from?" I mutter to Nitro.

"I wonder," he replies.

"You know I can hear you right?" she rolls her eyes.

We both chuckle, then, surprising us both she says, "Dad, can you pass me the ketchup?"

Nitro freezes for a moment.

Holy shit. Act natural…

He recovers quicky and leans over to pass her the bottle. "Smotherin' sauce all over your steak?" he laughs. "Nice."

She beams up at him like nothing happened. Like she didn't just light the fire inside him. I can tell by his eyes that he's overwhelmed with hearing her call him Dad for the first time, and I'm choked up she just said it so naturally.

She keeps on chatting as Nitro's eyes flick to mine. I roll my lips as he stares at me. So much love pours out of that very look. I feel it all the way down to my toes.

The warmth I feel right in this moment is like nothing I've ever felt before.

We may have a long road to go, but I'm here for it.

I glance across at them as she slaps his hand when he tries to steal a fry, and I know that no matter what happens between us, I'll always love him with all my heart.

Not just because he gave me our daughter, but because he's the only person in my life who lets me be who I am, without judgment.

He challenges me, pushes me to my limits, but it's what I need.

It's what I've always needed. And this.

Just the three of us.

Together.

NITRO

Three more weeks later…

I press my aching cock against her pussy as we make out on the couch. We're both fully clothed and tonight Raven is staying over at Angel and Brock's. She's made friends with Rawlings, who is a couple of years younger, but they've been playing together a lot.

It's been almost two months since we've had sex. This getting to know each other shit, and being a family is great and all, but I need to be with her physically. I need to show her how much I love her with my body.

"Need to tie you up and fuck you," I mutter in her ear.

We've been getting hot and heavy every time I come over, and I might finger fuck her and suck on her tits while she comes, but we've always got clothes on. And we're always on high alert in case Raven wakes up and comes down to bust us. Tonight, though, we've got the house to ourselves.

"Nitro," she gasps when I pull up her shirt and then yank her bra down. Her breast pops out and I lean down to suckle her.

"Need you so fuckin' bad," I growl.

I reach for one of her hands and press it down to my cock. She begins to massage it as I bite down on her neck.

Pushing up her skirt, I pull her panties down, sliding down off the couch to my knees as I spread her wide.

I pull her closer, reveling in the state of her messed up hair from our fully clothed romp. It's like we're teenagers again and are scared of getting caught.

I rip my shirt off as she stares at my body.

"Like what you see?" I laugh.

She nods, running her hands over my shoulders as I dip my head down, spreading her wider as I run my tongue through her folds. She's so fuckin' beautiful.

She grinds against me, trying to get friction, as I hold her legs apart when she tries to close them.

I do it again, swirling my tongue over her clit as she bucks off the couch. I play with her a little before I insert a finger, spreading her juices around as she moans and groans.

I latch onto her clit and suck as she grips my head with her hands and fully rides my face.

She comes quickly, calling out my name as I start to fuck her hole with my tongue. I can't get enough of her pussy.

Giving her another orgasm, I lick her juices until she's panting heavily and has discarded her top.

"Nitro." Her breathing hitches as she tries to catch

her breath.

I unzip my pants, free my cock, and waste no time in placing my knees on either side of her, spreading her legs as I hold her under her knees, and I shove my cock inside with one thrust.

"Fuck," I groan, as I start to move.

She stares as me as I smile wickedly, her face a mixture of pleasure and wonder.

I love shocking her. In fact, I can't get enough of it.

Looking down, I watch my cock disappearing inside her tight hole. Jesus Christ.

I close my eyes, if I keep watching I'll come too quick, and I want this to last.

"Yes…" she groans. "Oh, God, yes…"

I grind harder, my pubic bone brushing her clit as her orgasm builds. When she grabs my ass, and her nails dig into me, she lets go again, and I watch as her head tumbles back as I take her body nice and hard.

"Whose pussy is this?" I growl, not letting up.

"Yours!" she cries.

"I'll fuckin' take it when I want it from now on, got me?" She casts her eyes back on mine as I pull out and lean down. "Got me?"

"It's always been yours," she pants.

I kiss her chastely, then reach down and suckle each nipple into my mouth, enjoying the fullness of her tits as she gasps at every suck.

Flipping her over, I slap her ass as I reach around and cup her tits.

"Tell me how much you want it," I growl in her ear, pulling her nipples as she pushes her ass back into me.

"I need it so damn much," she sighs. "You don't know how much."

The truth is, I can't get close enough. I need her so damn much too.

Keeping her hands on the couch as she wiggles her ass again, I line up my cock and take her full tilt.

Luckily she's got a big ass couch so I can move how I want to.

I fuck her doggy style, rough, and she loves every second of it.

My release is building, and I know I'm not gonna last.

"So fuckin' horny for you," I mutter, my teeth clenched. "Makin' me wait for six fuckin' weeks and two days and four hours…"

"Ten minutes and thirty-five seconds," she finishes.

I smirk. That's my girl.

"Glad we've got all night, 'cause you're gonna need it."

She climaxes again, clenching my cock as I explode, stilling as I empty myself inside her. My cum spurts so violently, I take a second to compose myself when I'm done.

We collapse with me still on top of her.

"Jesus, Nitro, I forgot how good you were," she pants.

"Really?" I mutter, into her hair. "Though the last time we had sex, you were ridin' me in my truck, then again in my bed."

"Speaking of bed, we should really go…"

I'm reluctant to move, but I also am dying to fuck her in her own bed. And tonight, we can be as loud as we want.

I pull out of her, and while she gathers herself, I make my way to her bedroom naked.

She joins me a moment later, crawling into my lap as she sits on me and kisses me slowly.

It's so gentle and unnerving, I pull back and ask, "What was that for?"

"For being you, Nitro," she replies. "This last month and a half, it's been amazing."

I smile as she looks down at me, brushing my hair back off my face. "It has been pretty great. I've enjoyed it, gettin' to know both of you. Raven callin' me Dad…"

"That is pretty great," she admits. "You're so good with her, a natural."

"I couldn't ask for more." I brush her lips softly.

I've told her so much. About all the shit that went down that got me in jail. My relationship with my dad, even my suicide attempt when I was fifteen; the reason I have the cuff tattooed on my wrist to cover it up. Things I never thought I would ever talk about to another person. But she knows it all.

She sits naked in my lap as I rest my head against the headboard.

Tangled around her, this is exactly where I need to be.

"I never thought it could be like this," she whispers. "I couldn't dare to dream it."

"I could," I say. "But you're right, it was just a dream, for so long. We finally came together, that's all that matters."

She looks me right in the eye and says, "Thank you for forgiving me, for Raven, for…"

I hold a finger across her mouth. "It's water under the bridge, all that matters is right now."

"I love you, Nitro," she whispers. "I've always loved you, from the very first moment I saw you."

My heart lurches in my chest hearing those words. "I love you too, Doc," I say, cupping her face. "You're the only woman I'll ever want. It tore me up, all those years apart, but I'm gonna make it up to you, and to Raven. You're my girls, and I'll be here for the both of you, as long as you'll have me."

Tears build in her eyes as she buries her face in my shoulder, her body heaving as she sobs. I kiss her hair. "Don't cry," I say. "Babe, please don't, nothin' is ever gonna tear us apart."

She pulls back, and I wipe her tears away. "Don't ever

leave me again," she says. "I mean it. I won't recover from losing you again."

"Never," I whisper as our lips lock again. "I know where my future lies, babe, and it's with you and my baby girl. I'll never want anything more."

She kisses me back, then when we pull apart, she says, "Does this mean you're not gonna stalk me at the hospital anymore?" Her eyes flash with that spark of excitement.

We both know how overbearing I am, but she doesn't seem to mind it.

I grin, gripping her ass with my hands as she reaches between my legs. I slide her down onto my cock and she stills. "Nah, Doc, it only means I get to fuck you over your desk while your patients wait outside for you. And I'll take my sweet time about it, too."

She shakes her head as she smiles at me, pushing her body flush against mine. "Took the words right out of my mouth."

I grin against her lips. "That's not all I'm gonna take."

THREE MONTHS LATER

"Either way, you're fucked," I say to Gears as we lean on the fence post at Brock's farm. Watching Rawlings and Raven ride on the ponies. Angel and Frankie are out in the yard, chatting while they watch the girls.

"Not wrong there, brother." He stops talking as Amelia sidles up beside us.

We're discussing how he's gonna be in two places at once because Hutch has been especially hard on him for the last few months. Which kind of tells me Gears is close to being patched in.

Jax has been our longest prospect and one day he might make the grade, though he seems pretty happy shit-kicking. I can't say the same for Gears. He's got an edge to him that I see a lot of my younger self in. I hope he doesn't implode like I did, though.

Anger only lands you in jail, and that ain't any place I'm going back to.

"Hey, boys," she says as I roll my eyes at Gears.

"Hey, Amelia," I say as Gears gives her a nod.

He's been staying well away from Brock and Axton's little sister, and for good reason. She's a whole world of trouble, despite the 'legal-secretary' persona she puts on.

"What ya'll doing?" she coos.

"I'm about to go bang my ol' lady against a hay bale," I say with a chagrin. "While Angel keeps the kids distracted." I can't get enough of her in her riding gear.

"Eww, TMI," she says with a wince.

"Leave you to it, brother." I pat him on the shoulder as I leave, but the frown on his face tells me he's not comfortable being left alone with her without adult supervision.

I chuckle as I leave.

Then I hear her say, "I've always wanted to learn to ride a horse…"

Jesus. He's fucked.

I make my way over to the girls, and just as I do, Raven's pony trots up to me.

"Dad!" she cries out, all excited. "Did you see me?"

I pull her into my arms and give her a kiss and a hug, then settle her back on the horse.

"I did, honey, and I'm so proud of you."

I'll never get sick of her calling me that, it's like music to my ears. We've grown so close these last few months; I couldn't honestly wish for anything more, well, maybe one other thing…more babies. We've talked about it, and she wants at least one more. Yeah, I could do this kid thing, and imagining Frankie barefoot and pregnant with another kid, one that I get to be part of this time from the start, has me really wanting to go find that hay bale.

Just as I think it, an arm slides around my waist and Frankie cuddles into my side as Raven takes off again, laughing as she does.

She's gonna be even more excited in a few days time when she gets the new dog we've organized from Faux Paws, courtesy of Steel. According to him we're not a complete family until we adopt a pup.

"How'd I get so lucky?" I muse, looking down at my woman's face.

"Could have something to do with that brilliant doctor you stalked," she replies, beaming up at me.

I kiss her on the nose, then move my mouth to her ear. "Wanna do it on a hay bale?"

She smacks me on the ass as I purse my lips and give her eyes. "Behave."

"How can I behave when you have that gear on." I pull her closer and kiss her hard.

"Mom! Dad! Ewww!" Raven calls out. As we both look up at the same time, she's covering one face with one hand.

I laugh, and so does Frankie. "You sure you want more kids?" Frankie asks.

"Absofuckin'lutely." I smooth her hair back. "I wanna practice first, though, with you bent over with those ridin' boots on and nothin' else."

She shakes her head, smiling while trying to push me back. "Babe, not here!"

"Spoilsport." I kiss the top of her head and look out at my little girl on her pony, laughing like she hasn't a care in the world.

My girls' happiness, that's all I want. Whatever else life has in store for me, I'm here for it.

Now and forever.

It was worth the wait.

THE END

403

ACKNOWLEDGMENTS

Firstly, I'm so grateful to all my readers around the world, without you wanting more of my Bracken Ridge bikers, none of this would be possible. I hope you enjoy Nitro, he's a very different character to anyone I've ever written before. He and Frankie spoke to me so effortlessly, I absolutely loved being in their world and I'm sad to see it end!

Thank you to my amazing team, Savannah and Brianna at Peachy Keen Author Services (peachykeenas) for all your help. I love working with you so much.

To my sister D, hugs for always keeping me going and being my #1 supporter.

Thank you to my Alpha reader Michelle (the outgoing bookworm) and my Beta reader Alana for all your hard work, especially at such short notice. I promise I will get better at getting you the manuscript on time!

A big round of applause to my ARC readers for taking the time to read and review and for sharing my blog tour posts and spreading the word. Much appreciated.

Thanks once again for all my blogger friends, fellow authors, and all the amazing people on my journey. I'm so grateful for your support.

Special thanks to my editor Mackenzie @ nicegirlnaughtyedits for all that you do x

Thanks LJ from Mayhem Cover Creations for the cover design for another fantastic cover.

A big shout out to Wander Aguiar Photography for an amazing cover model photo (Alex C) he is the perfect fit for Nitro. I love your work!

If you can spare the time to leave a review on GR and/or Amazon if you loved Nitro or any of my books that would be greatly appreciated and helps me so much as an indie author. Links are on the following pages.

I can't wait for you to meet Gears; he will be the next up in the series. His book is scheduled for January 2023.

Be sure to check out my private facebook group (links below) as I update this page regularly before anything gets released on other social media channels.

Love from Australia, MF xx

FIND ME AT

Facebook: https://www.facebook.com/mackenzy.foxauthor.5

Instagram: https://www.instagram.com/mackenzyfoxbooks/

Tiktok: https://www.tiktok.com/@mackenzyfoxauthor

Linktree: https://linktr.ee/mackenzyfox

Goodreads: https://bit.ly/2TKp7ck

https://books2read.com/Steel-BRR

Website: https://mackenzyfox.com

Join my private Facebook group for all the juicy gossip, giveaways and spicy reveals first at The Den - A Mackenzy Fox Reader Group - https://bit.ly/3dgQfKk

ABOUT THE AUTHOR

Mackenzy Fox is an author of contemporary, romantic and erotic themed romance novels. When she's not writing she loves vegan cooking, walking her beloved pooch's, reading books and is an expert on online shopping.

She's slightly obsessed with drinking tea, testing bubbly Moscato, watching home decorating shows and has a black belt in origami. She strives to live a quiet and introverted life in Western Australia's North West with her hubby, twin sister and her dogs.

ALSO BY
MACKENZY FOX

Bracken Ridge Rebels MC:
Steel
Gunner
Brock
Colt
Rubble
Bones
Axton
Nitro
Gears
Knox

Medici Mafia:
Fortress of the King
Fortress of the Queen
Fortress of the Heart
Fortress of the Soul
Fortress of the Damned
Fortress of the Brave

Bad Boys of New York:
Jaxon

Standalone:
Broken Wings